You're Invited
to a
Birthday Party!

The Misadventures of
SALEM HYDE

2

Big Birthday Bash

Frank Cammuso

AMULET BOOKS
NEW YORK

Hardcover ISBN: 978-1-4197-1025-4
Paperback ISBN: 978-1-4197-1026-1

Text and illustrations copyright © 2014 Frank Cammuso
Book design by Frank Cammuso and Sara Corbett

Published in 2014 by Amulet Books, an imprint of ABRAMS.

Printed and bound in China
10 9 8 7 6 5 4 3 2

Amulet Books are available at special discounts when purchased in quantity for premiums and promotions as well as fundraising or educational use. Special editions can also be created to specification. For details, contact specialsales@abramsbooks.com or the address below.

ABRAMS

THE ART OF BOOKS SINCE 1949

115 West 18th Street
New York, NY 10011
www.abramsbooks.com

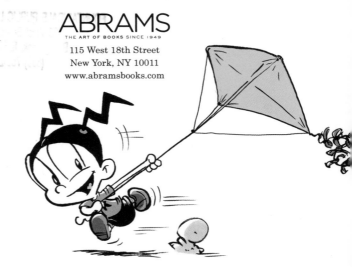

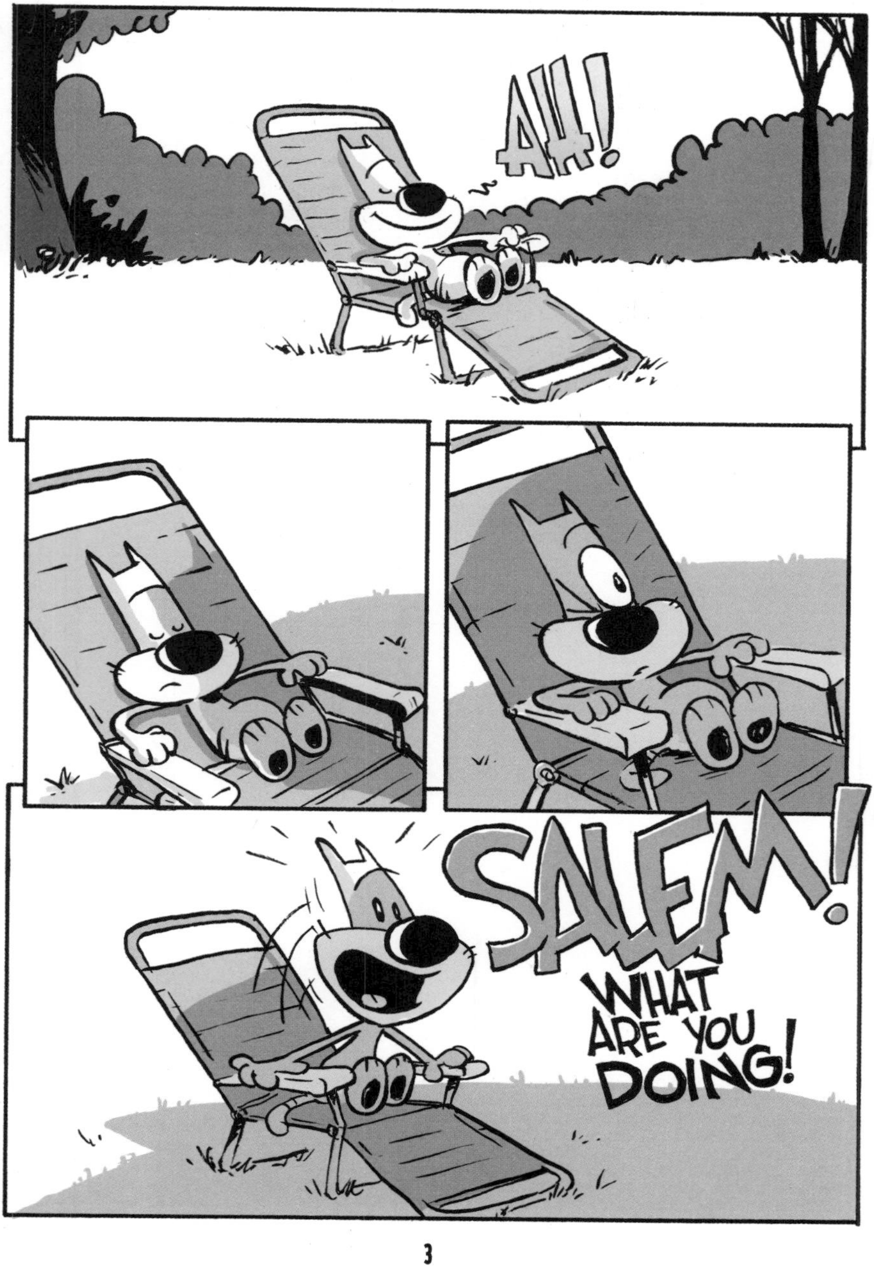
AH!
SALEM!
WHAT ARE YOU DOING!

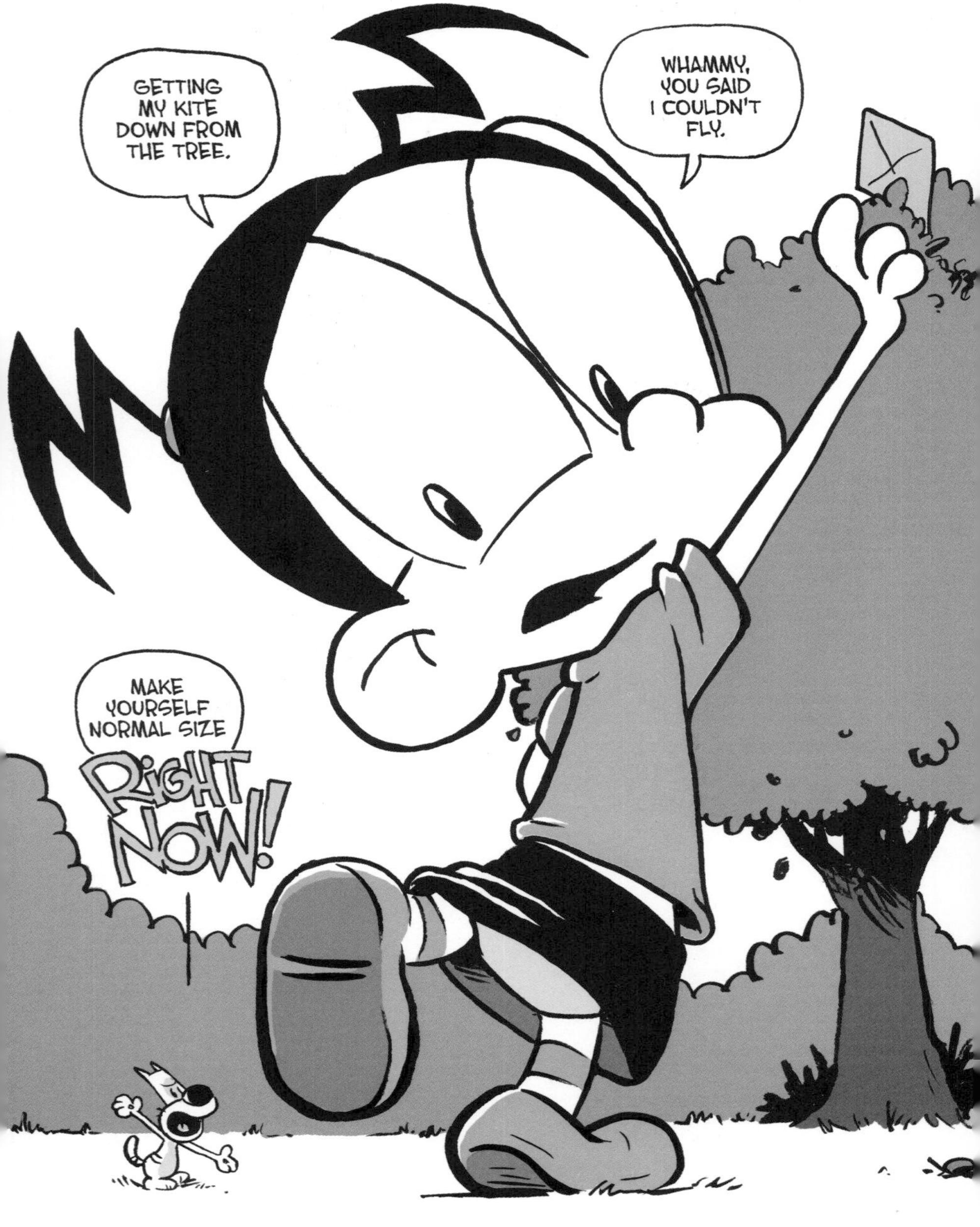

GETTING MY KITE DOWN FROM THE TREE.
WHAMMY, YOU SAID I COULDN'T FLY.
MAKE YOURSELF NORMAL SIZE RIGHT NOW!

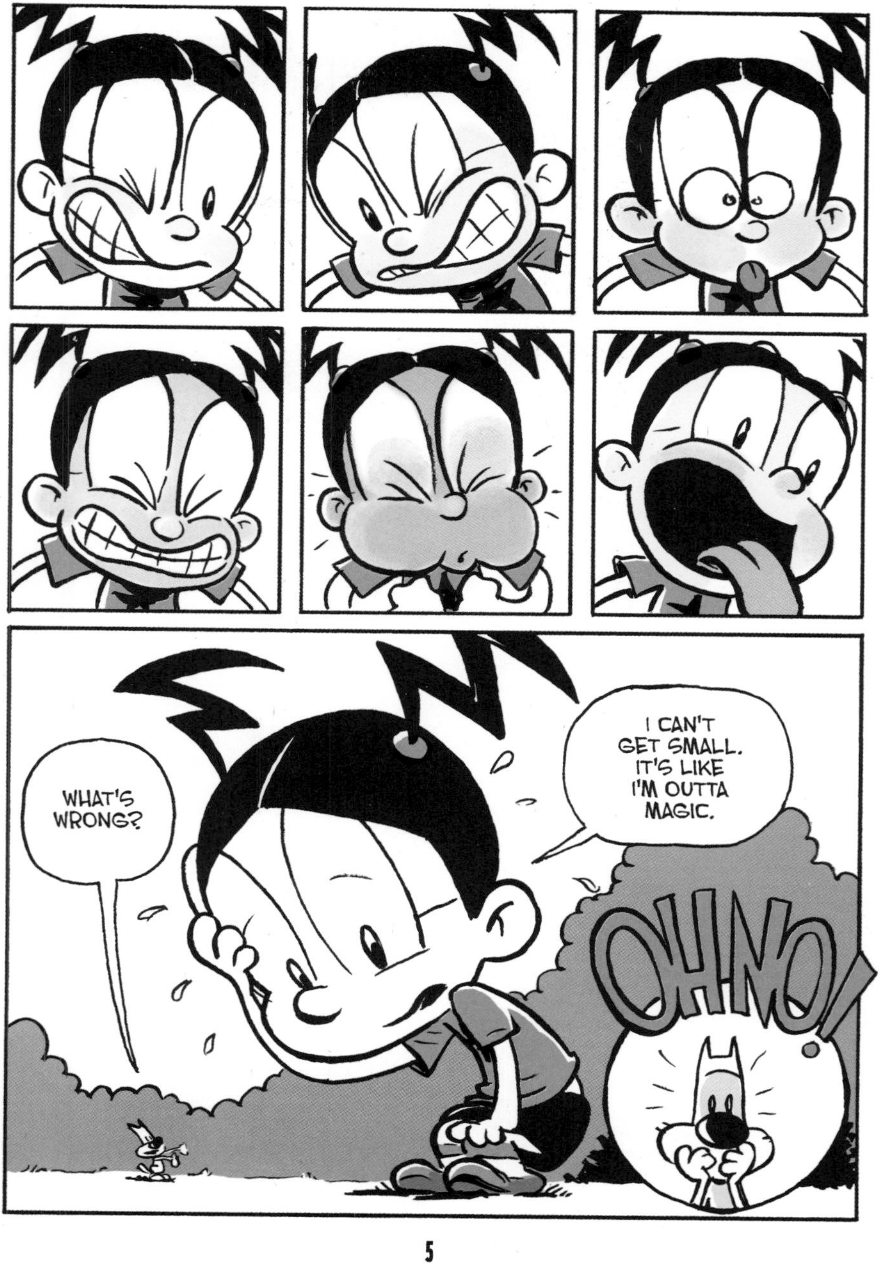
WHAT'S WRONG?
I CAN'T GET SMALL. IT'S LIKE I'M OUTTA MAGIC.
OH NO!

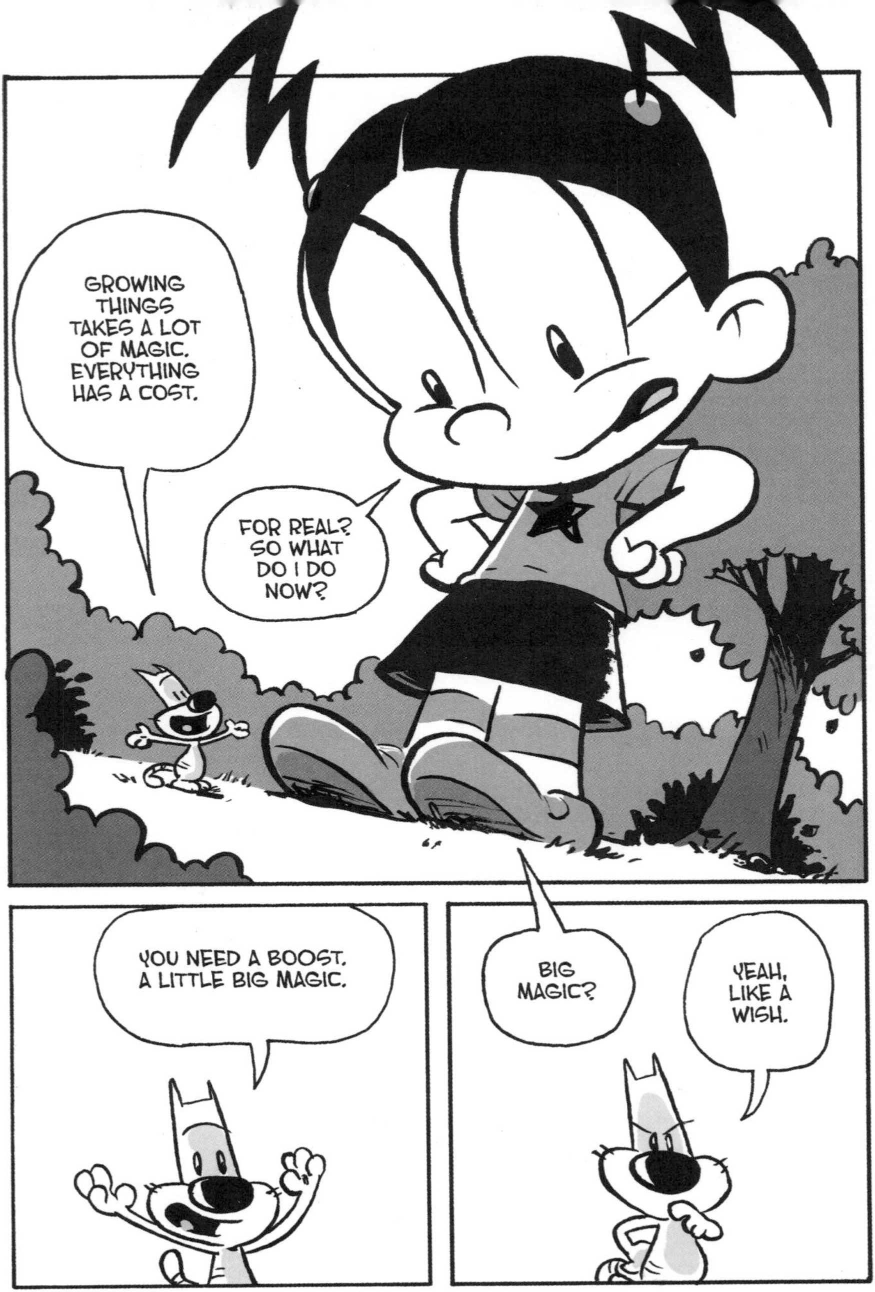
GROWING THINGS TAKES A LOT OF MAGIC. EVERYTHING HAS A COST.
FOR REAL? SO WHAT DO I DO NOW?
YOU NEED A BOOST. A LITTLE BIG MAGIC.
BIG MAGIC?
YEAH, LIKE A WISH.

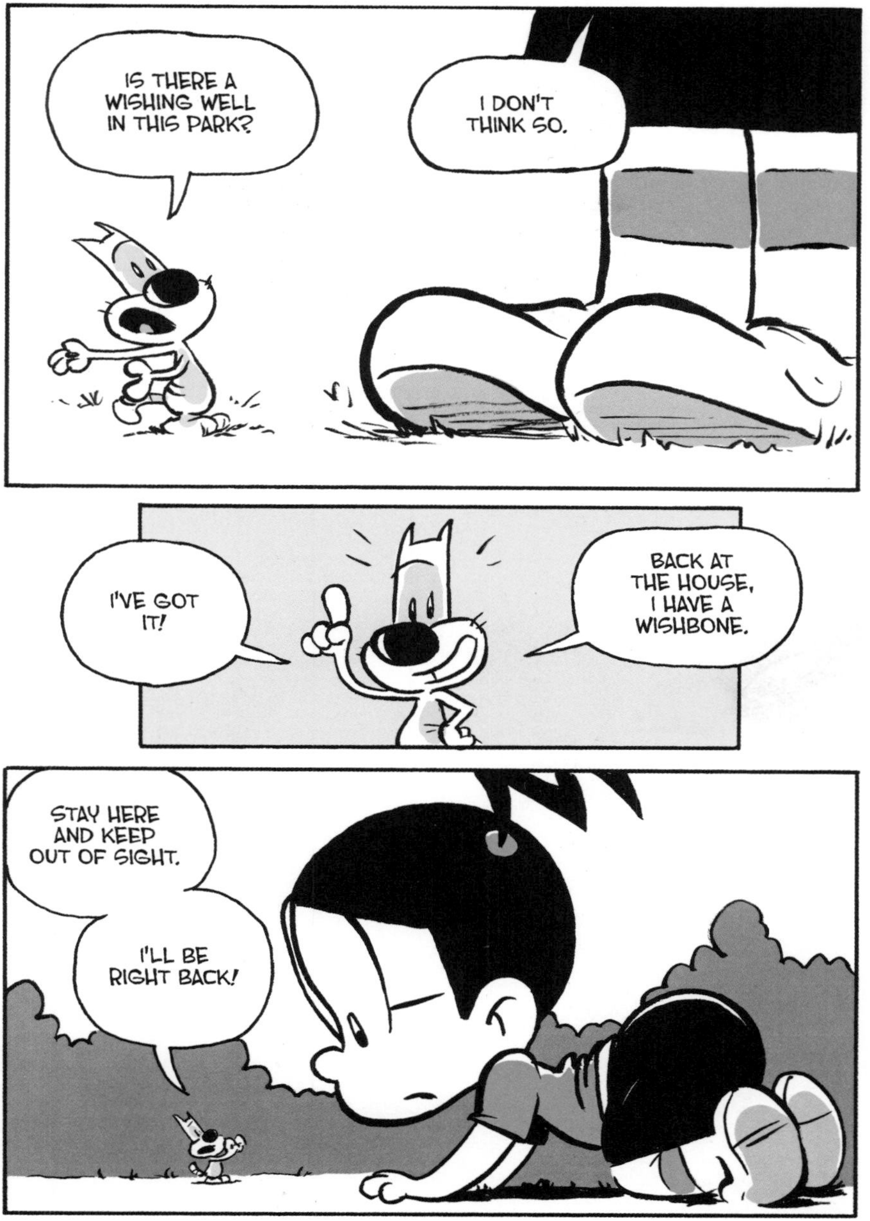
IS THERE A WISHING WELL IN THIS PARK?
I DON'T THINK SO.
I'VE GOT IT!
BACK AT THE HOUSE, I HAVE A WISHBONE.
STAY HERE AND KEEP OUT OF SIGHT.
I'LL BE RIGHT BACK!

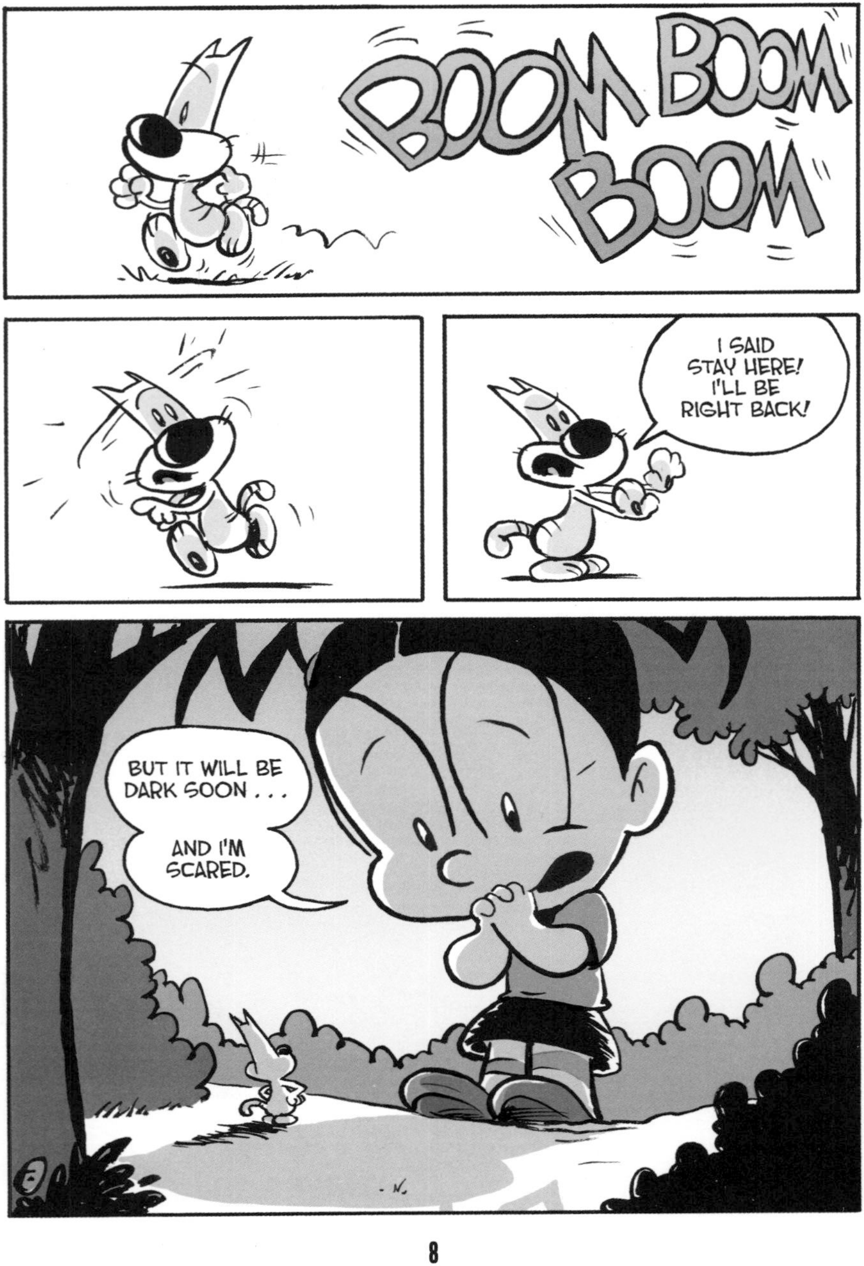
BOOM BOOM BOOM
I SAID STAY HERE! I'LL BE RIGHT BACK!
BUT IT WILL BE DARK SOON . . .
AND I'M SCARED.

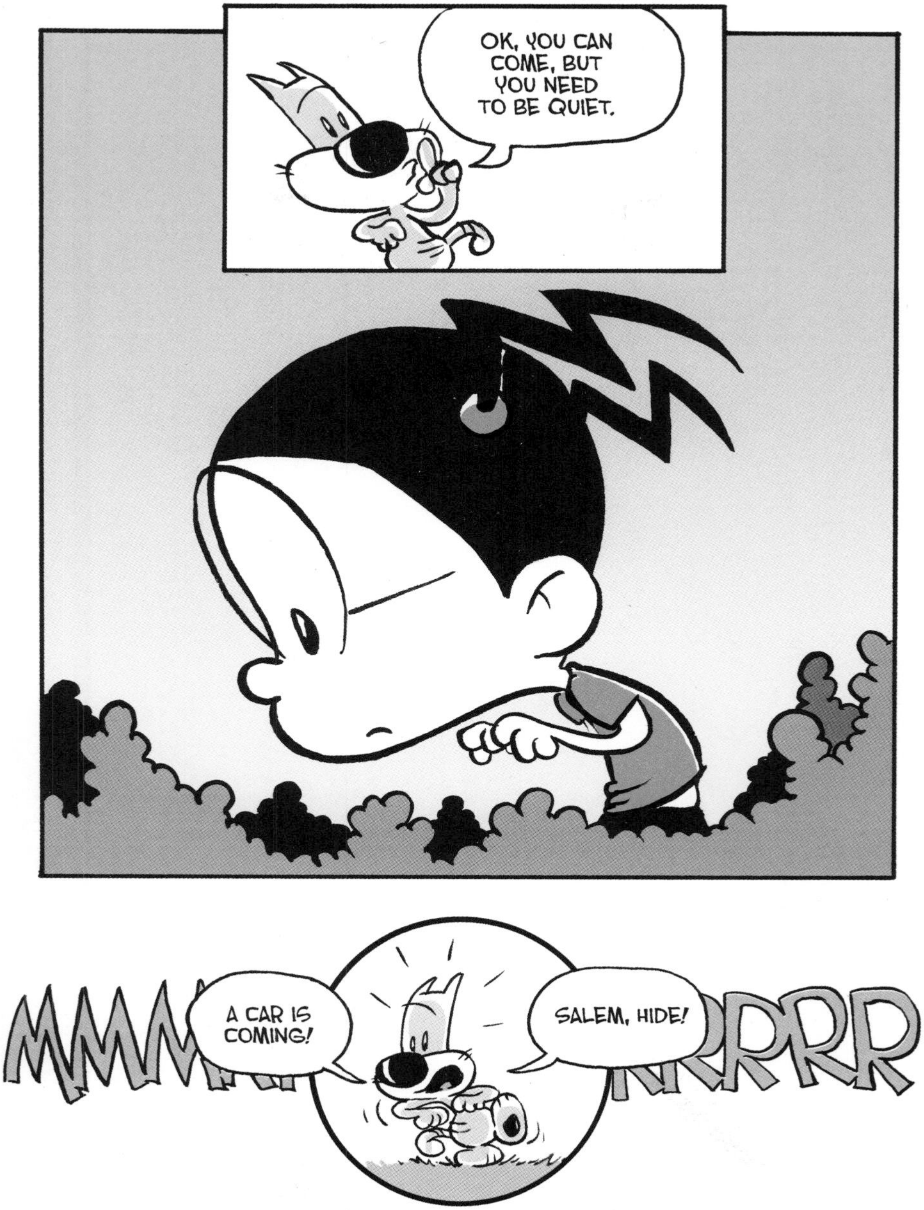
OK, YOU CAN COME, BUT YOU NEED TO BE QUIET.
A CAR IS COMING!
SALEM, HIDE!

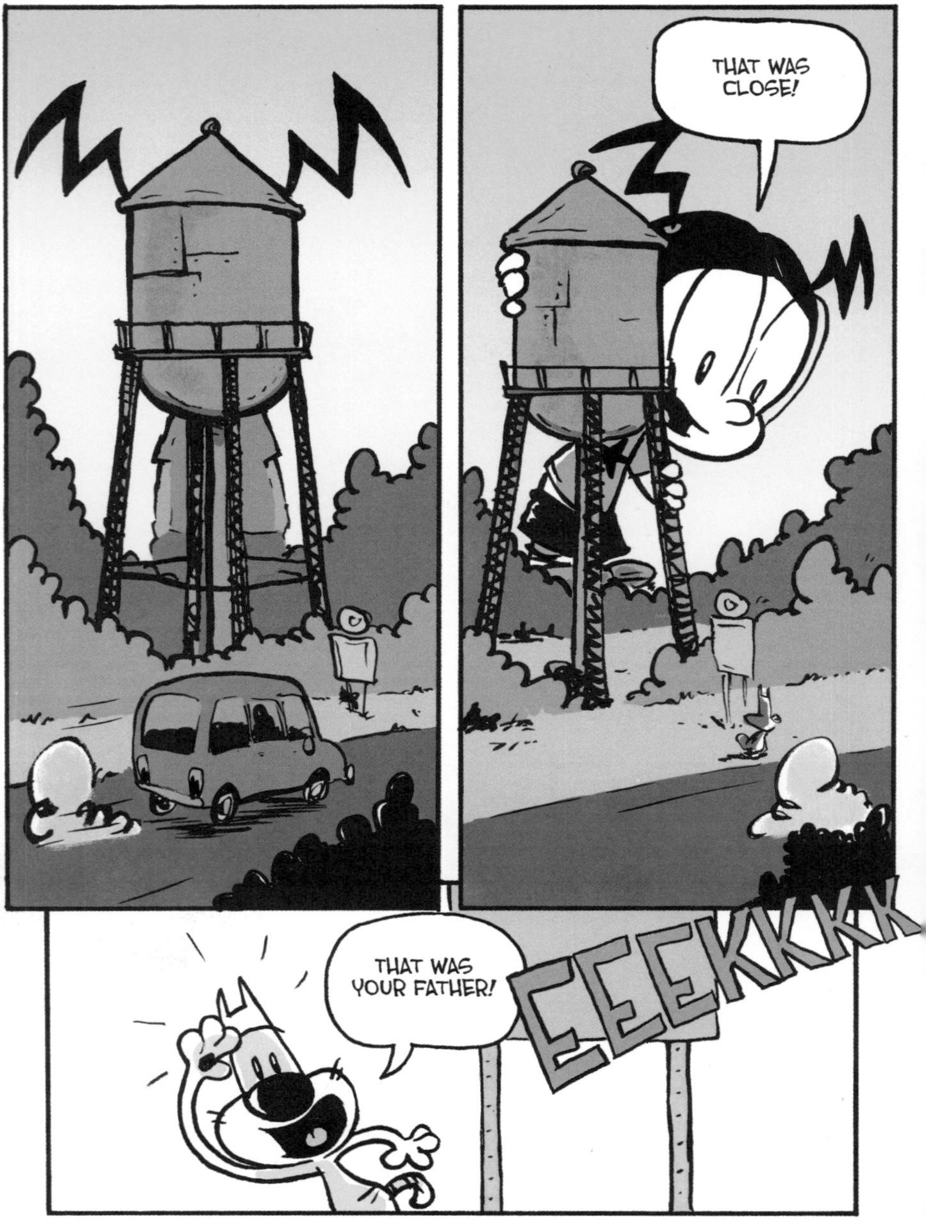
THAT WAS CLOSE!
THAT WAS YOUR FATHER!
EEEKKKK

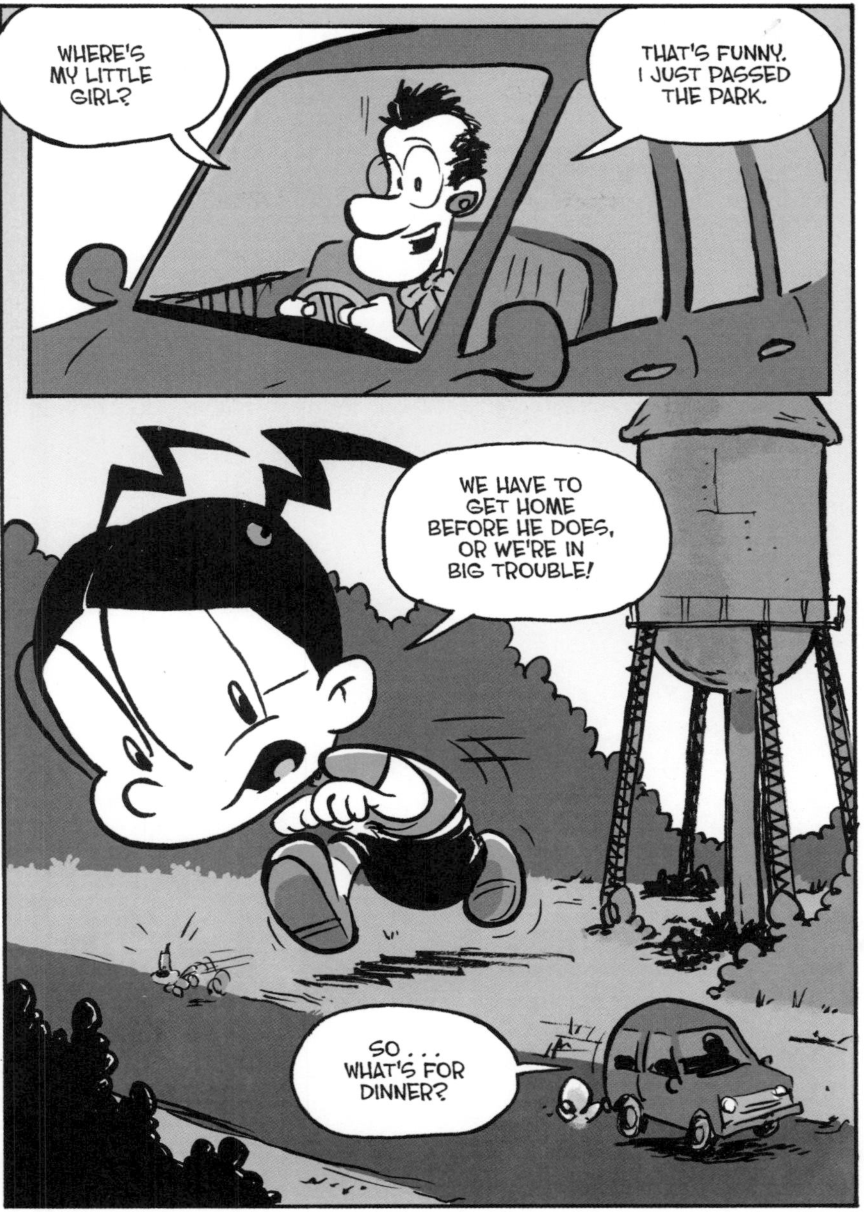
WHERE'S MY LITTLE GIRL?
THAT'S FUNNY. I JUST PASSED THE PARK.
WE HAVE TO GET HOME BEFORE HE DOES, OR WE'RE IN BIG TROUBLE!
SO . . . WHAT'S FOR DINNER?

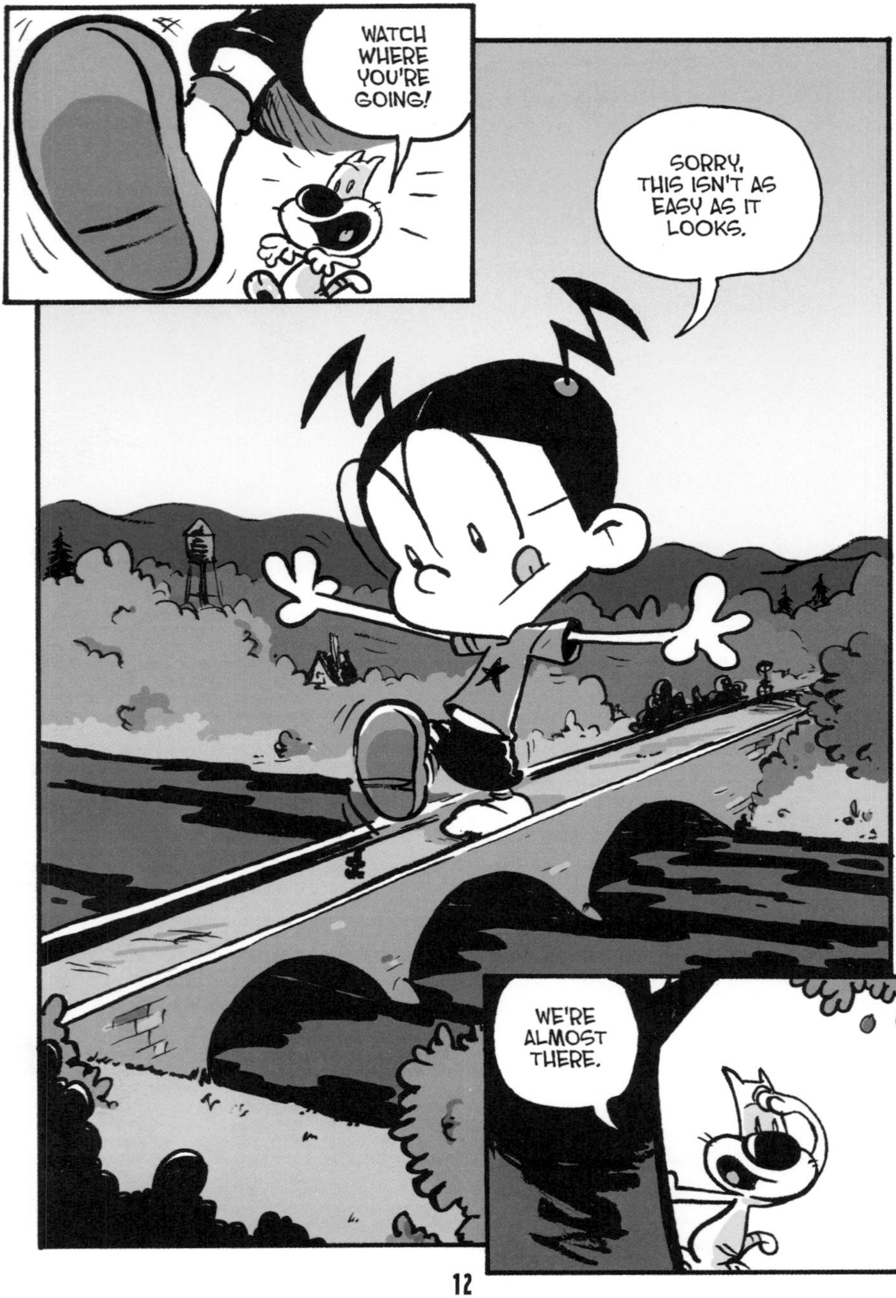
WATCH WHERE YOU'RE GOING!
SORRY, THIS ISN'T AS EASY AS IT LOOKS.
WE'RE ALMOST THERE.

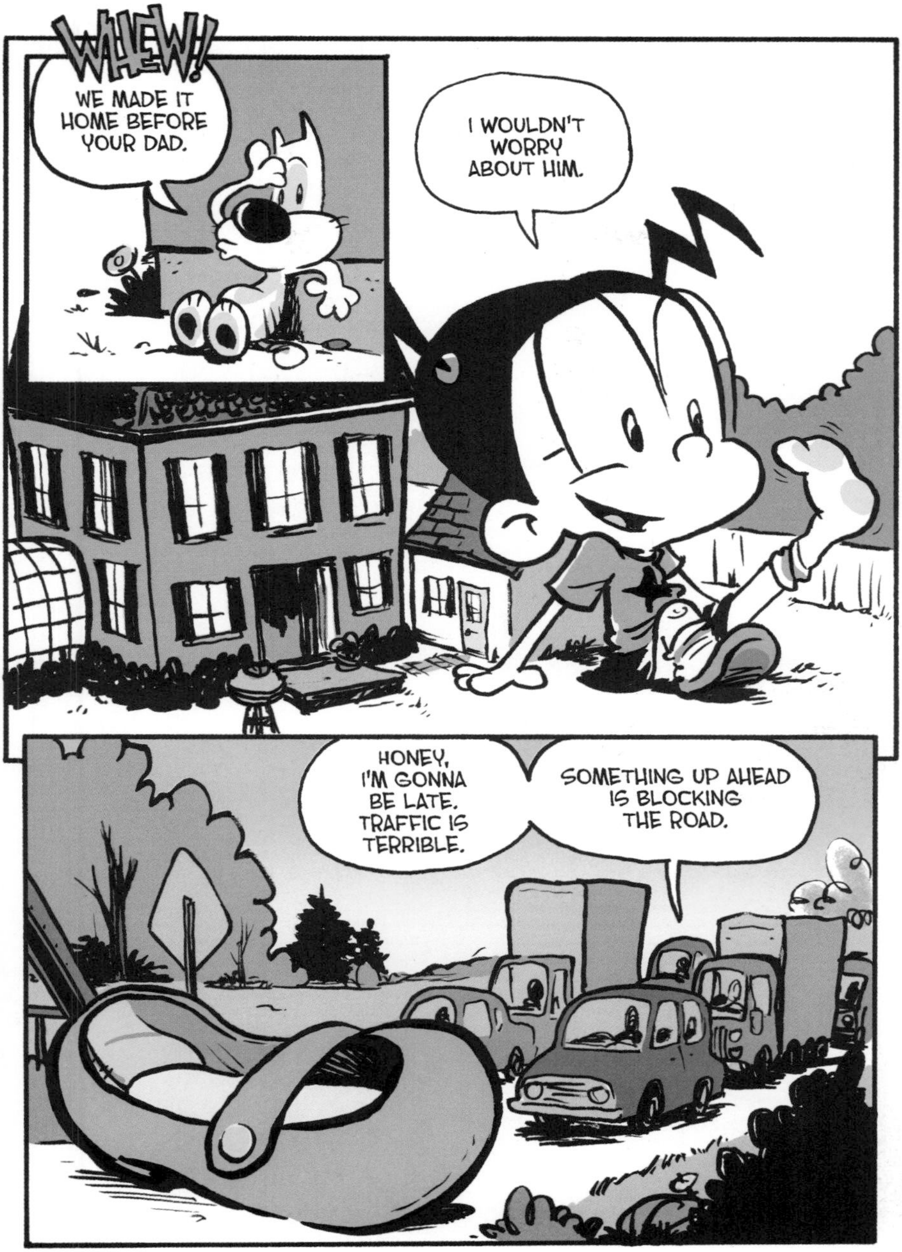
WHEW!
WE MADE IT HOME BEFORE YOUR DAD.
I WOULDN'T WORRY ABOUT HIM.
HONEY, I'M GONNA BE LATE. TRAFFIC IS TERRIBLE.
SOMETHING UP AHEAD IS BLOCKING THE ROAD.

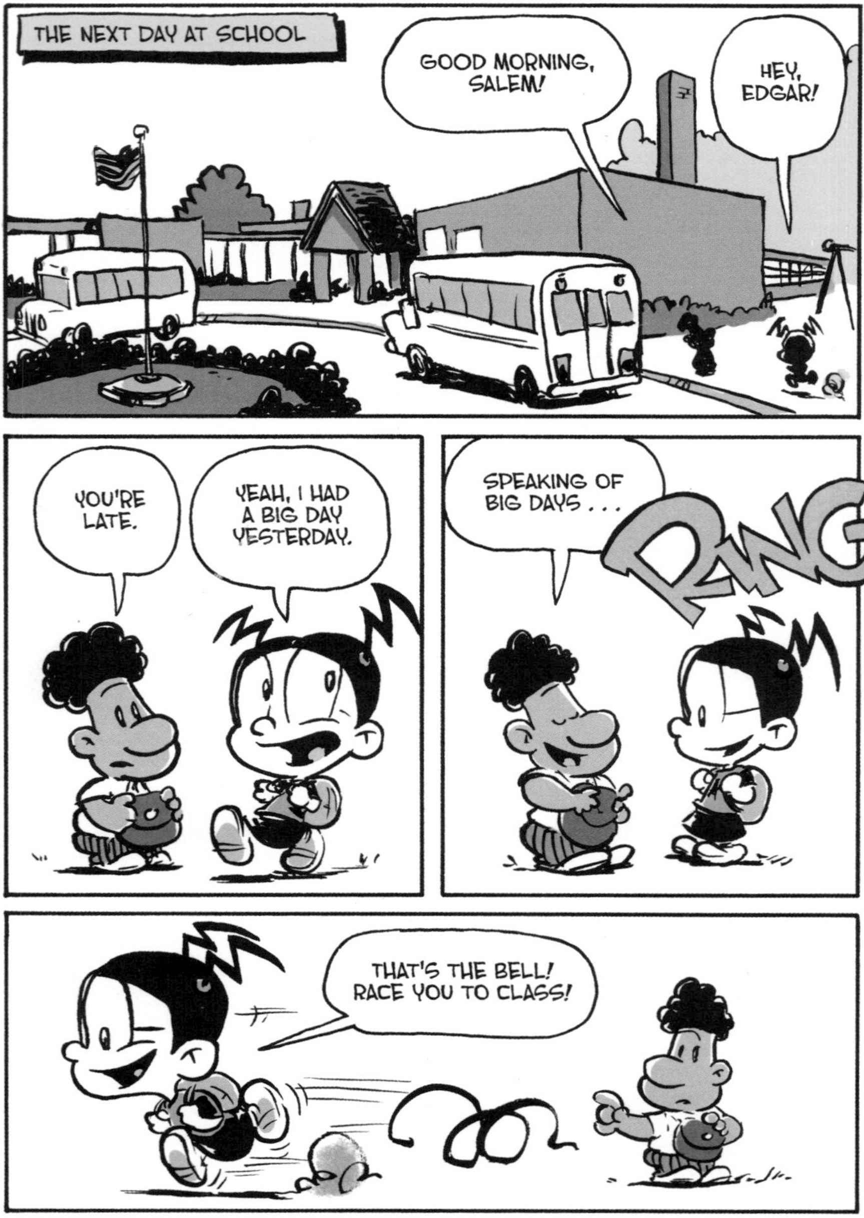
THE NEXT DAY AT SCHOOL
GOOD MORNING, SALEM!
HEY, EDGAR!
YOU'RE LATE.
YEAH, I HAD A BIG DAY YESTERDAY.
SPEAKING OF BIG DAYS . . .
RING
THAT'S THE BELL! RACE YOU TO CLASS!

Getting to Know Edgar

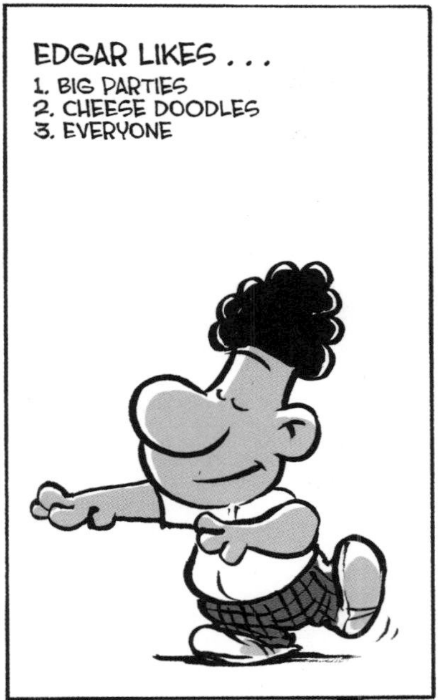
EDGAR LIKES . . .
1. BIG PARTIES
2. CHEESE DOODLES
3. EVERYONE

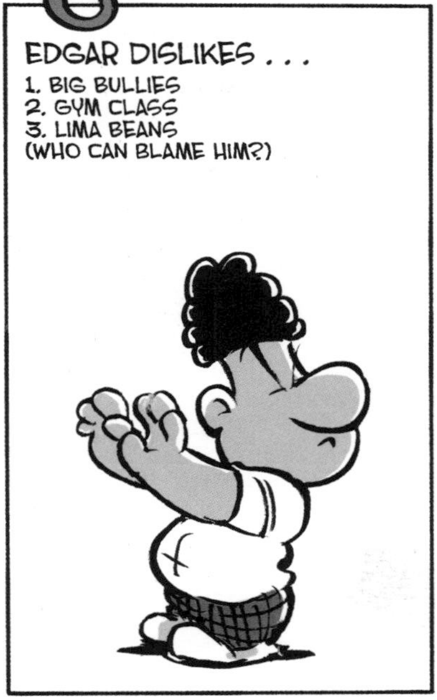
EDGAR DISLIKES . . .
1. BIG BULLIES
2. GYM CLASS
3. LIMA BEANS
(WHO CAN BLAME HIM?)

POWERS

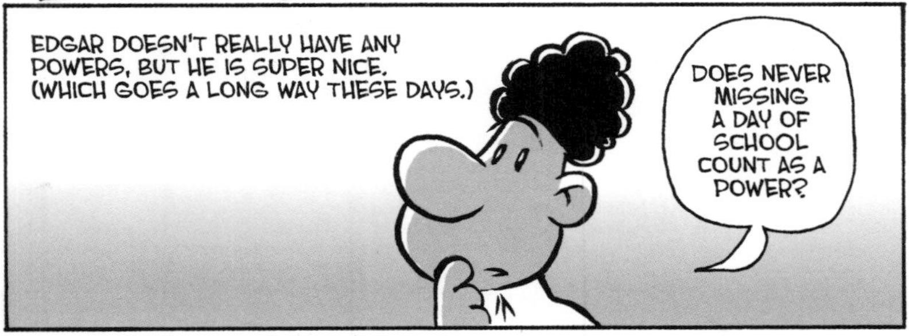
EDGAR DOESN'T REALLY HAVE ANY POWERS, BUT HE IS SUPER NICE. (WHICH GOES A LONG WAY THESE DAYS.)
DOES NEVER MISSING A DAY OF SCHOOL COUNT AS A POWER?

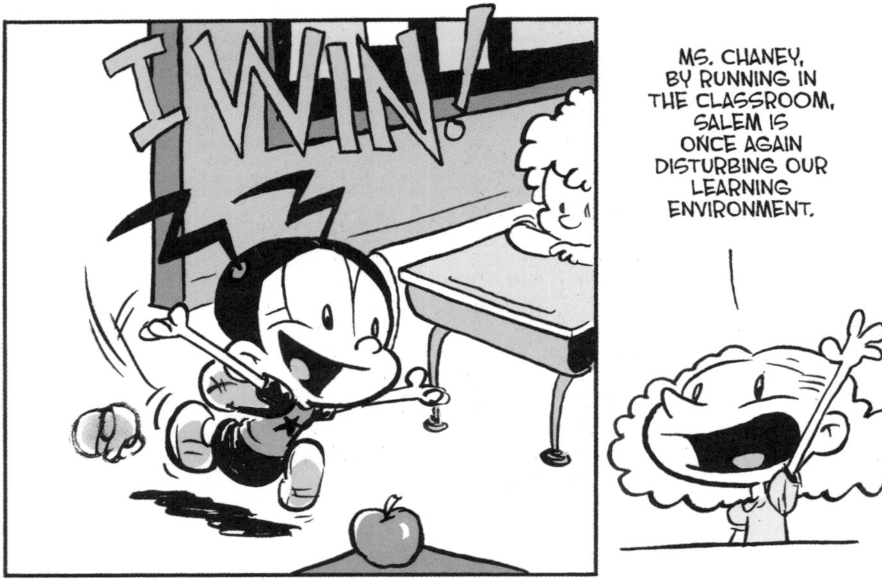
I WIN!
MS. CHANEY, BY RUNNING IN THE CLASSROOM, SALEM IS ONCE AGAIN DISTURBING OUR LEARNING ENVIRONMENT.

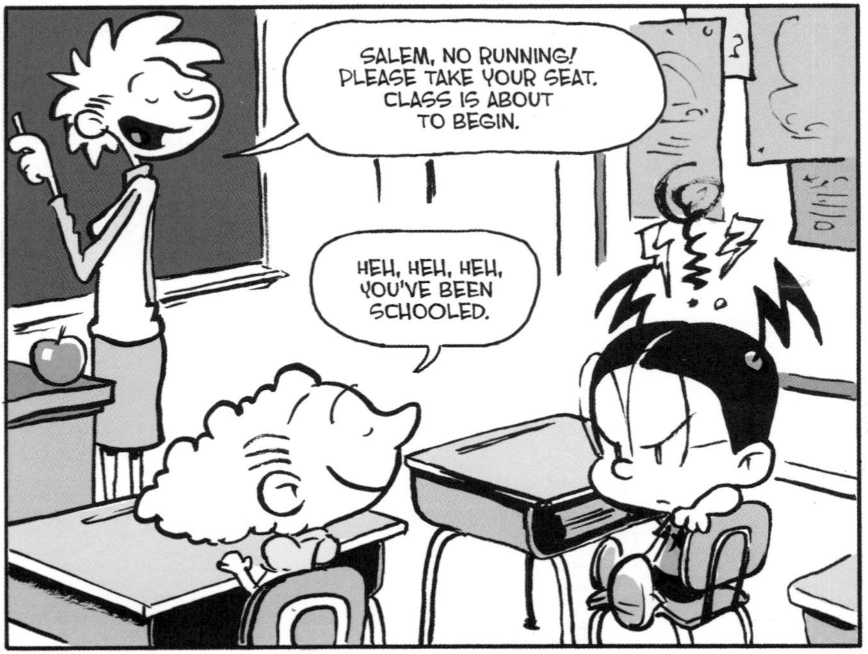
SALEM, NO RUNNING! PLEASE TAKE YOUR SEAT. CLASS IS ABOUT TO BEGIN.
HEH, HEH, HEH, YOU'VE BEEN SCHOOLED.

Getting to KNOW Shelly (AS IF YOU'D WANT TO)

SHELLY LIKES . . .
1. SHELLY
2. BEING THE CENTER OF ATTENTION!
3. TELLING ON OTHER KIDS

SHELLY DISLIKES . . .
1. SALEM
2. SHARING
3. ANYONE WHO ISN'T SHELLY

POWERS

SHELLY HAS THE POWER TO ACT INNOCENT, ESPECIALLY WHEN SHE HAS DONE SOMETHING WRONG.

I'M TELLING ON YOU!

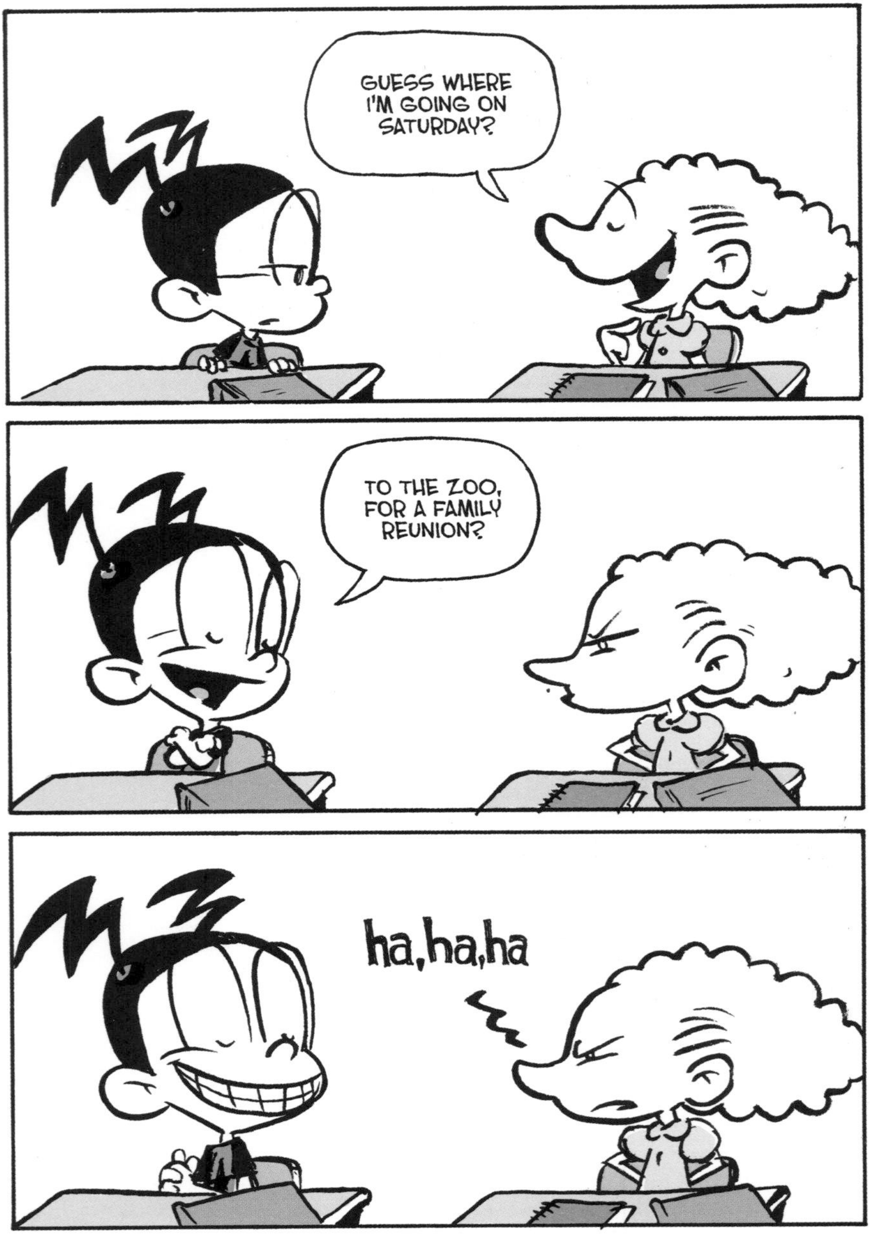
GUESS WHERE I'M GOING ON SATURDAY?
TO THE ZOO, FOR A FAMILY REUNION?
ha,ha,ha

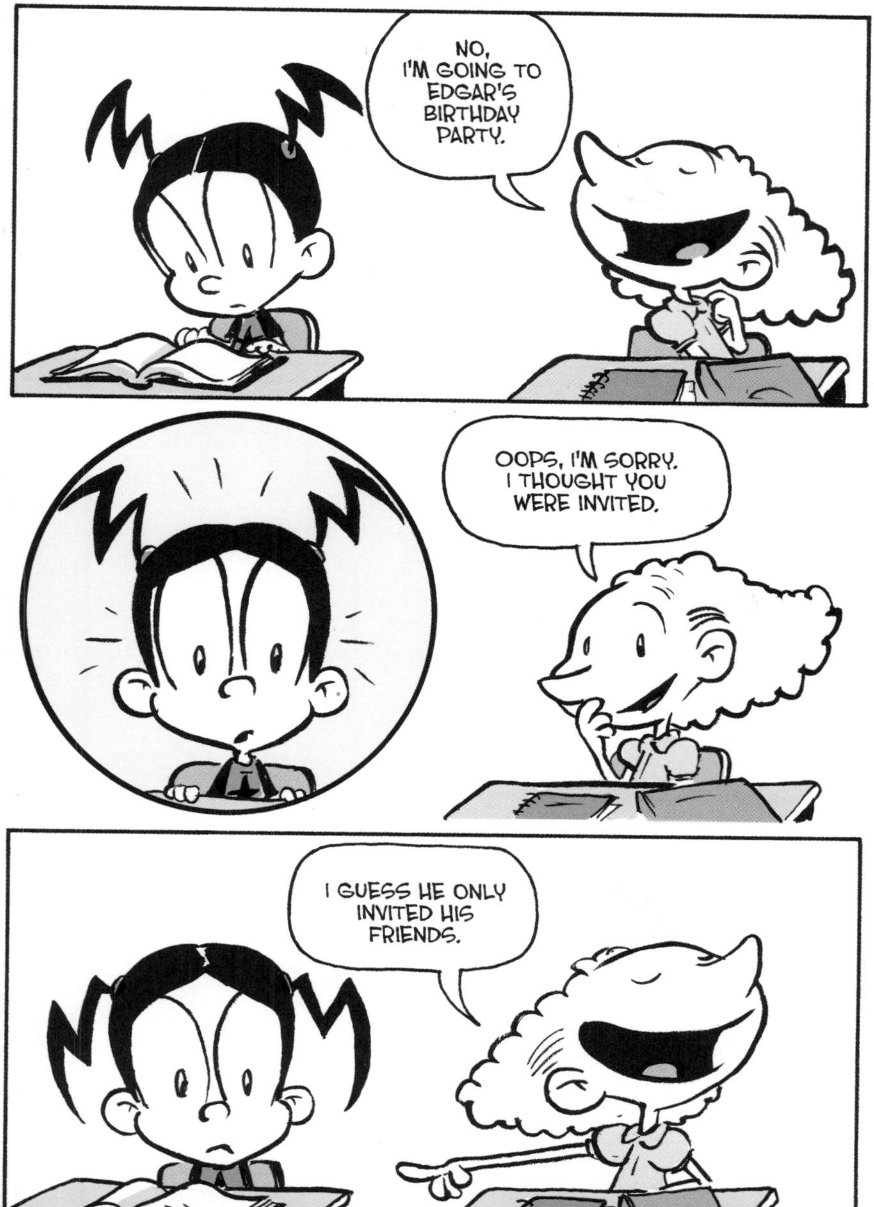
NO, I'M GOING TO EDGAR'S BIRTHDAY PARTY.
OOPS, I'M SORRY. I THOUGHT YOU WERE INVITED.
I GUESS HE ONLY INVITED HIS FRIENDS.

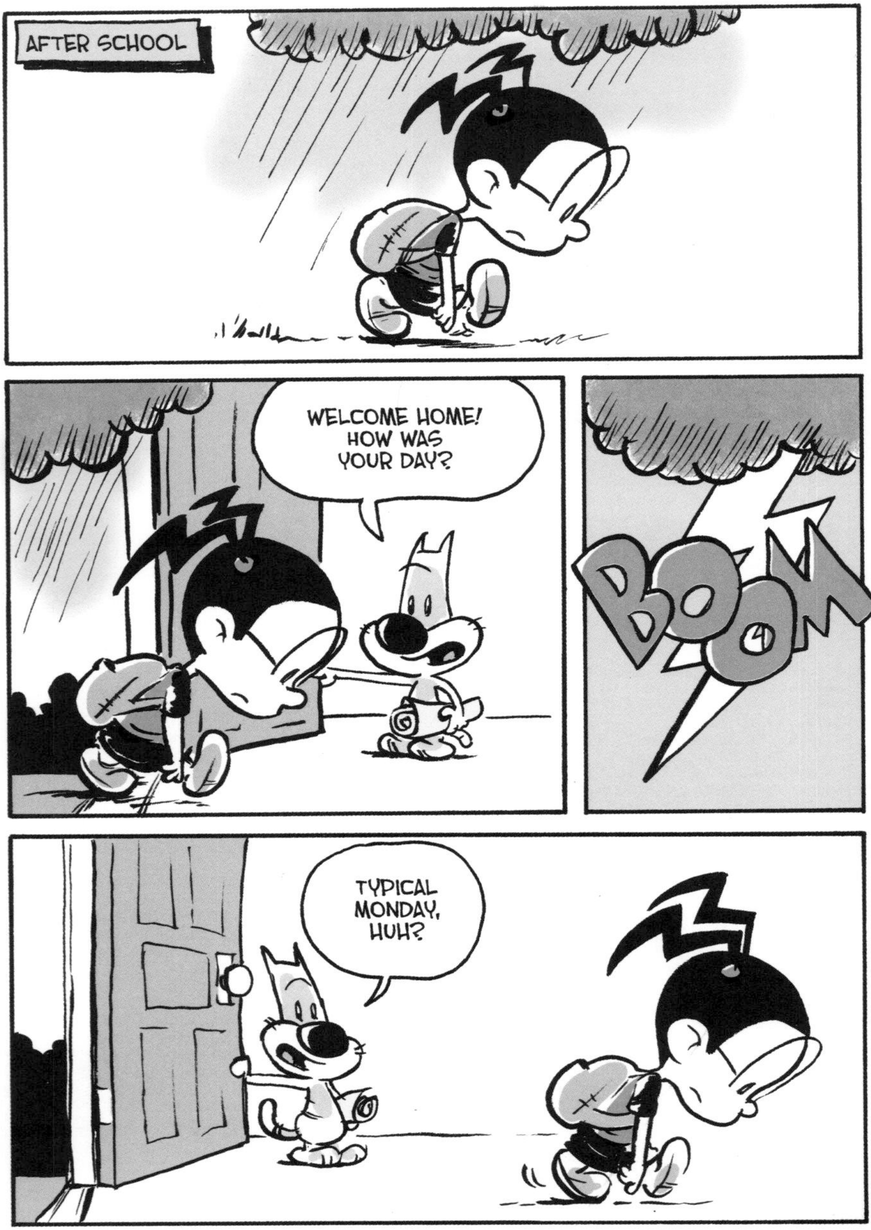
AFTER SCHOOL
WELCOME HOME! HOW WAS YOUR DAY?
BOOM
TYPICAL MONDAY, HUH?

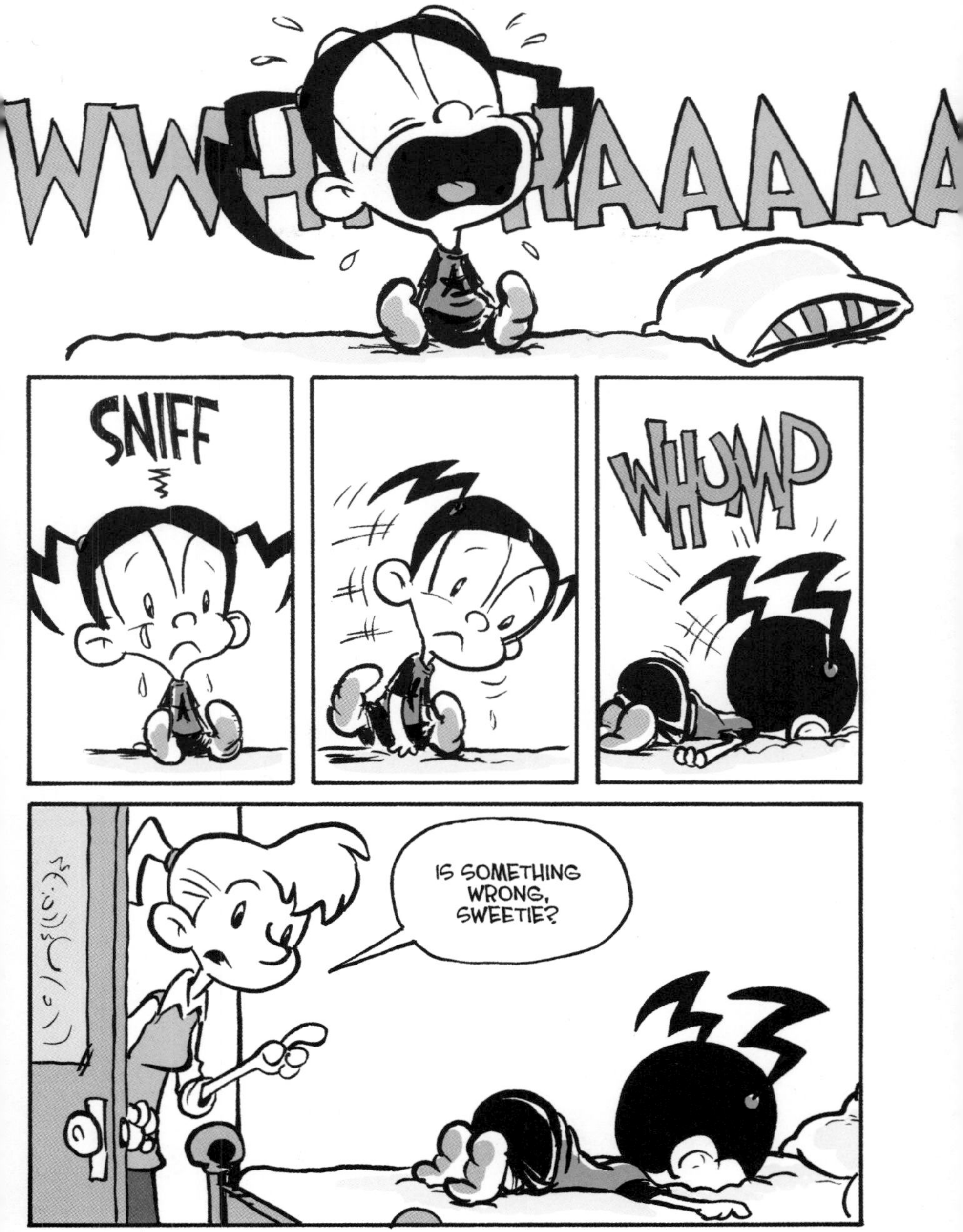
WWHHAAAAAA
SNIFF
WHUMP
IS SOMETHING WRONG, SWEETIE?

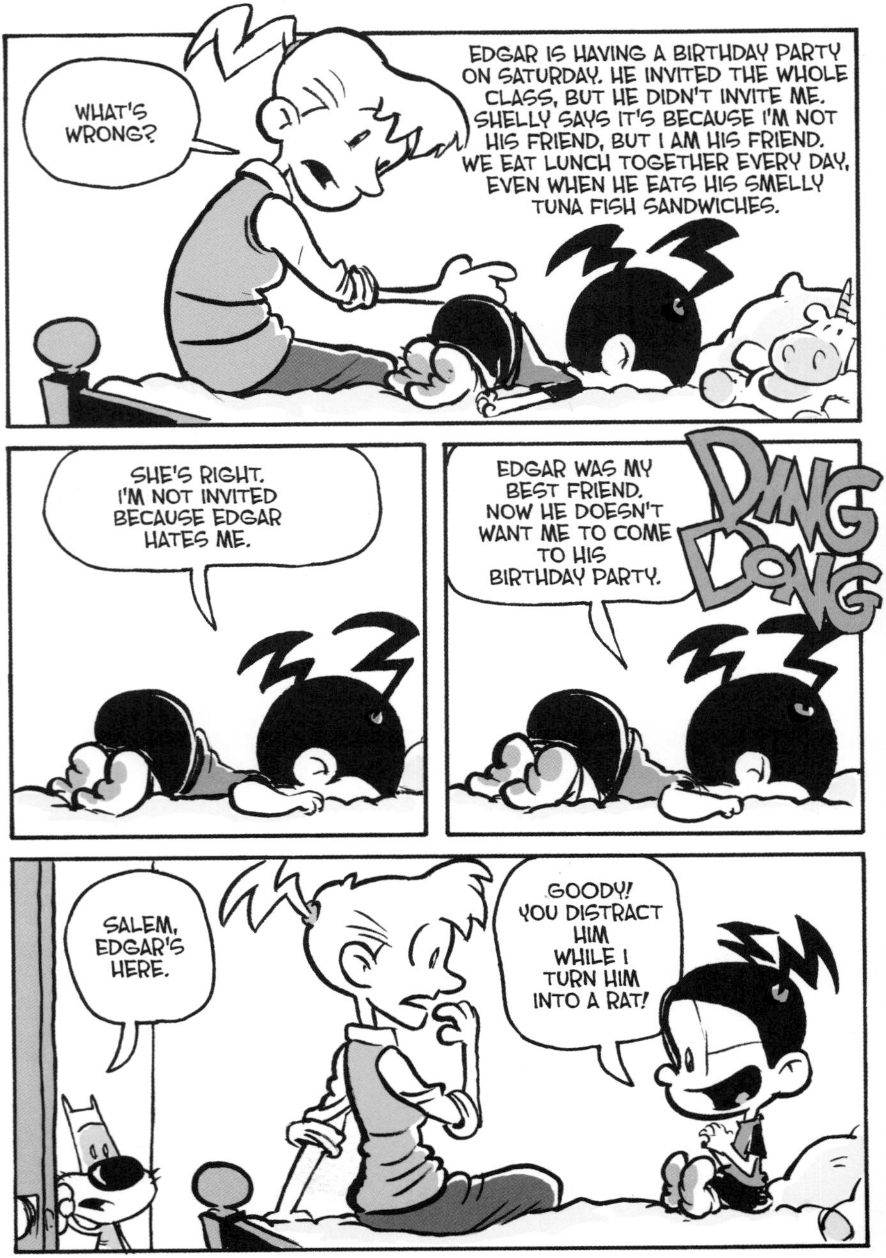
EDGAR IS HAVING A BIRTHDAY PARTY ON SATURDAY. HE INVITED THE WHOLE CLASS, BUT HE DIDN'T INVITE ME. SHELLY SAYS IT'S BECAUSE I'M NOT HIS FRIEND, BUT I AM HIS FRIEND. WE EAT LUNCH TOGETHER EVERY DAY, EVEN WHEN HE EATS HIS SMELLY TUNA FISH SANDWICHES.
WHAT'S WRONG?
SHE'S RIGHT. I'M NOT INVITED BECAUSE EDGAR HATES ME.
EDGAR WAS MY BEST FRIEND. NOW HE DOESN'T WANT ME TO COME TO HIS BIRTHDAY PARTY.
DING DONG
SALEM, EDGAR'S HERE.
GOODY! YOU DISTRACT HIM WHILE I TURN HIM INTO A RAT!

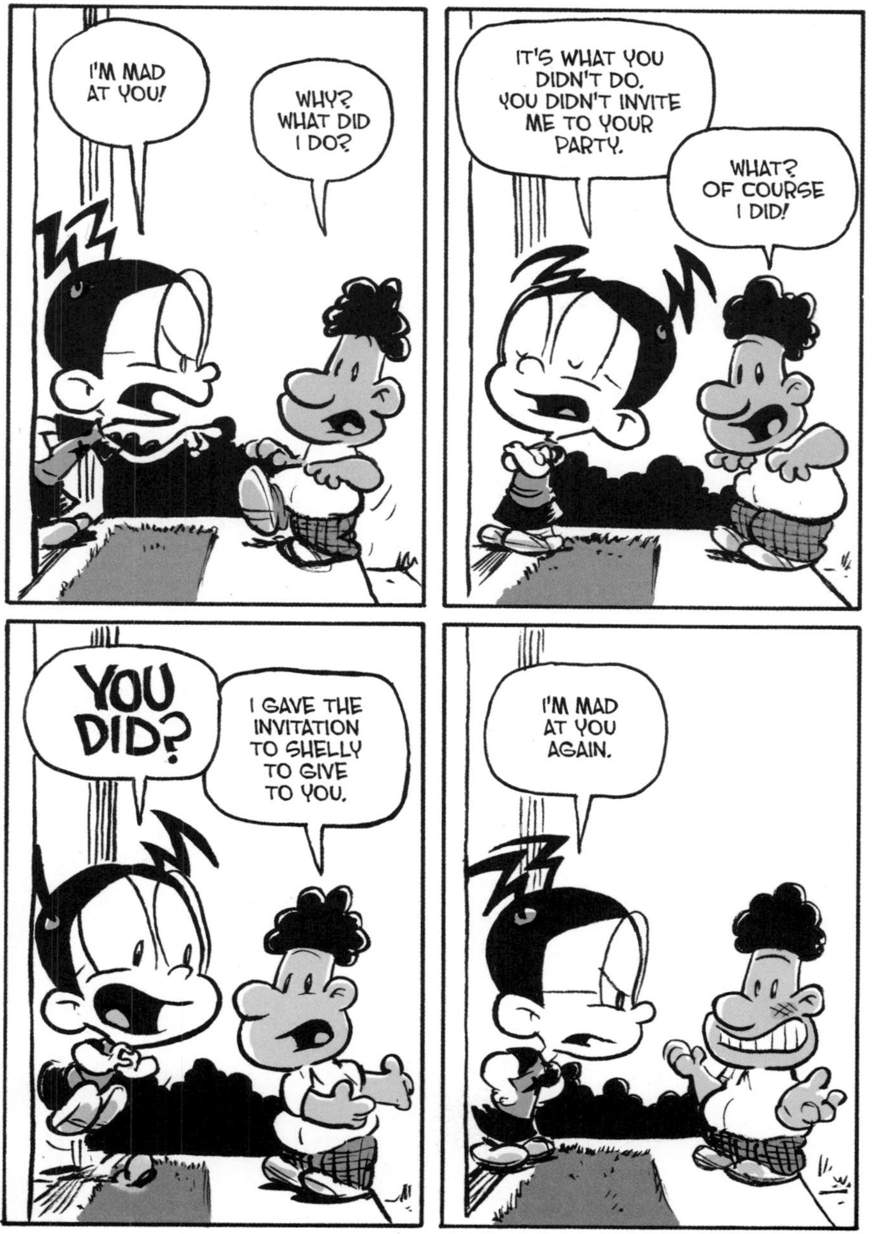
I'M MAD AT YOU!
WHY? WHAT DID I DO?
IT'S WHAT YOU DIDN'T DO. YOU DIDN'T INVITE ME TO YOUR PARTY.
WHAT? OF COURSE I DID!
YOU DID?
I GAVE THE INVITATION TO SHELLY TO GIVE TO YOU.
I'M MAD AT YOU AGAIN.

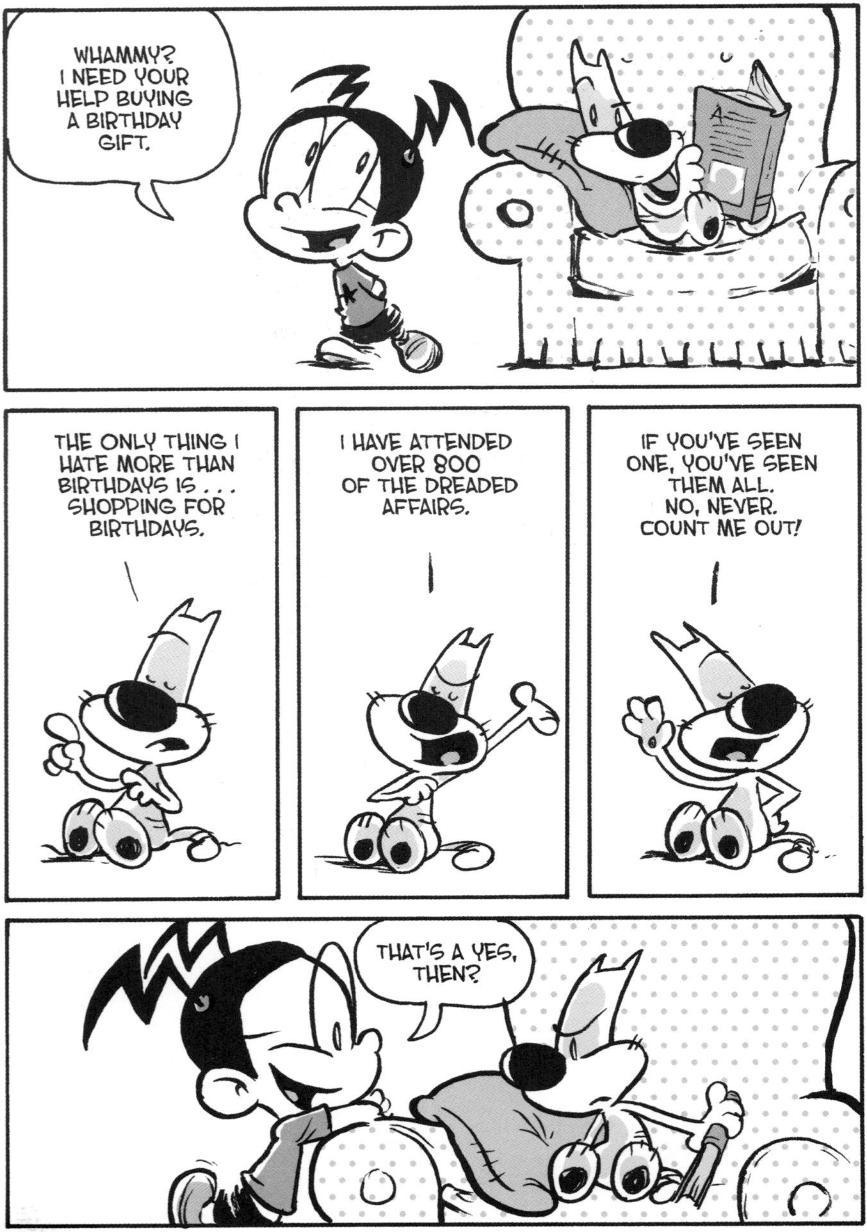
WHAMMY? I NEED YOUR HELP BUYING A BIRTHDAY GIFT.
THE ONLY THING I HATE MORE THAN BIRTHDAYS IS . . . SHOPPING FOR BIRTHDAYS.
I HAVE ATTENDED OVER 800 OF THE DREADED AFFAIRS.
IF YOU'VE SEEN ONE, YOU'VE SEEN THEM ALL. NO, NEVER. COUNT ME OUT!
THAT'S A YES, THEN?

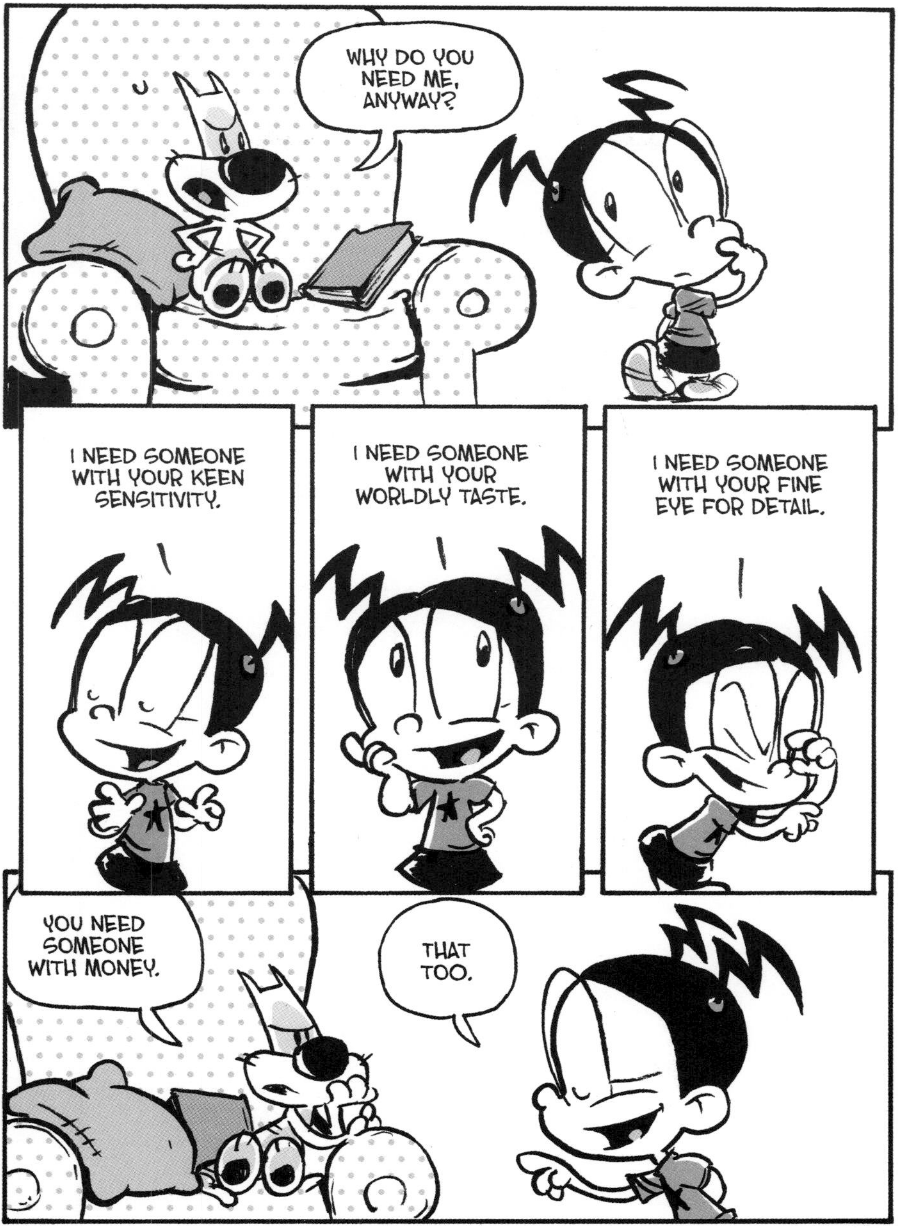
WHY DO YOU NEED ME, ANYWAY?
I NEED SOMEONE WITH YOUR KEEN SENSITIVITY.
I NEED SOMEONE WITH YOUR WORLDLY TASTE.
I NEED SOMEONE WITH YOUR FINE EYE FOR DETAIL.
YOU NEED SOMEONE WITH MONEY.
THAT TOO.

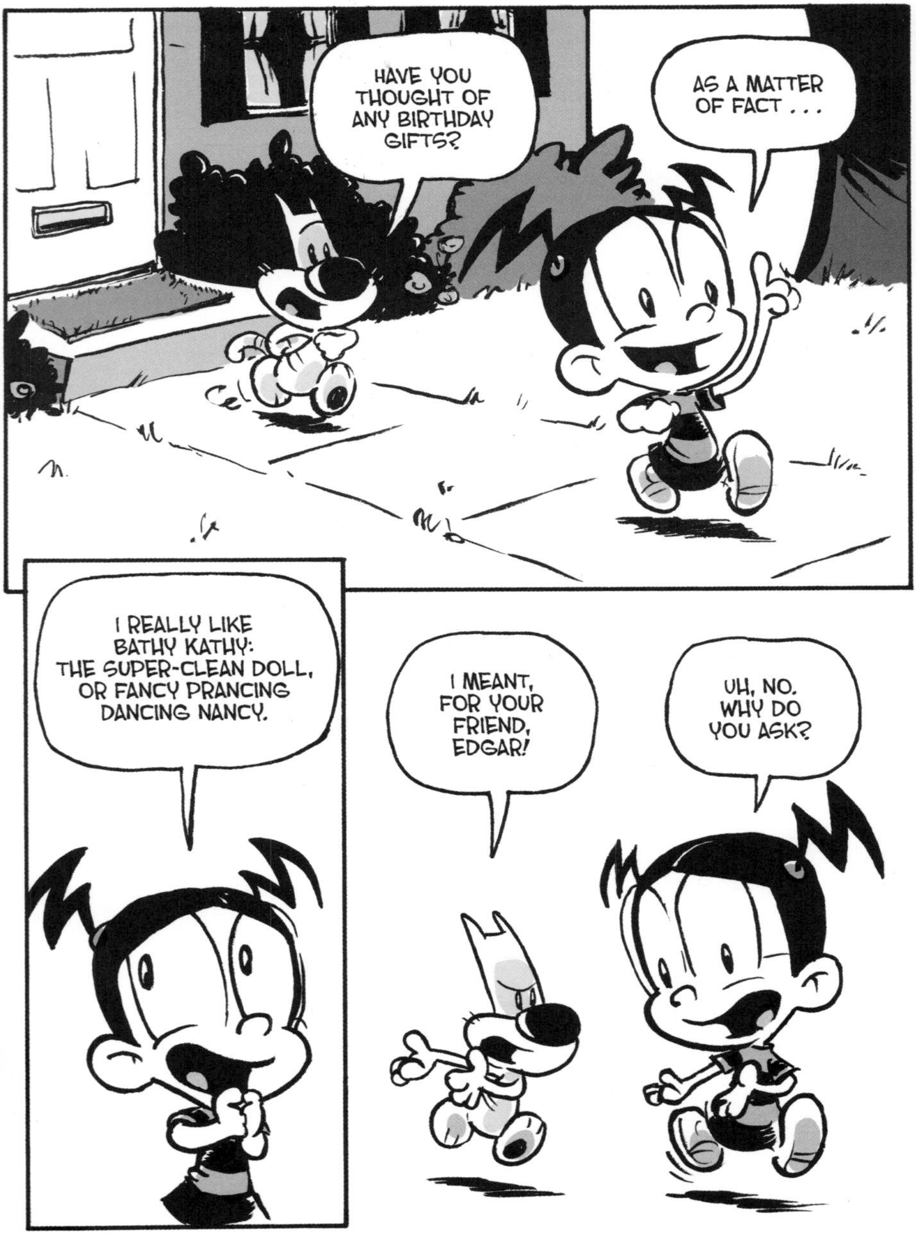
HAVE YOU THOUGHT OF ANY BIRTHDAY GIFTS?
AS A MATTER OF FACT . . .
I REALLY LIKE BATHY KATHY: THE SUPER-CLEAN DOLL, OR FANCY PRANCING DANCING NANCY.
UH, NO. WHY DO YOU ASK?
I MEANT, FOR YOUR FRIEND, EDGAR!

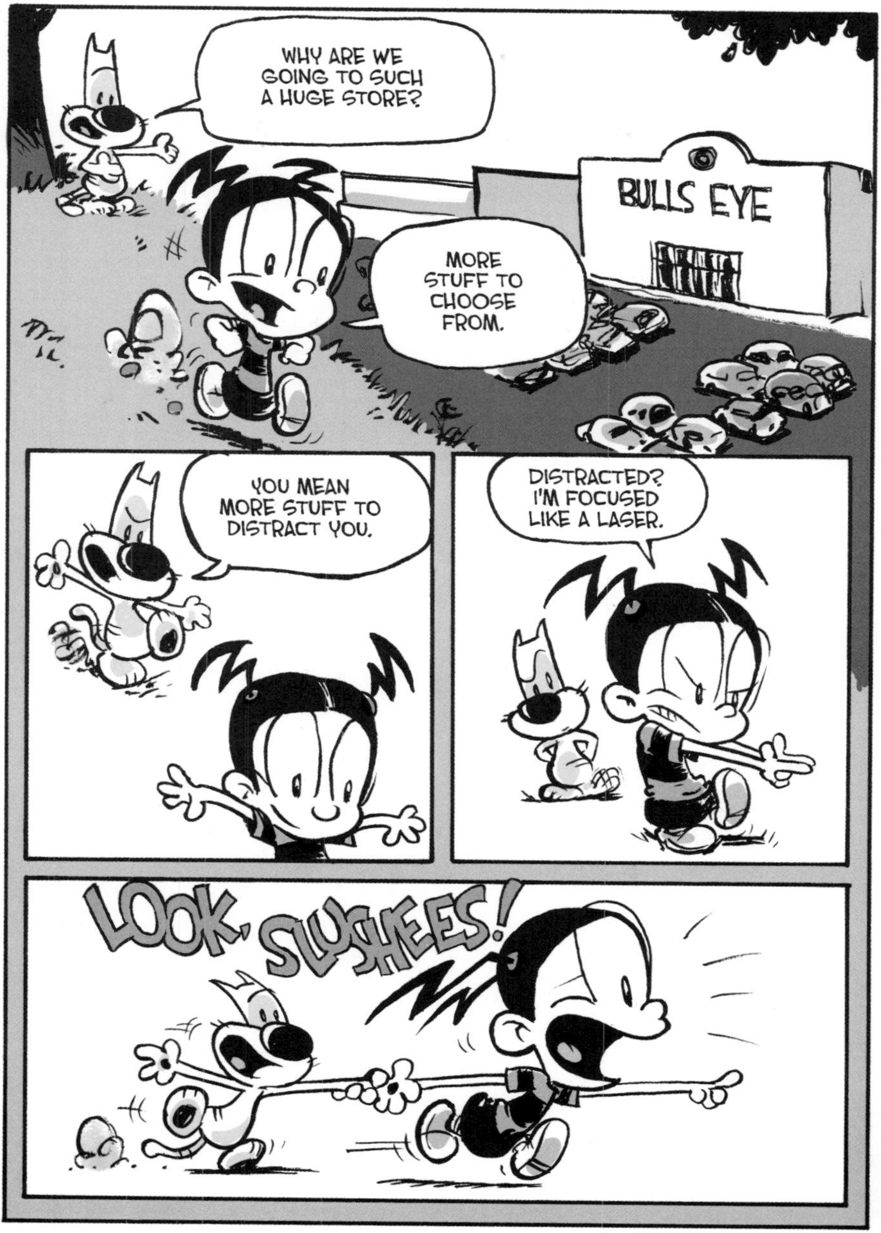
WHY ARE WE GOING TO SUCH A HUGE STORE?
BULLS EYE
MORE STUFF TO CHOOSE FROM.
YOU MEAN MORE STUFF TO DISTRACT YOU.
DISTRACTED? I'M FOCUSED LIKE A LASER.
LOOK, SLUSHEES!

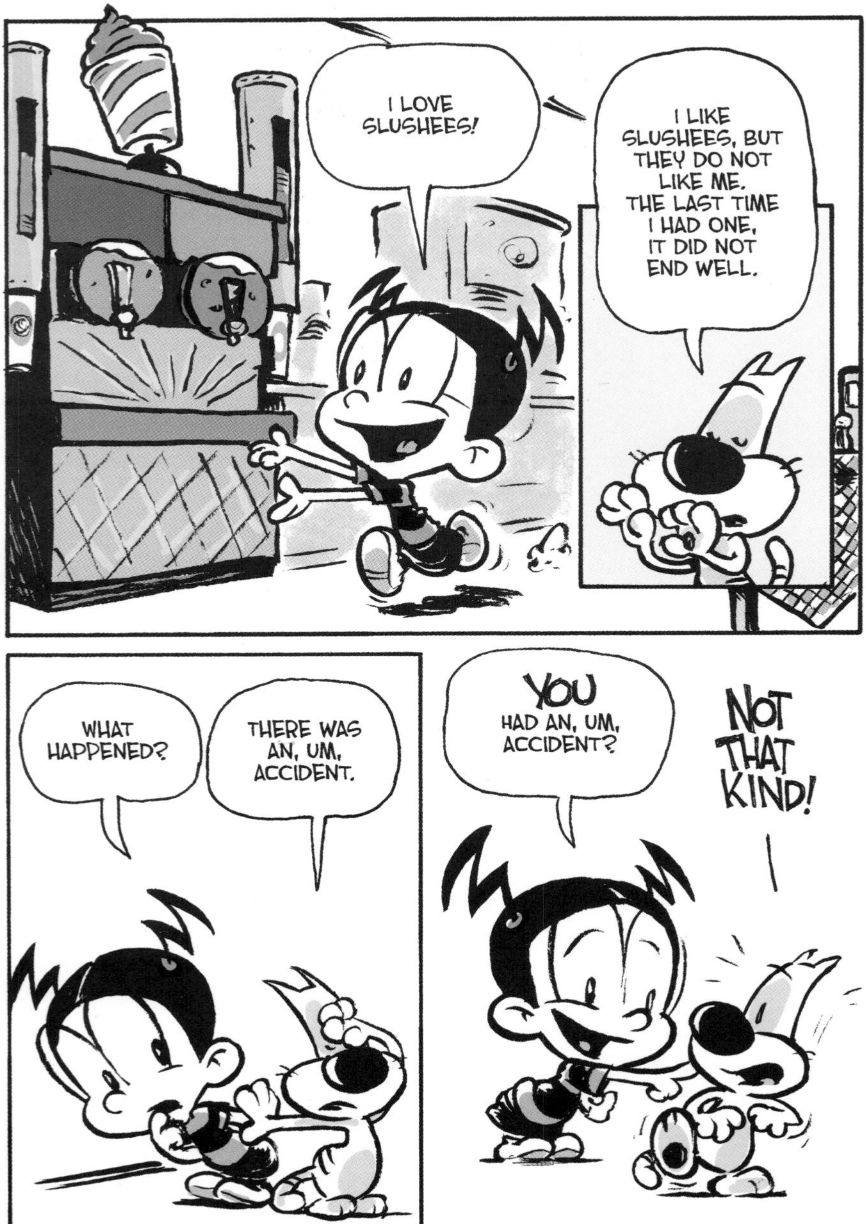
I LOVE SLUSHEES!
I LIKE SLUSHEES, BUT THEY DO NOT LIKE ME. THE LAST TIME I HAD ONE, IT DID NOT END WELL.
WHAT HAPPENED?
THERE WAS AN, UM, ACCIDENT.
YOU HAD AN, UM, ACCIDENT?
NOT THAT KIND!

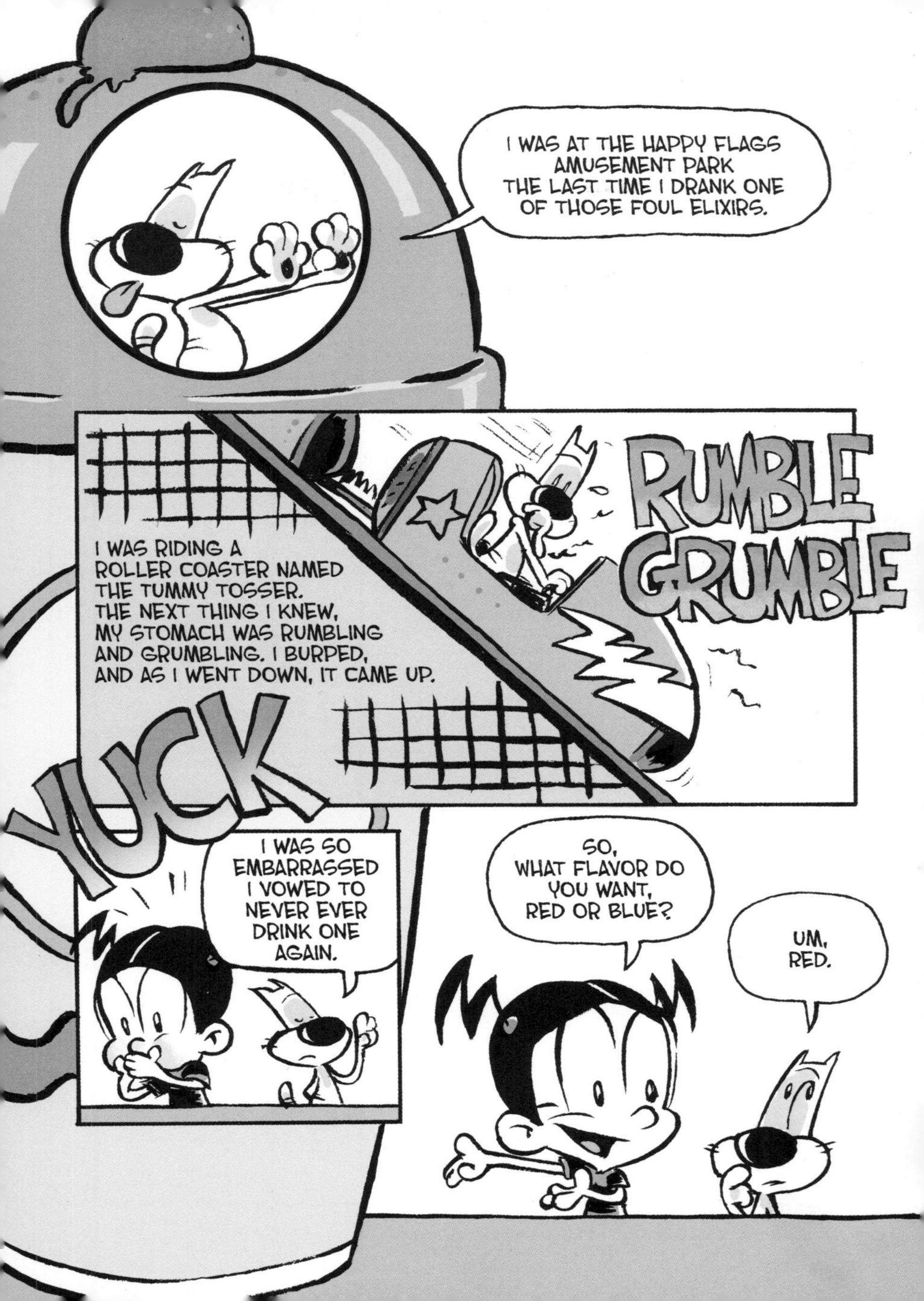
I WAS AT THE HAPPY FLAGS AMUSEMENT PARK THE LAST TIME I DRANK ONE OF THOSE FOUL ELIXIRS.
RUMBLE
GRUMBLE
I WAS RIDING A ROLLER COASTER NAMED THE TUMMY TOSSER. THE NEXT THING I KNEW, MY STOMACH WAS RUMBLING AND GRUMBLING. I BURPED, AND AS I WENT DOWN, IT CAME UP.
YUCK
I WAS SO EMBARRASSED I VOWED TO NEVER EVER DRINK ONE AGAIN.
SO, WHAT FLAVOR DO YOU WANT, RED OR BLUE?
UM, RED.

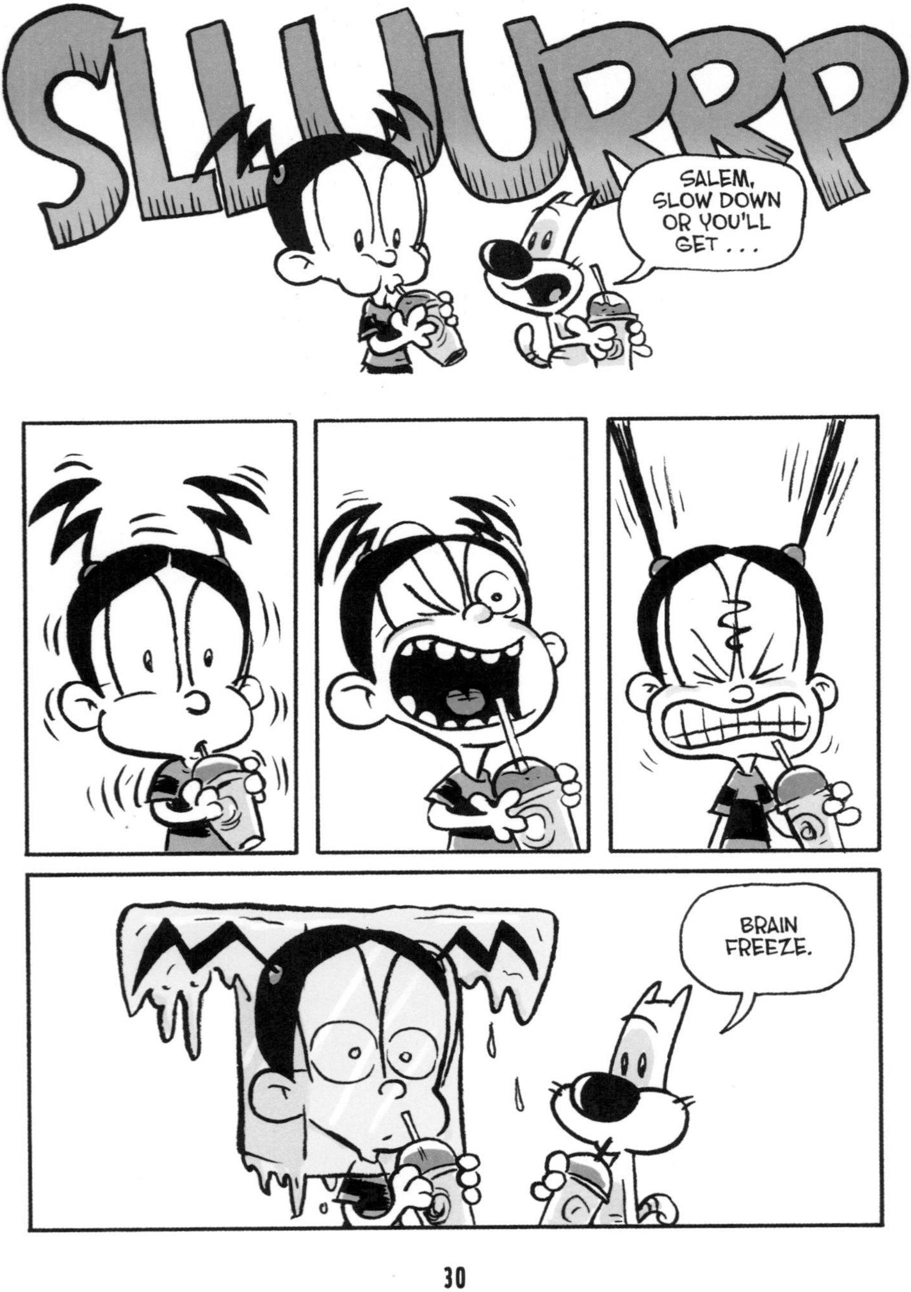
SLLLUURRRP
SALEM, SLOW DOWN OR YOU'LL GET . . .
BRAIN FREEZE.

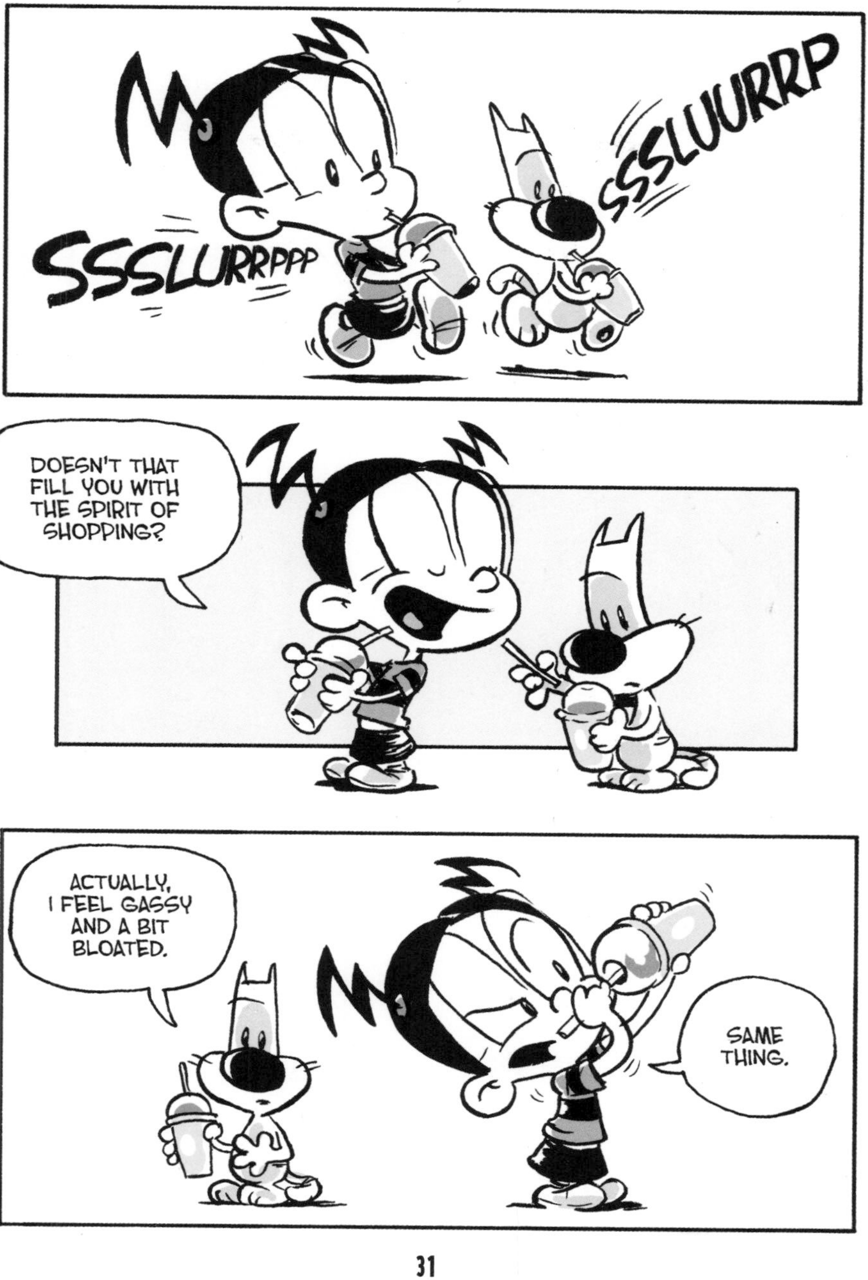
SSSLURRPPP
SSSLUURRP
DOESN'T THAT FILL YOU WITH THE SPIRIT OF SHOPPING?
ACTUALLY, I FEEL GASSY AND A BIT BLOATED.
SAME THING.

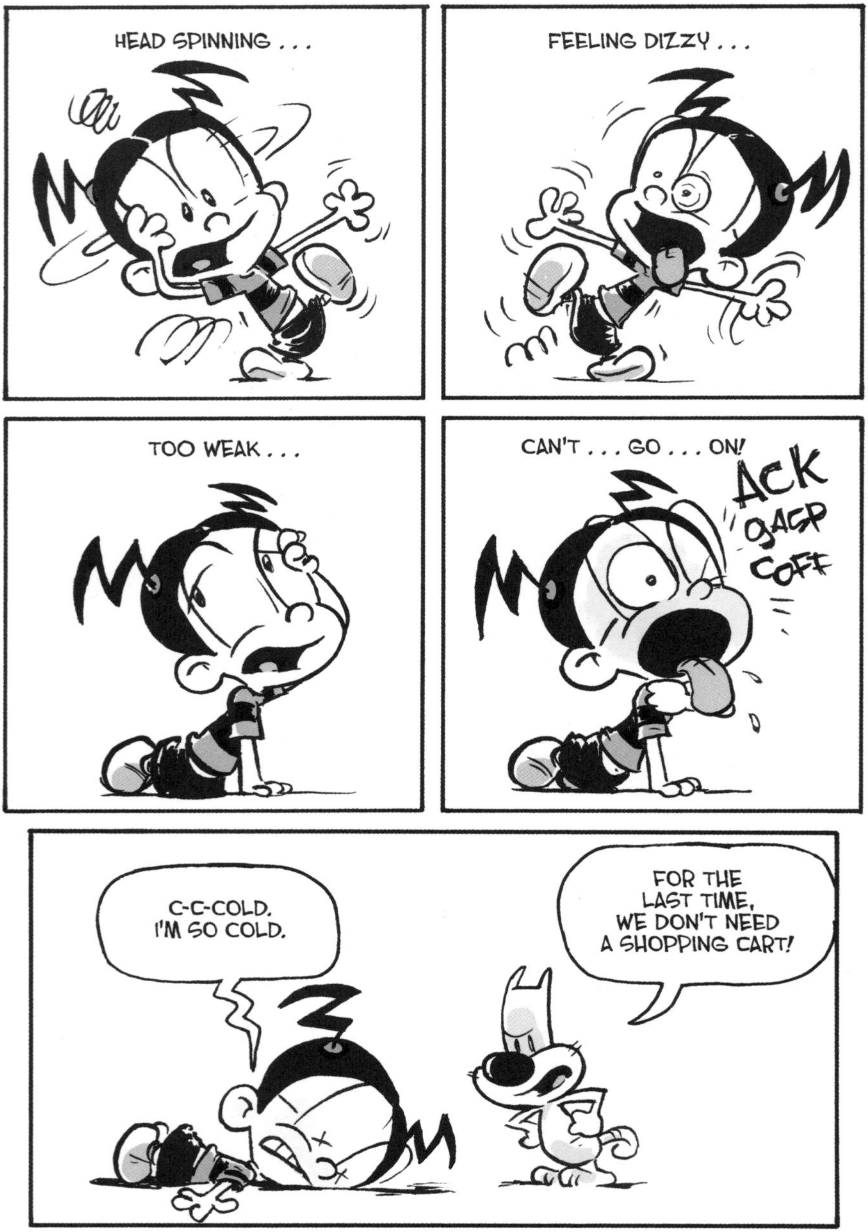
HEAD SPINNING . . .
FEELING DIZZY . . .
TOO WEAK . . .
CAN'T . . . GO . . . ON!
ACK
GASP
COFF
C-C-COLD. I'M SO COLD.
FOR THE LAST TIME, WE DON'T NEED A SHOPPING CART!

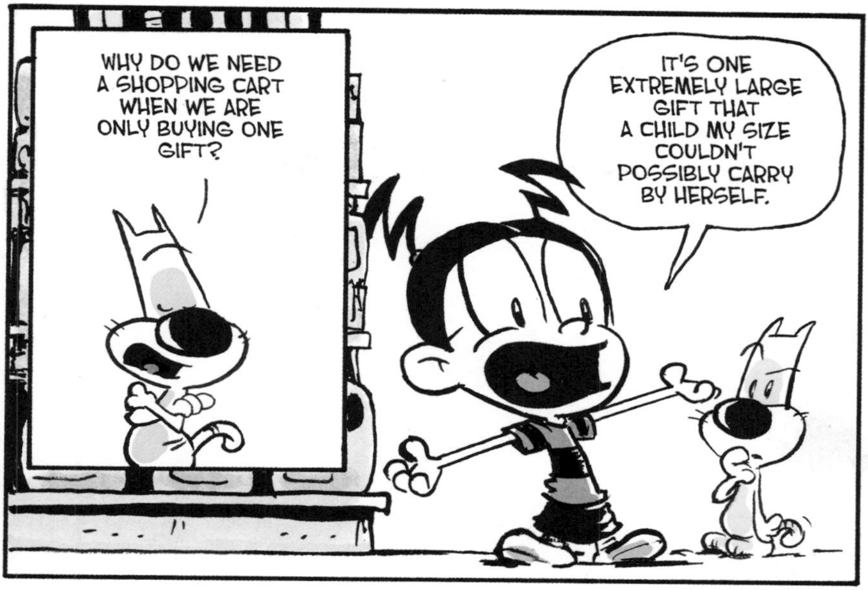
WHY DO WE NEED A SHOPPING CART WHEN WE ARE ONLY BUYING ONE GIFT?
IT'S ONE EXTREMELY LARGE GIFT THAT A CHILD MY SIZE COULDN'T POSSIBLY CARRY BY HERSELF.

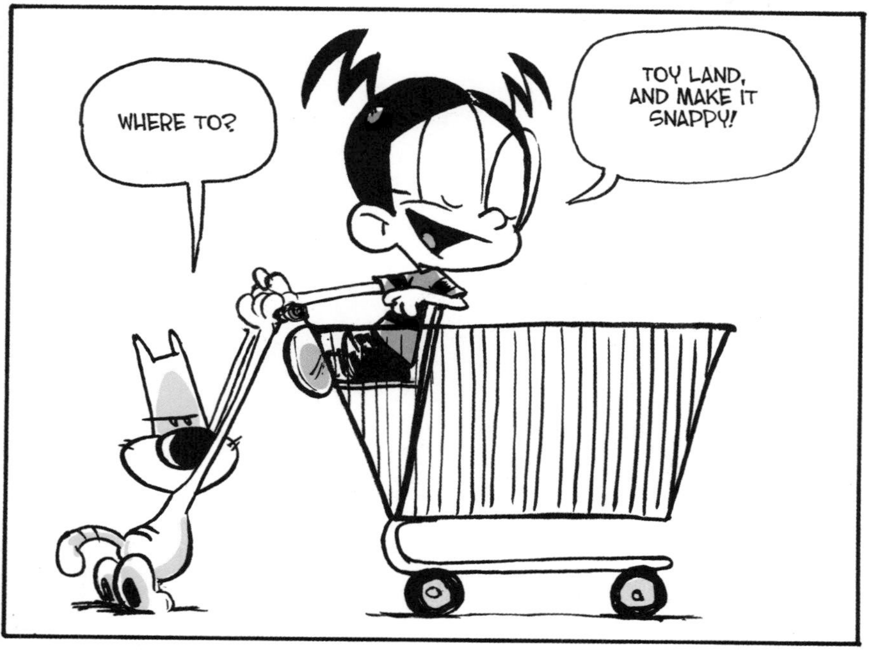
WHERE TO?
TOY LAND, AND MAKE IT SNAPPY!

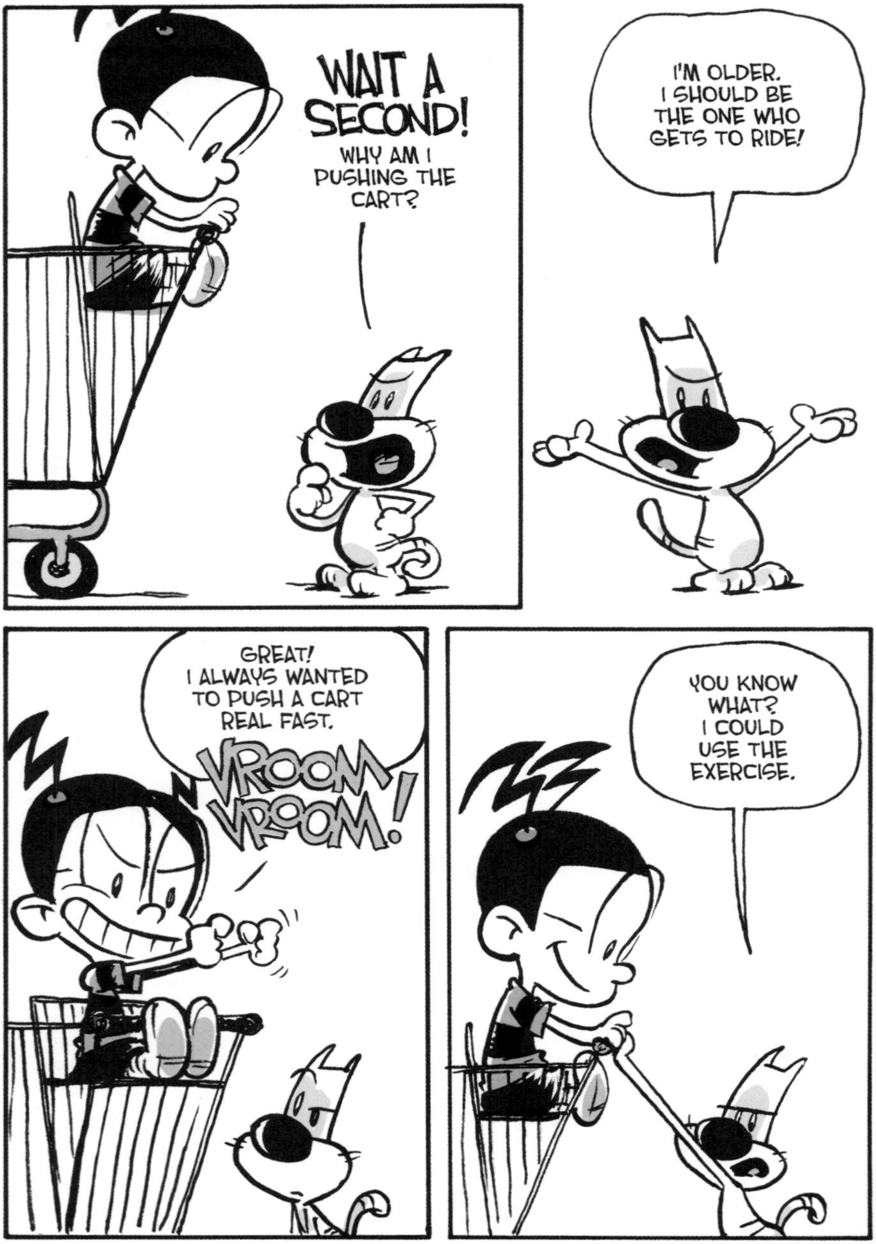
WAIT A SECOND!
WHY AM I PUSHING THE CART?
I'M OLDER. I SHOULD BE THE ONE WHO GETS TO RIDE!
GREAT! I ALWAYS WANTED TO PUSH A CART REAL FAST.
VROOM VROOM!
YOU KNOW WHAT? I COULD USE THE EXERCISE.

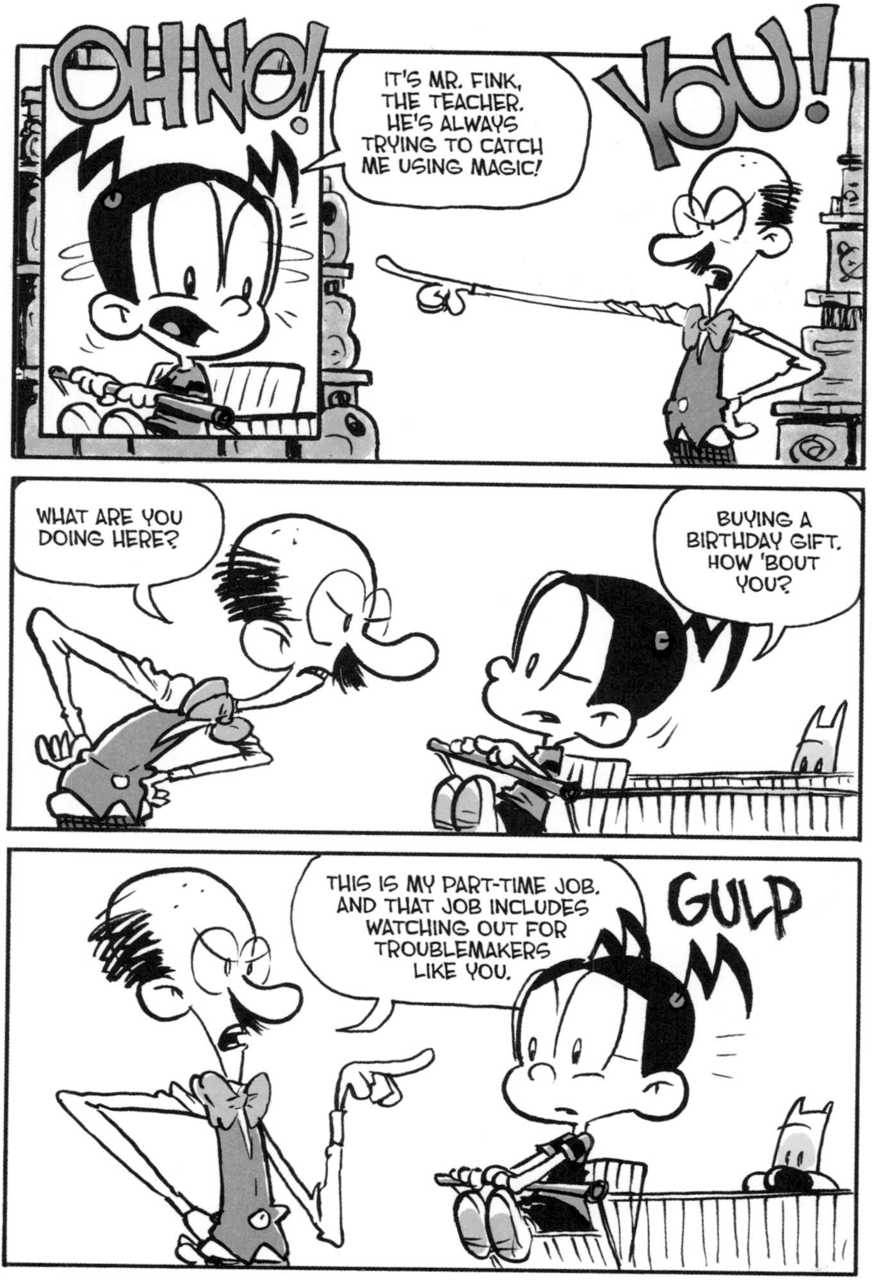
OH NO!
IT'S MR. FINK, THE TEACHER. HE'S ALWAYS TRYING TO CATCH ME USING MAGIC!
YOU!
WHAT ARE YOU DOING HERE?
BUYING A BIRTHDAY GIFT. HOW 'BOUT YOU?
THIS IS MY PART-TIME JOB. AND THAT JOB INCLUDES WATCHING OUT FOR TROUBLEMAKERS LIKE YOU.
GULP

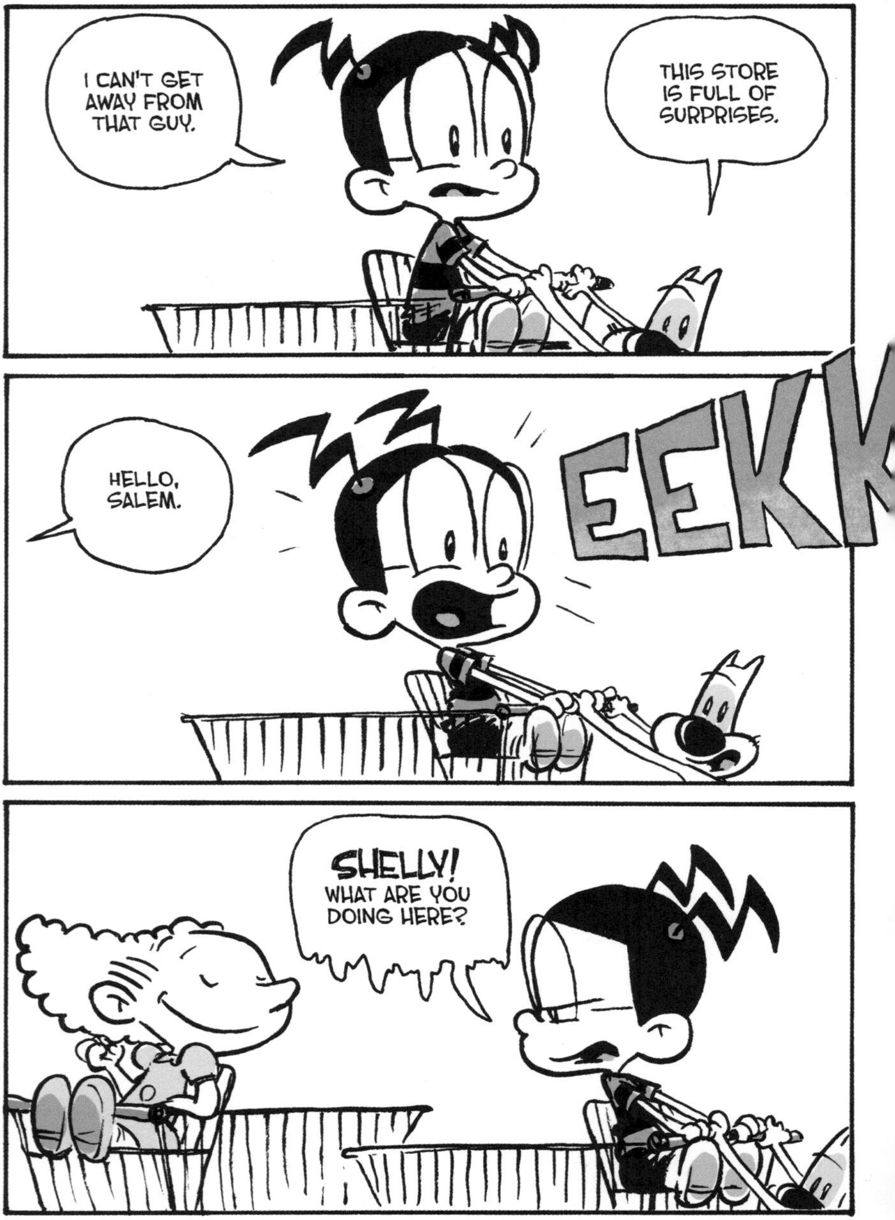
I CAN'T GET AWAY FROM THAT GUY.
THIS STORE IS FULL OF SURPRISES.
HELLO, SALEM.
EEKK
SHELLY! WHAT ARE YOU DOING HERE?

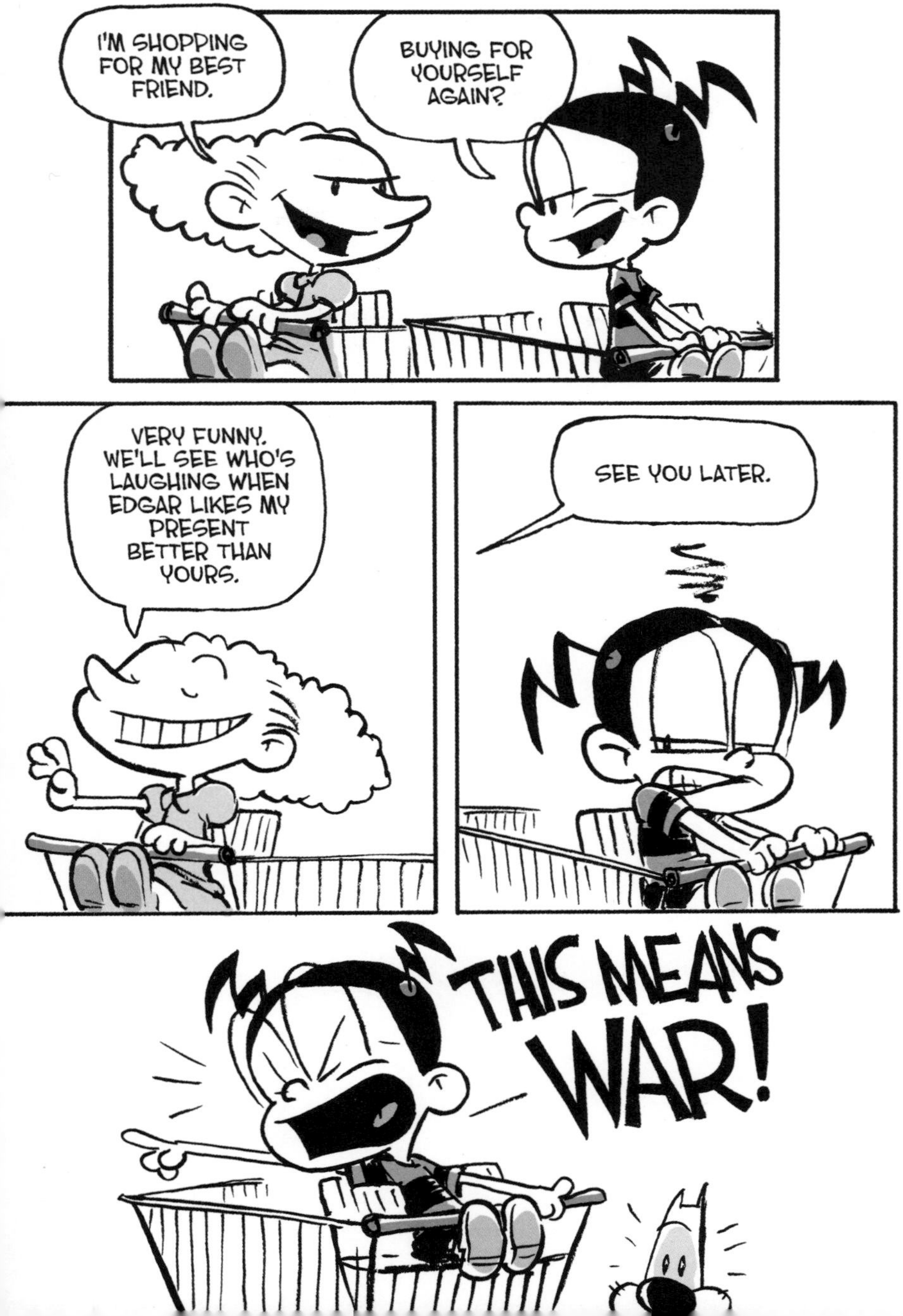
I'M SHOPPING FOR MY BEST FRIEND.
BUYING FOR YOURSELF AGAIN?
VERY FUNNY. WE'LL SEE WHO'S LAUGHING WHEN EDGAR LIKES MY PRESENT BETTER THAN YOURS.
SEE YOU LATER.
THIS MEANS WAR!

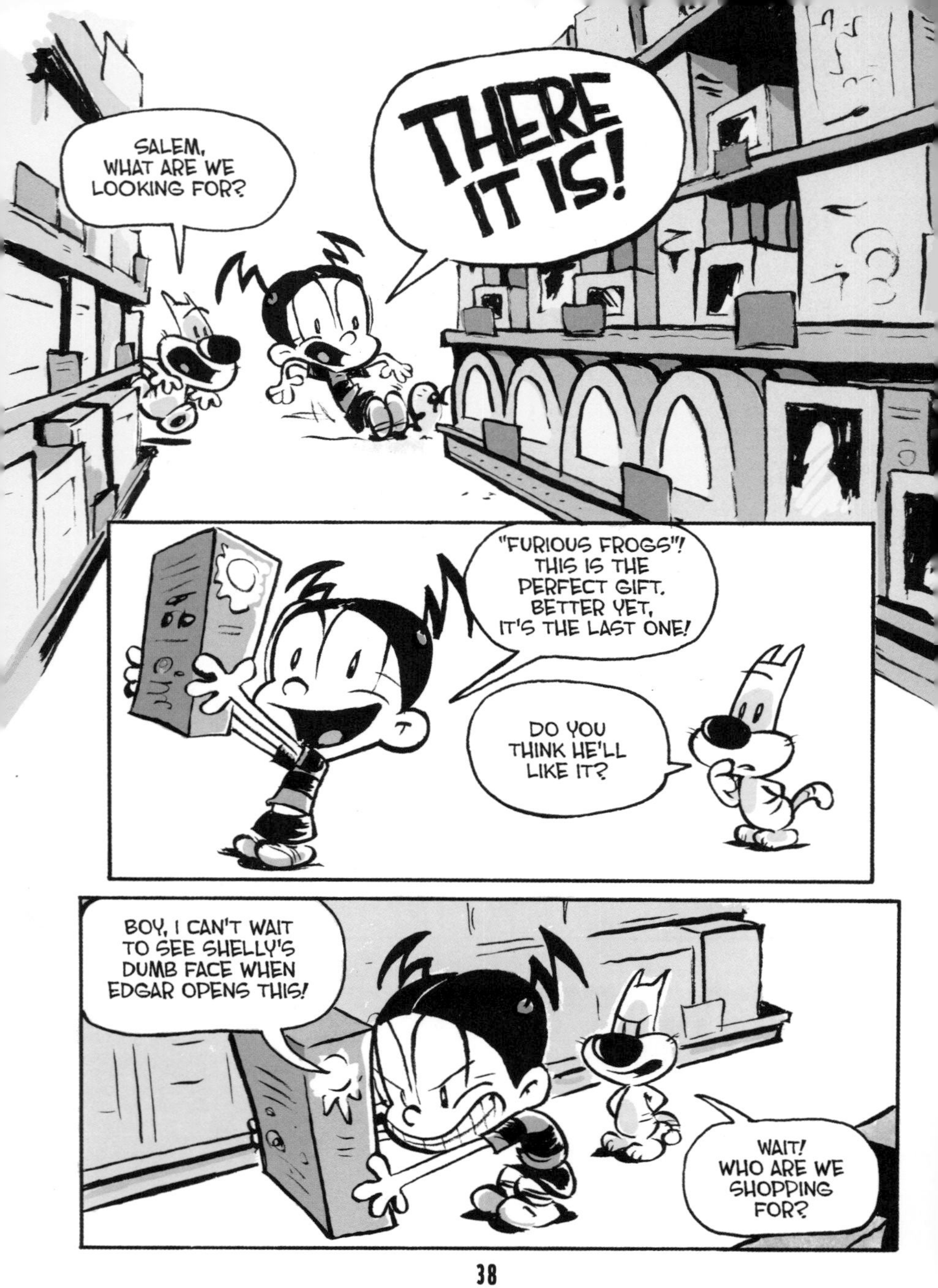
SALEM, WHAT ARE WE LOOKING FOR?
THERE IT IS!
"FURIOUS FROGS"! THIS IS THE PERFECT GIFT. BETTER YET, IT'S THE LAST ONE!
DO YOU THINK HE'LL LIKE IT?
BOY, I CAN'T WAIT TO SEE SHELLY'S DUMB FACE WHEN EDGAR OPENS THIS!
WAIT! WHO ARE WE SHOPPING FOR?

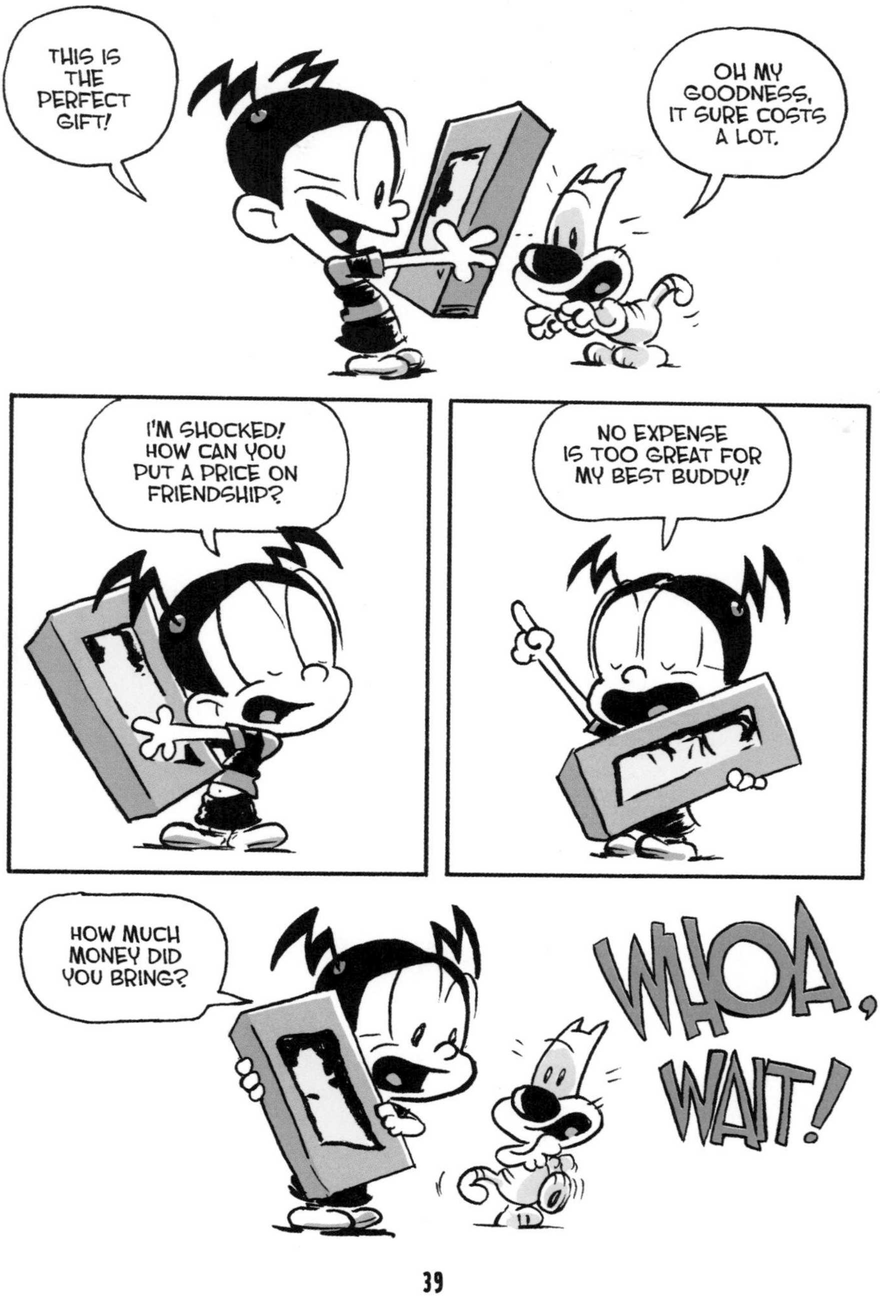

THIS IS THE PERFECT GIFT!
OH MY GOODNESS, IT SURE COSTS A LOT.
I'M SHOCKED! HOW CAN YOU PUT A PRICE ON FRIENDSHIP?
NO EXPENSE IS TOO GREAT FOR MY BEST BUDDY!
HOW MUCH MONEY DID YOU BRING?
WHOA, WAIT!

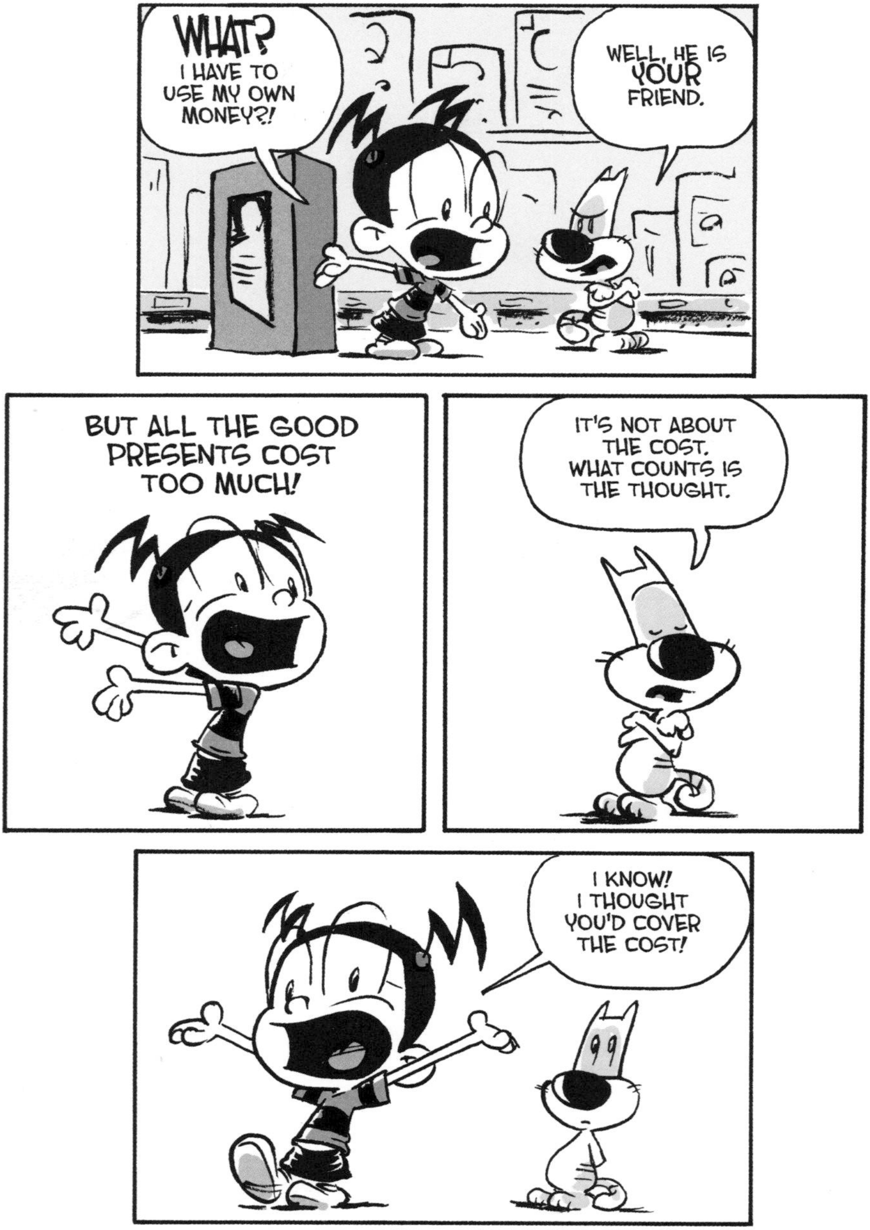
WHAT? I HAVE TO USE MY OWN MONEY?!
WELL, HE IS YOUR FRIEND.
BUT ALL THE GOOD PRESENTS COST TOO MUCH!
IT'S NOT ABOUT THE COST. WHAT COUNTS IS THE THOUGHT.
I KNOW! I THOUGHT YOU'D COVER THE COST!

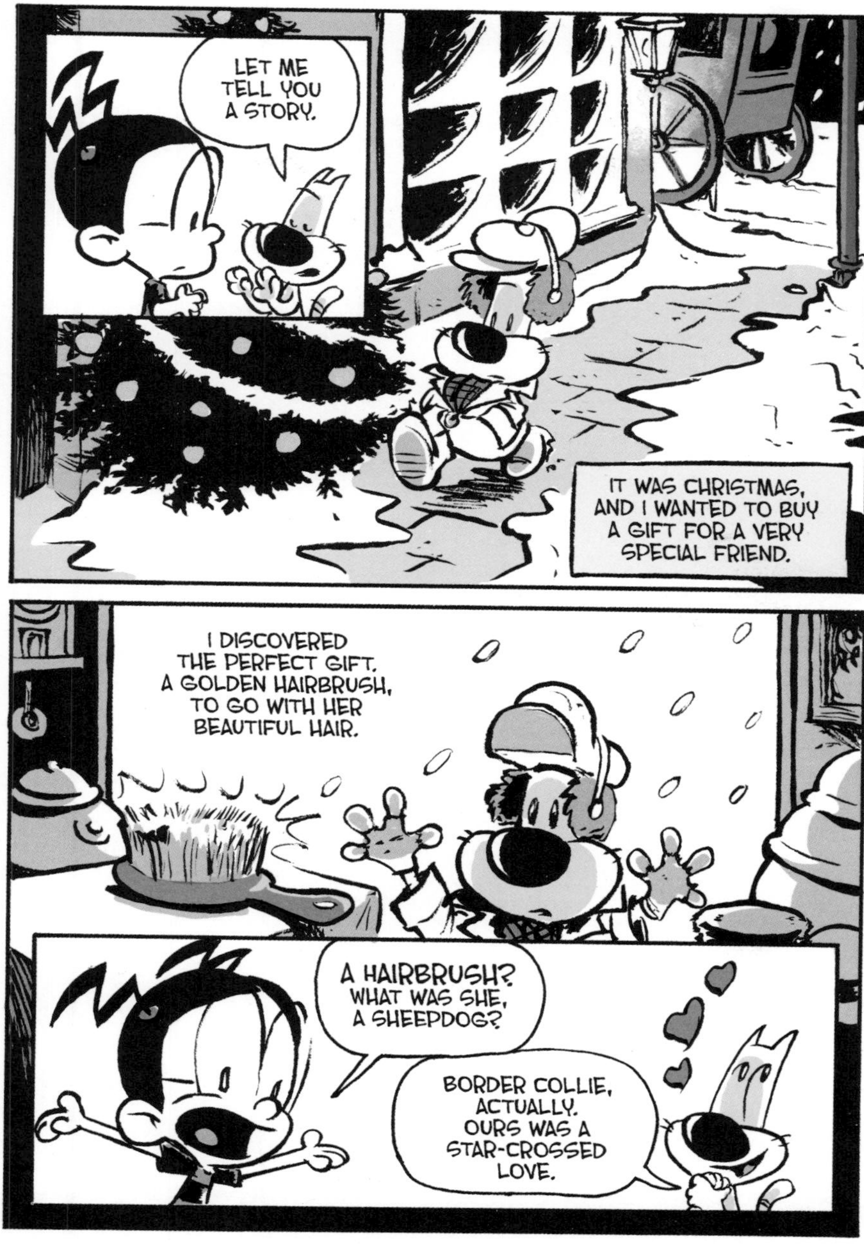

LET ME TELL YOU A STORY.
IT WAS CHRISTMAS, AND I WANTED TO BUY A GIFT FOR A VERY SPECIAL FRIEND.
I DISCOVERED THE PERFECT GIFT. A GOLDEN HAIRBRUSH, TO GO WITH HER BEAUTIFUL HAIR.
A HAIRBRUSH? WHAT WAS SHE, A SHEEPDOG?
BORDER COLLIE, ACTUALLY. OURS WAS A STAR-CROSSED LOVE.

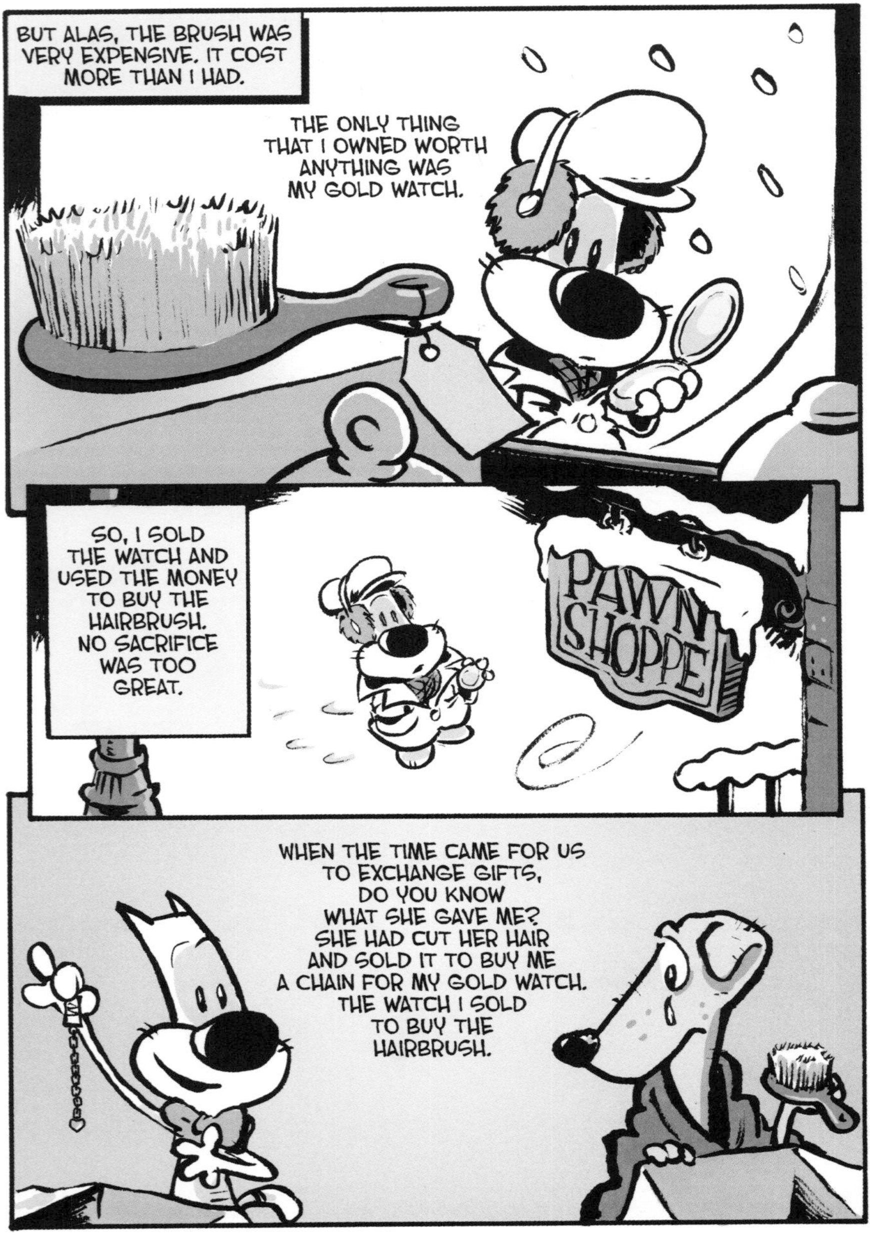
BUT ALAS, THE BRUSH WAS VERY EXPENSIVE. IT COST MORE THAN I HAD.
THE ONLY THING THAT I OWNED WORTH ANYTHING WAS MY GOLD WATCH.
SO, I SOLD THE WATCH AND USED THE MONEY TO BUY THE HAIRBRUSH. NO SACRIFICE WAS TOO GREAT.
PAWN SHOPPE
WHEN THE TIME CAME FOR US TO EXCHANGE GIFTS, DO YOU KNOW WHAT SHE GAVE ME? SHE HAD CUT HER HAIR AND SOLD IT TO BUY ME A CHAIN FOR MY GOLD WATCH. THE WATCH I SOLD TO BUY THE HAIRBRUSH.

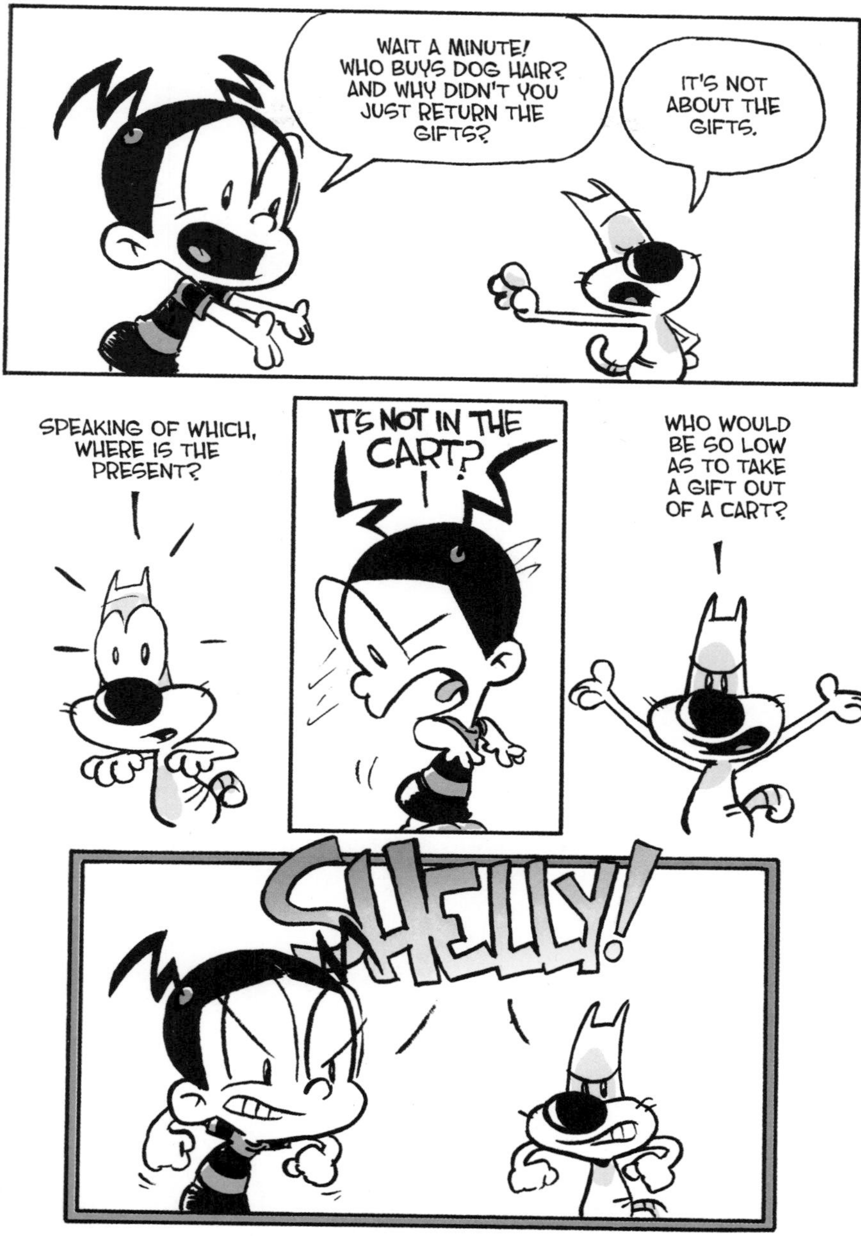
WAIT A MINUTE! WHO BUYS DOG HAIR? AND WHY DIDN'T YOU JUST RETURN THE GIFTS?
IT'S NOT ABOUT THE GIFTS.
SPEAKING OF WHICH, WHERE IS THE PRESENT?
IT'S NOT IN THE CART?
WHO WOULD BE SO LOW AS TO TAKE A GIFT OUT OF A CART?
SHELLY!

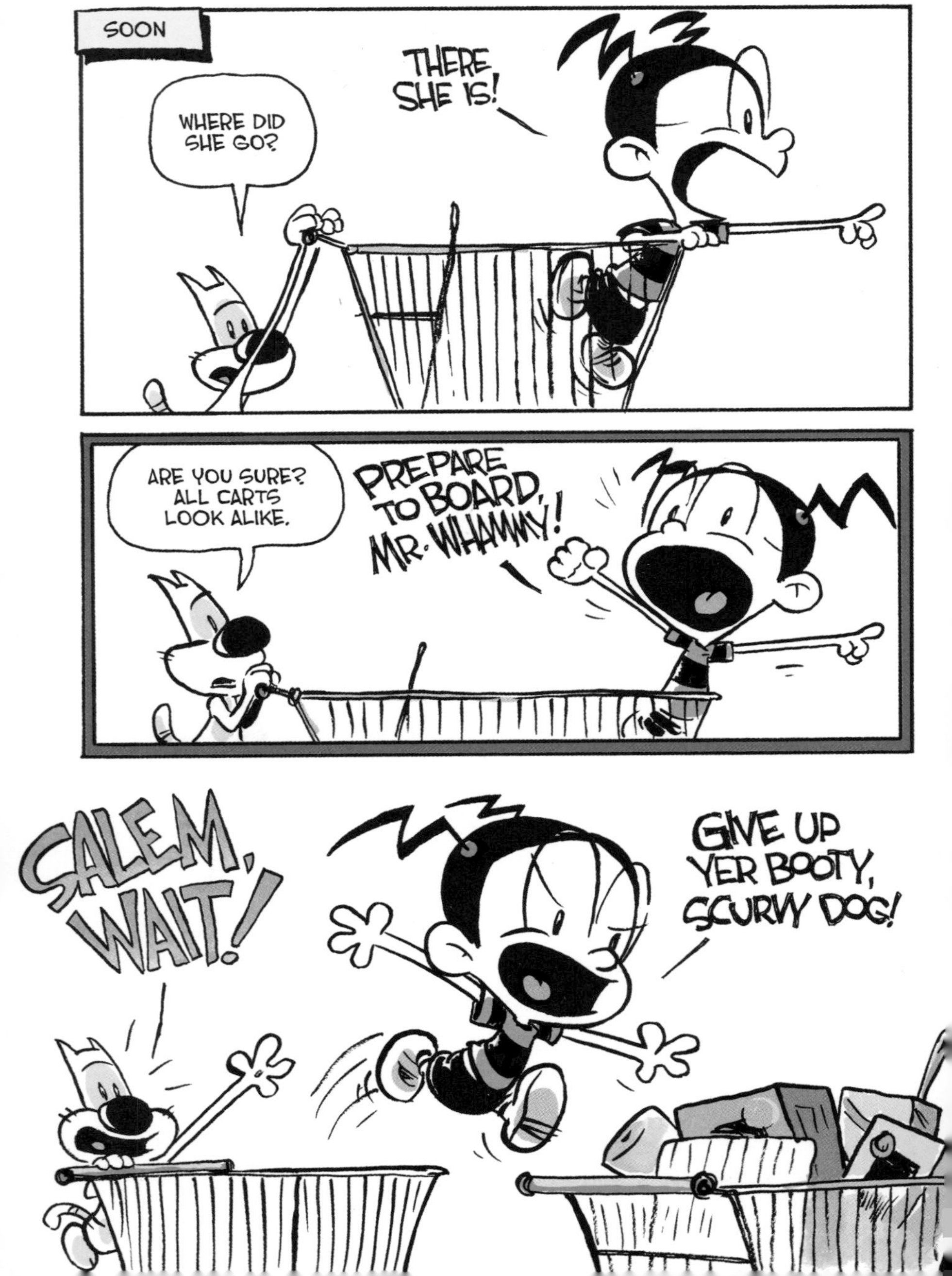
SOON
WHERE DID SHE GO?
THERE SHE IS!
ARE YOU SURE? ALL CARTS LOOK ALIKE.
PREPARE TO BOARD, MR. WHAMMY!
SALEM, WAIT!
GIVE UP YER BOOTY, SCURVY DOG!

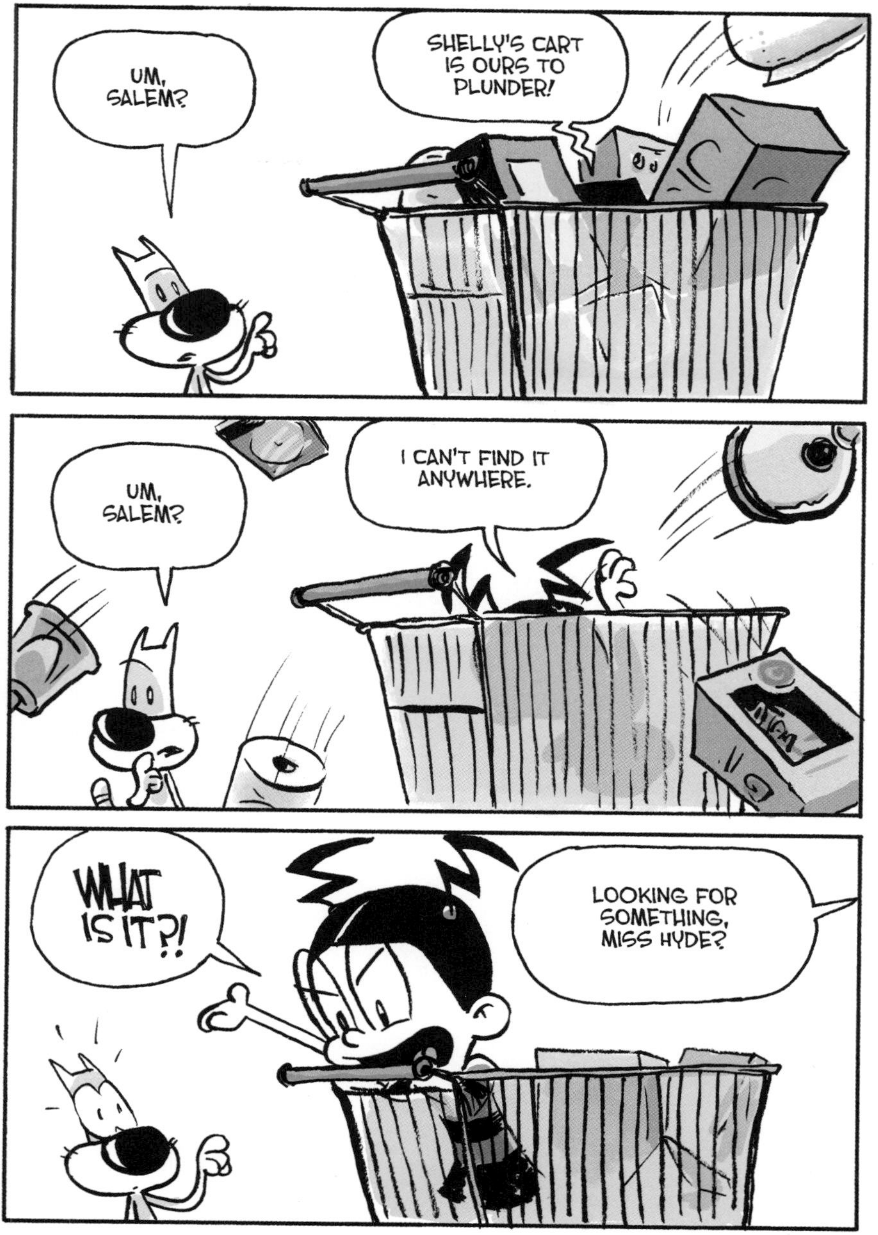
UM, SALEM?
SHELLY'S CART IS OURS TO PLUNDER!
UM, SALEM?
I CAN'T FIND IT ANYWHERE.
WHAT IS IT?!
LOOKING FOR SOMETHING, MISS HYDE?

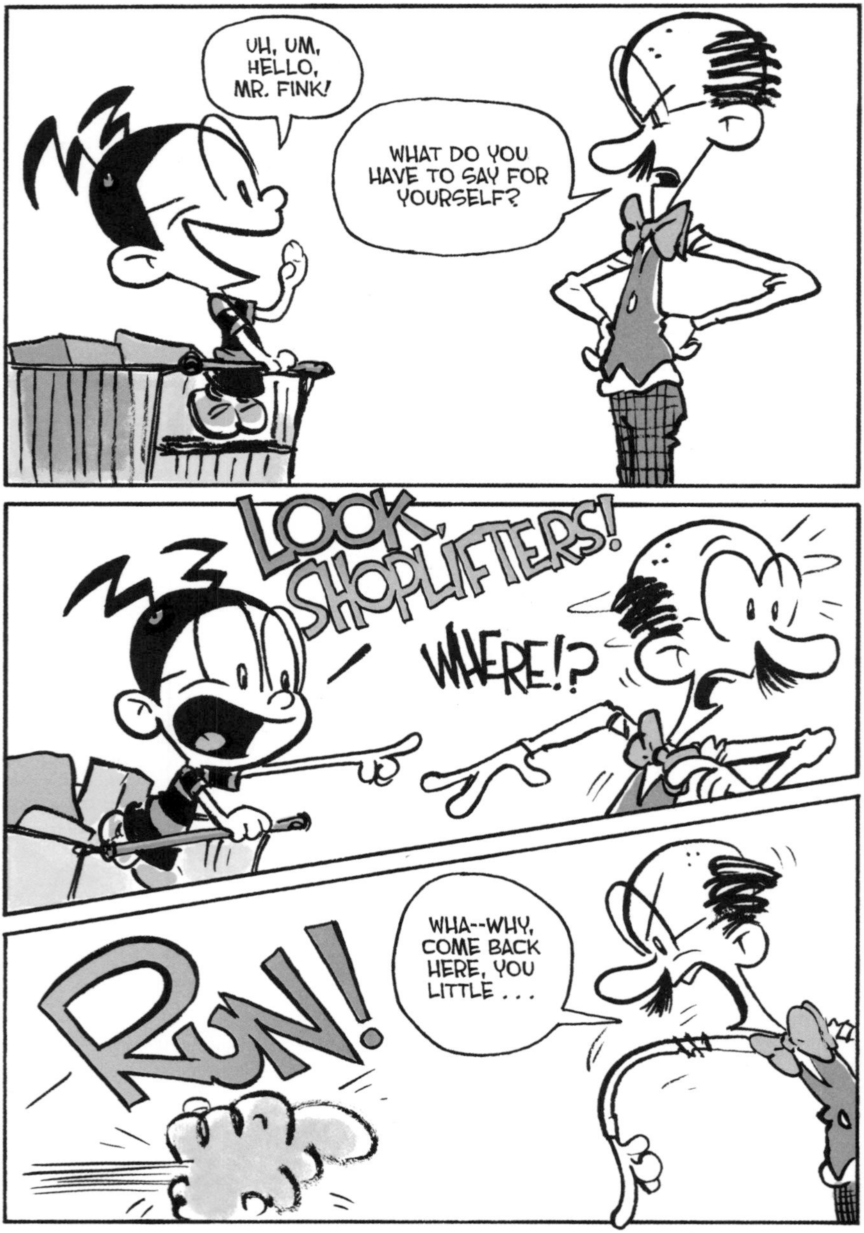
UH, UM, HELLO, MR. FINK!
WHAT DO YOU HAVE TO SAY FOR YOURSELF?
LOOK, SHOPLIFTERS!
WHERE!?
RUN!
WHA--WHY, COME BACK HERE, YOU LITTLE . . .

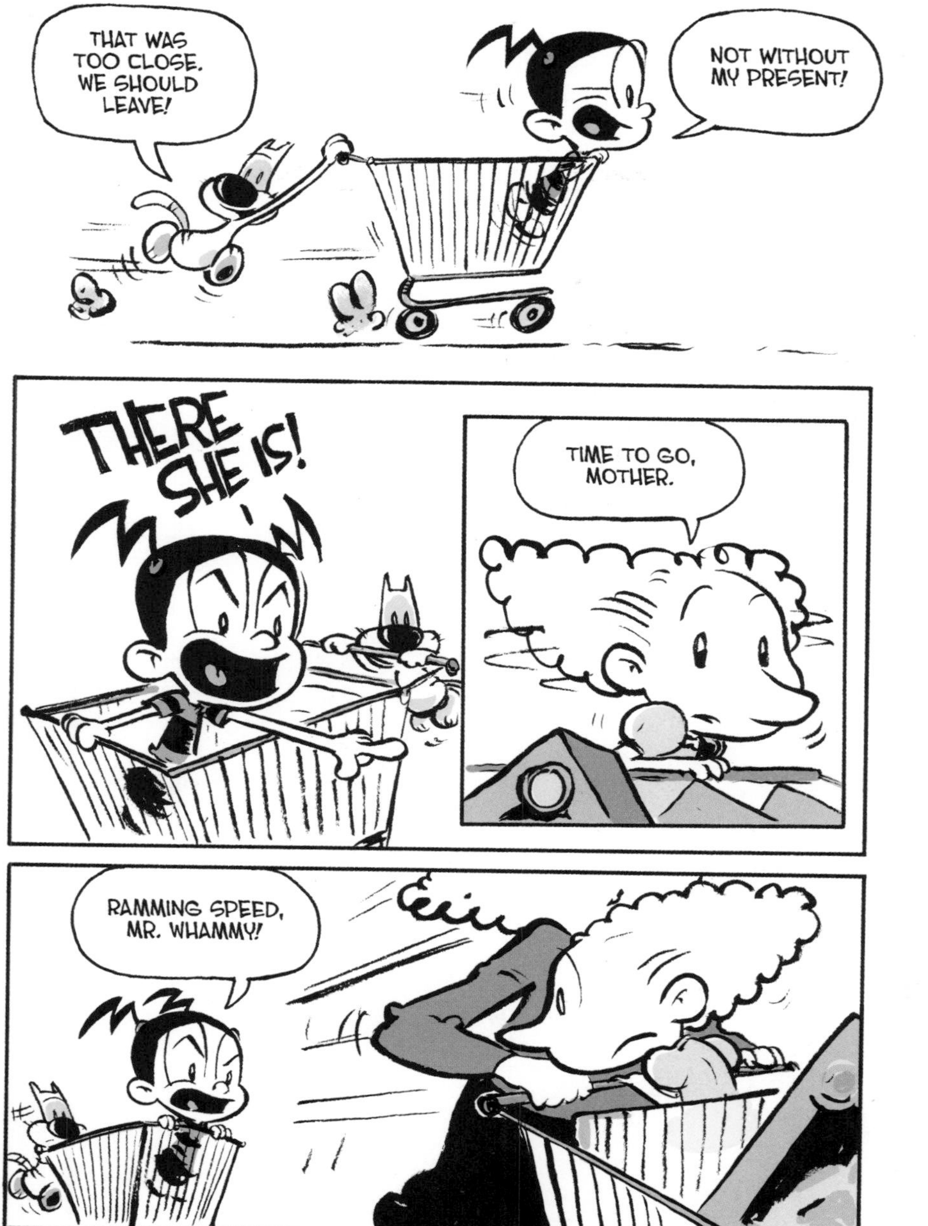
THAT WAS TOO CLOSE. WE SHOULD LEAVE!
NOT WITHOUT MY PRESENT!
THERE SHE IS!
TIME TO GO, MOTHER.
RAMMING SPEED, MR. WHAMMY!

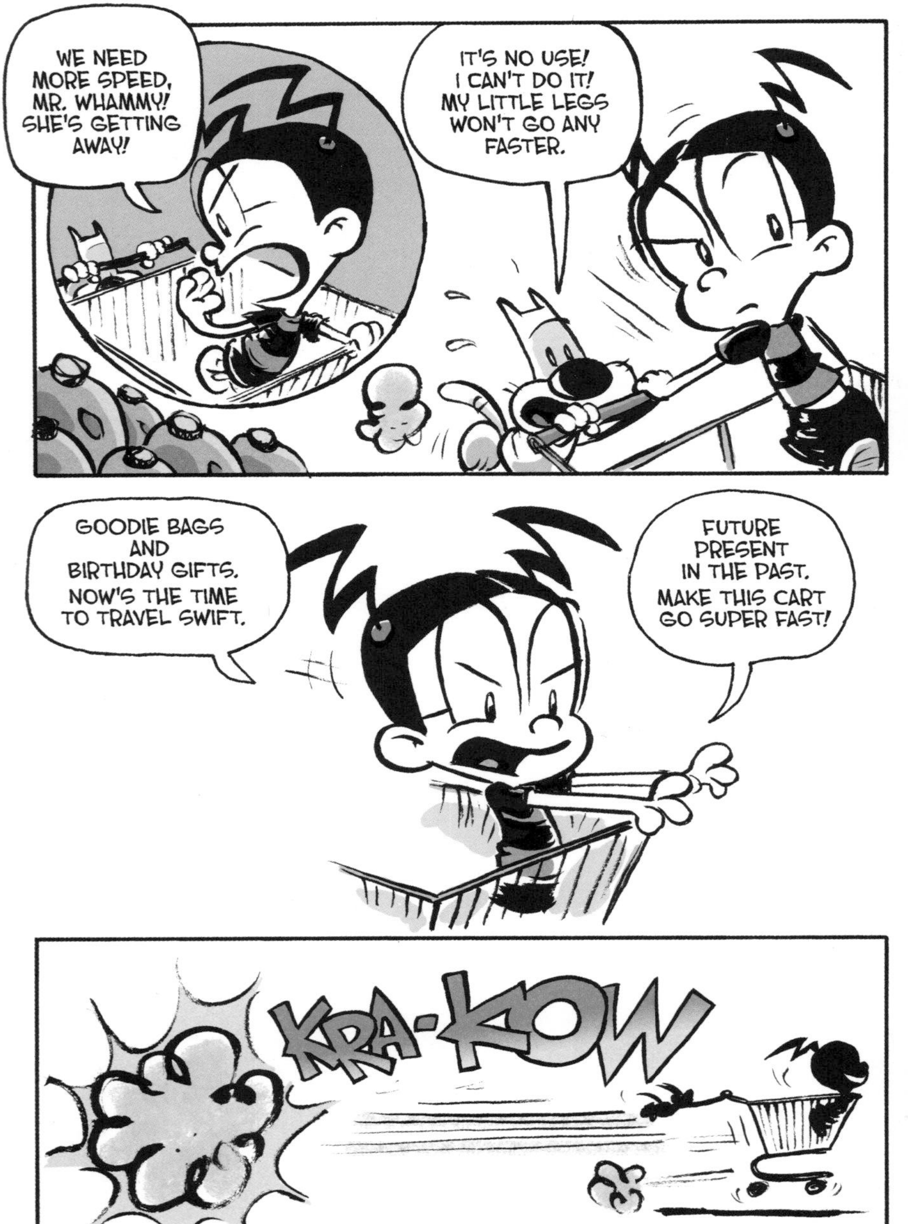
WE NEED MORE SPEED, MR. WHAMMY! SHE'S GETTING AWAY!
IT'S NO USE! I CAN'T DO IT! MY LITTLE LEGS WON'T GO ANY FASTER.
GOODIE BAGS AND BIRTHDAY GIFTS. NOW'S THE TIME TO TRAVEL SWIFT.
FUTURE PRESENT IN THE PAST. MAKE THIS CART GO SUPER FAST!
KRA-KOW

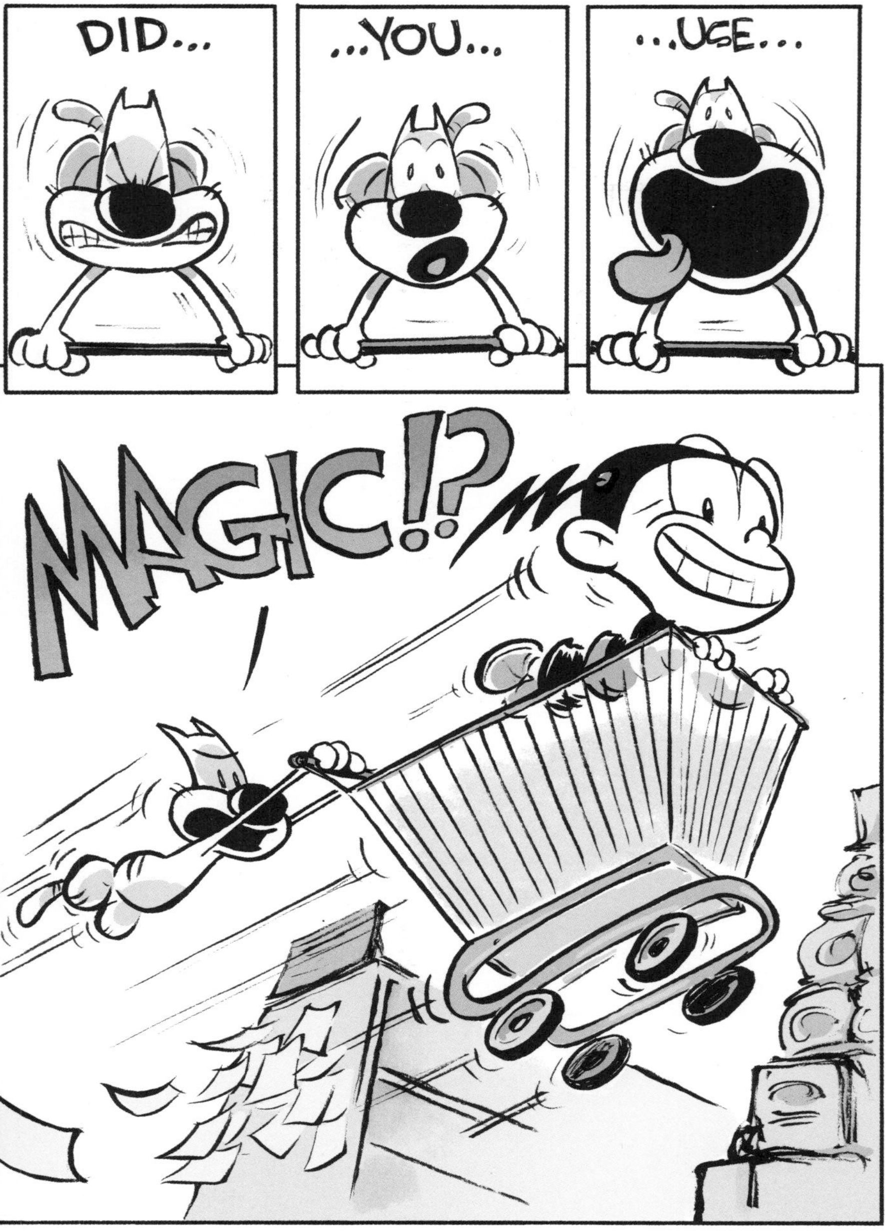
DID...
...YOU...
...USE...
MAGIC!?

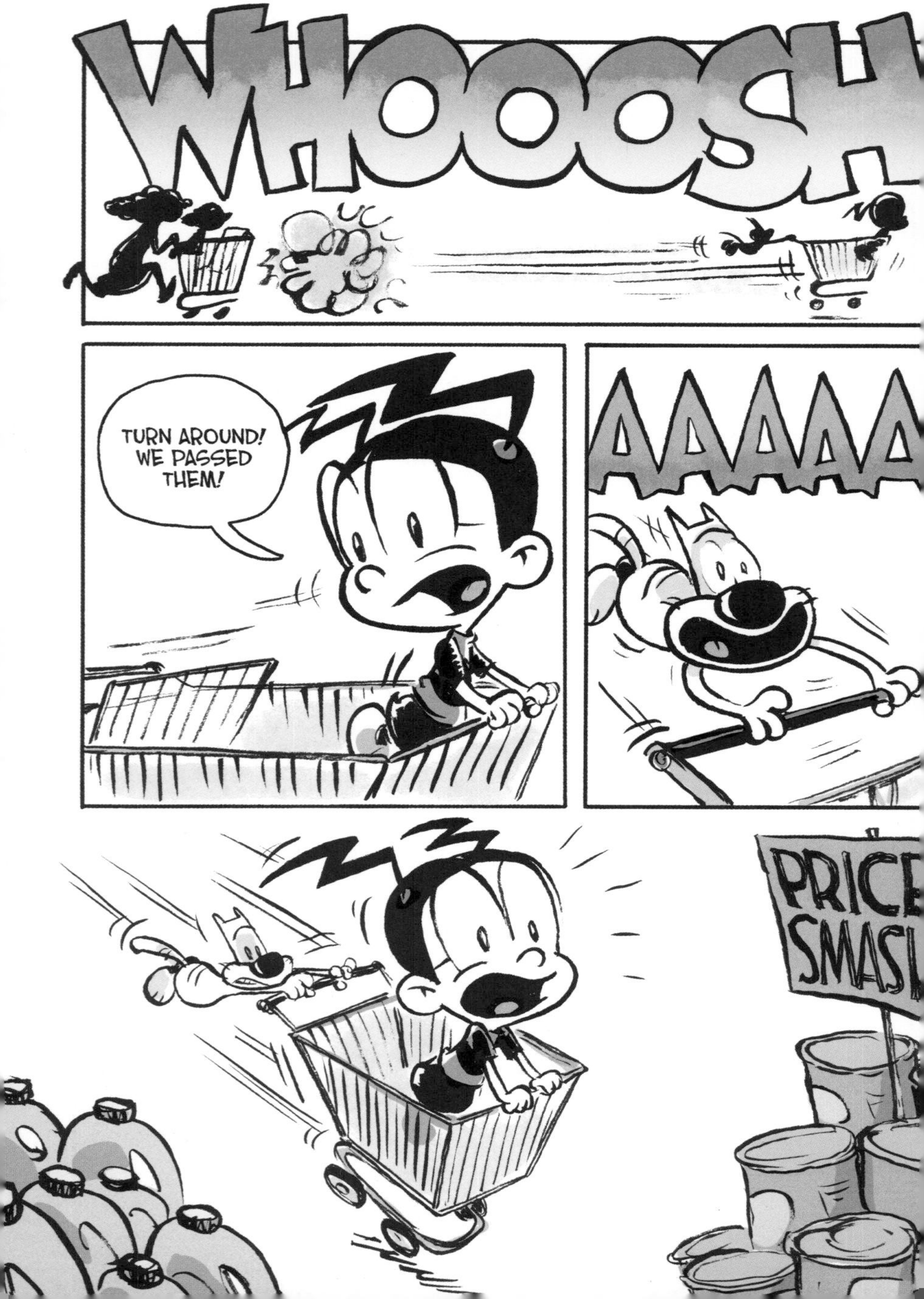
WHOOOSH
TURN AROUND! WE PASSED THEM!
AAAAA
PRICE
SMAS

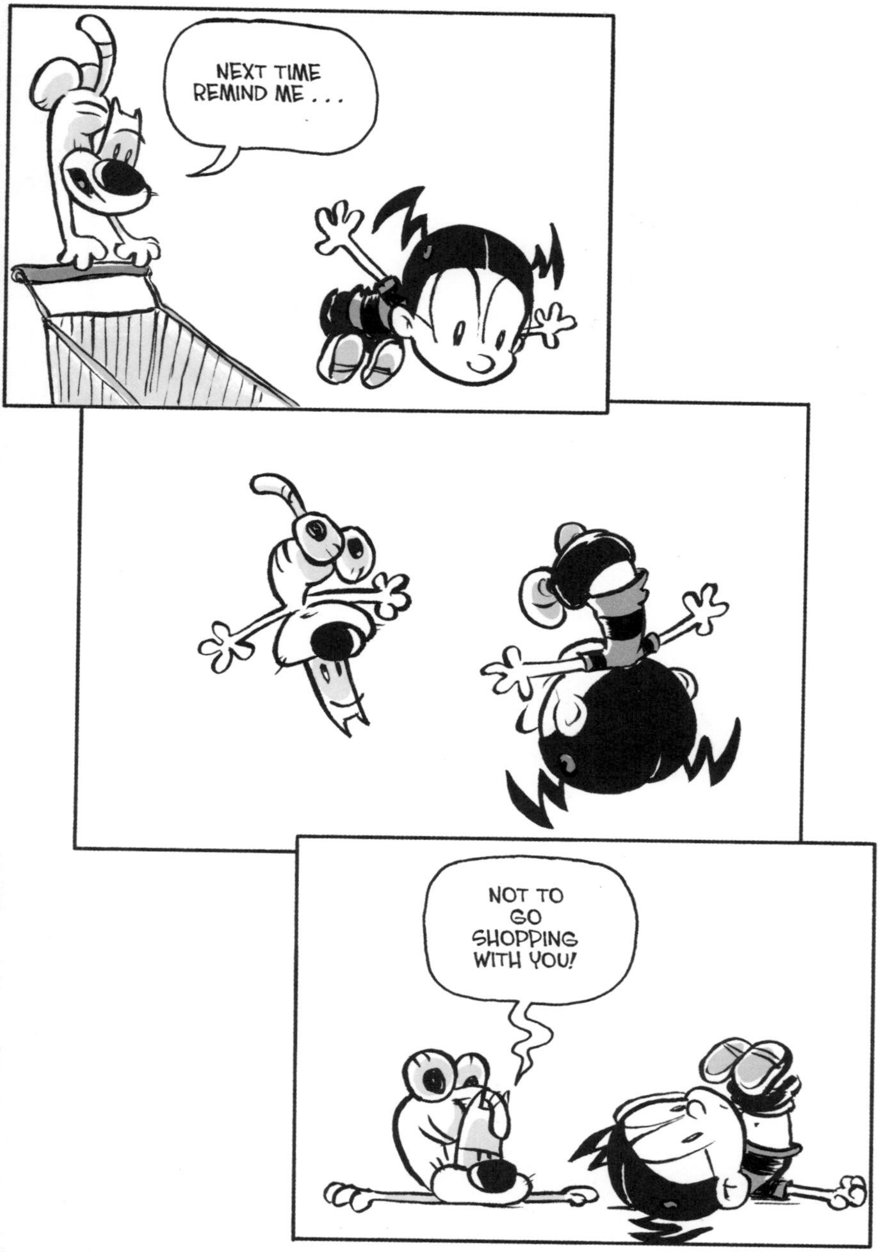
NEXT TIME
REMIND ME . . .
NOT TO
GO
SHOPPING
WITH YOU!

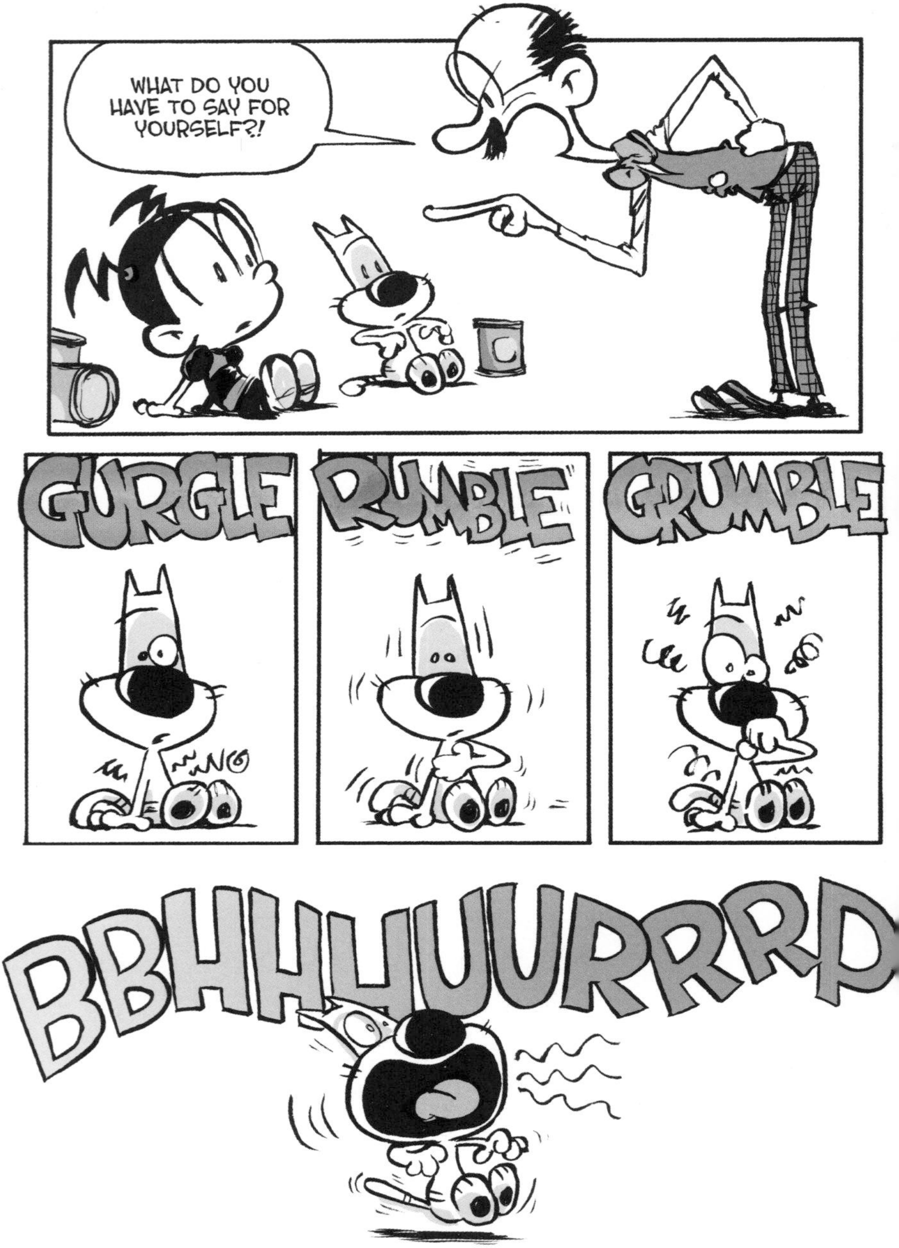
WHAT DO YOU HAVE TO SAY FOR YOURSELF?!
GURGLE
RUMBLE
GRUMBLE
BBHHUURRRP

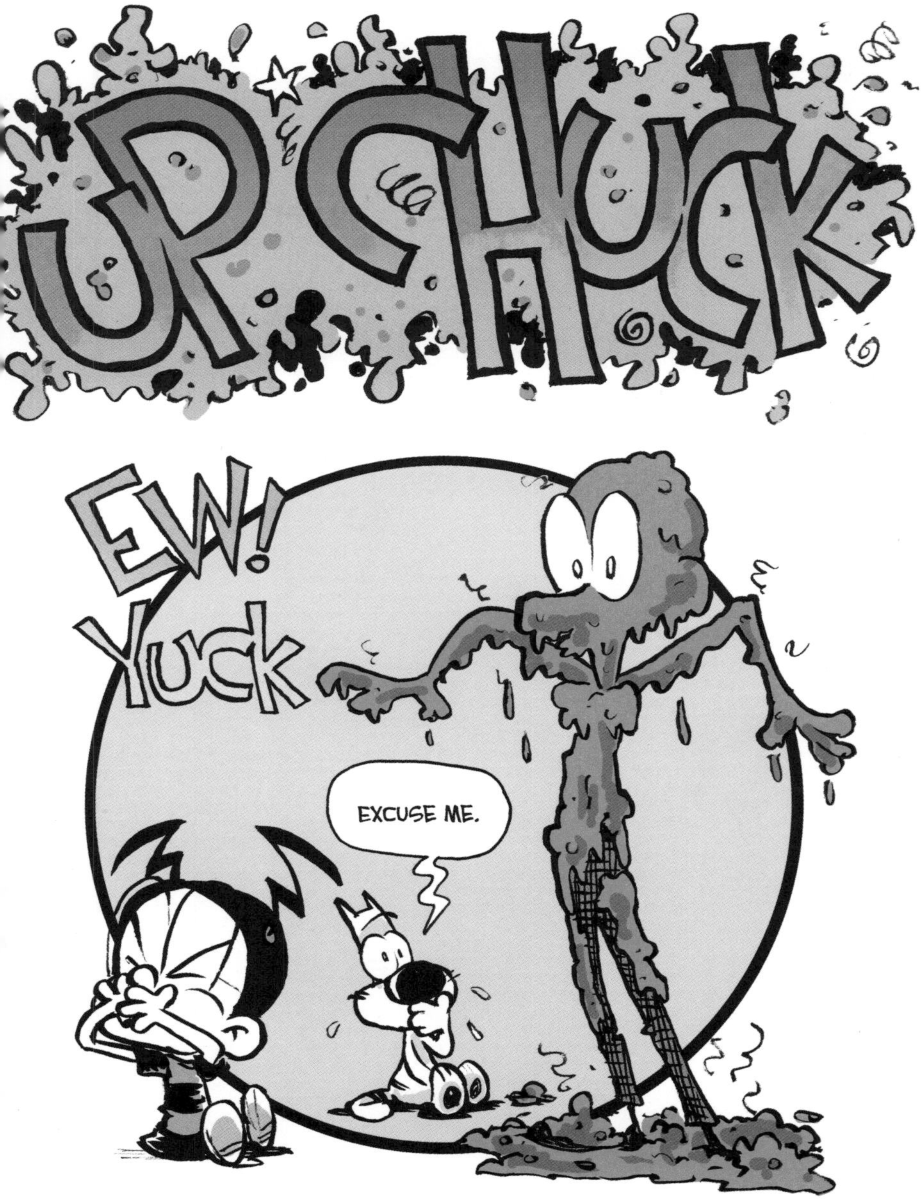
UP CHUCK
EW!
YUCK
EXCUSE ME.

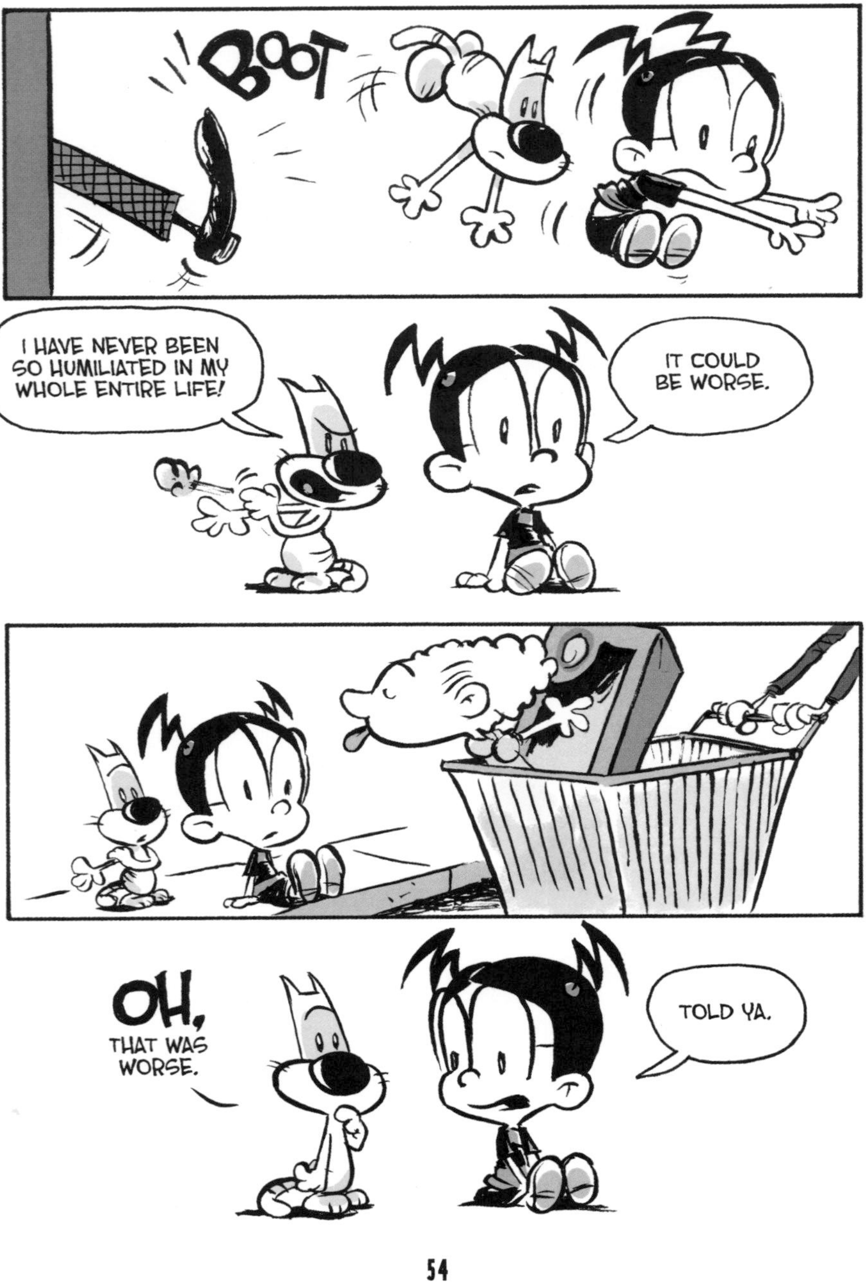
BOOT
I HAVE NEVER BEEN SO HUMILIATED IN MY WHOLE ENTIRE LIFE!
IT COULD BE WORSE.
OH, THAT WAS WORSE.
TOLD YA.

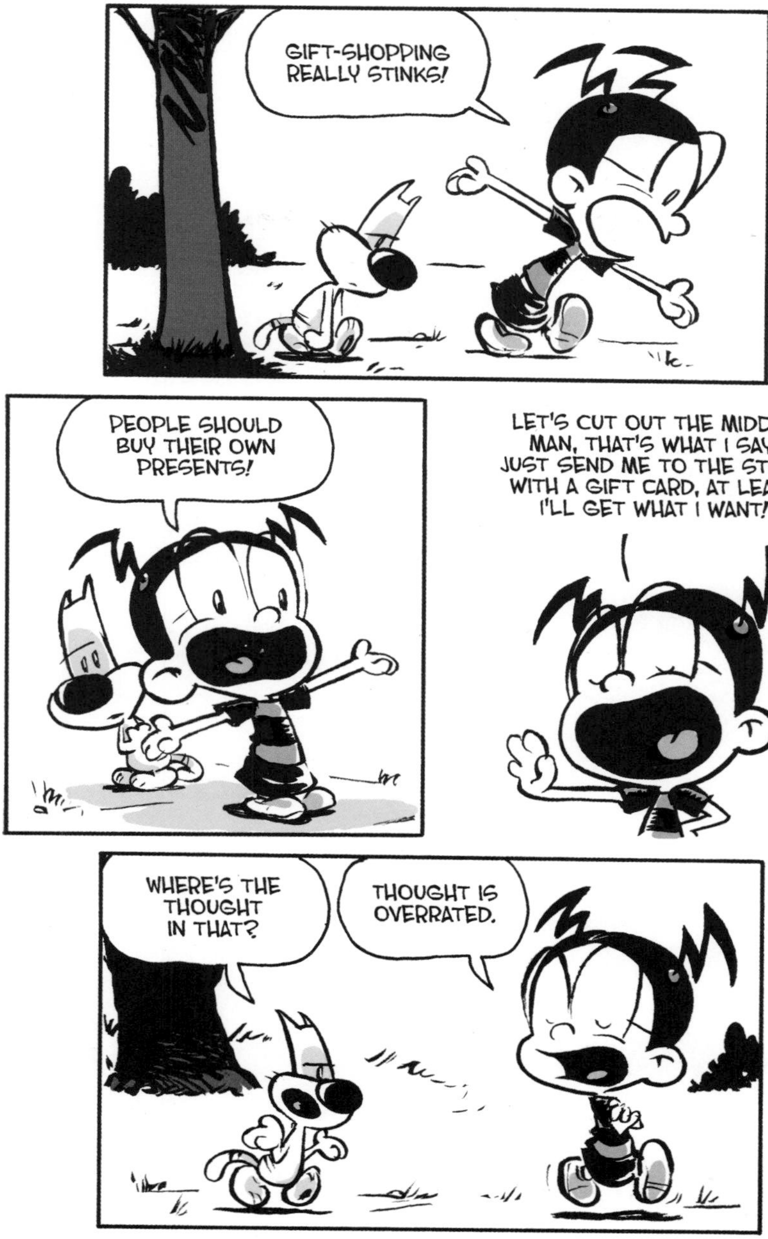
GIFT-SHOPPING REALLY STINKS!
PEOPLE SHOULD BUY THEIR OWN PRESENTS!
LET'S CUT OUT THE MIDDLE MAN, THAT'S WHAT I SAY! JUST SEND ME TO THE STORE WITH A GIFT CARD, AT LEAST I'LL GET WHAT I WANT!
WHERE'S THE THOUGHT IN THAT?
THOUGHT IS OVERRATED.

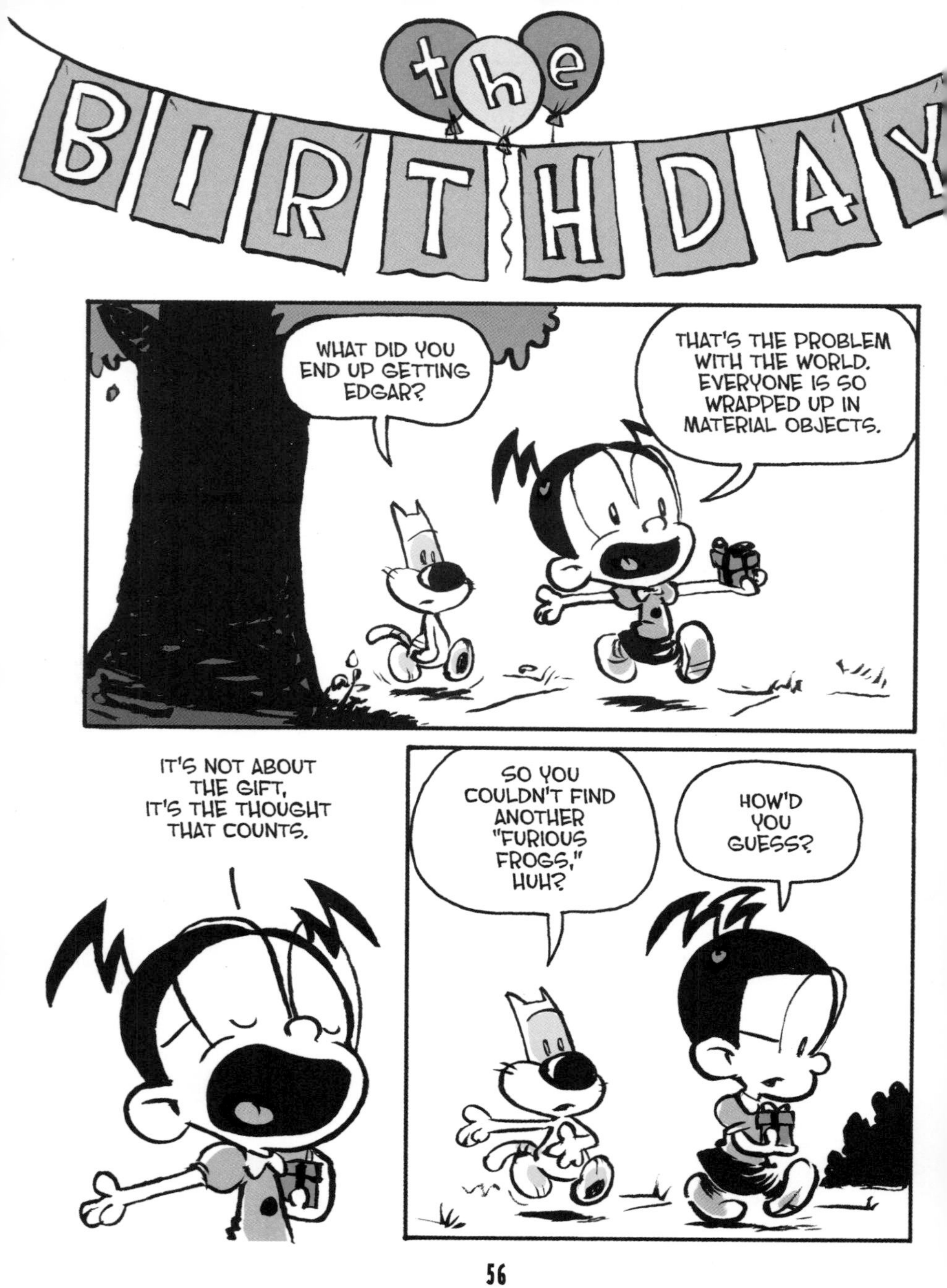
the BIRTHDAY
WHAT DID YOU END UP GETTING EDGAR?
THAT'S THE PROBLEM WITH THE WORLD. EVERYONE IS SO WRAPPED UP IN MATERIAL OBJECTS.
IT'S NOT ABOUT THE GIFT, IT'S THE THOUGHT THAT COUNTS.
SO YOU COULDN'T FIND ANOTHER "FURIOUS FROGS," HUH?
HOW'D YOU GUESS?

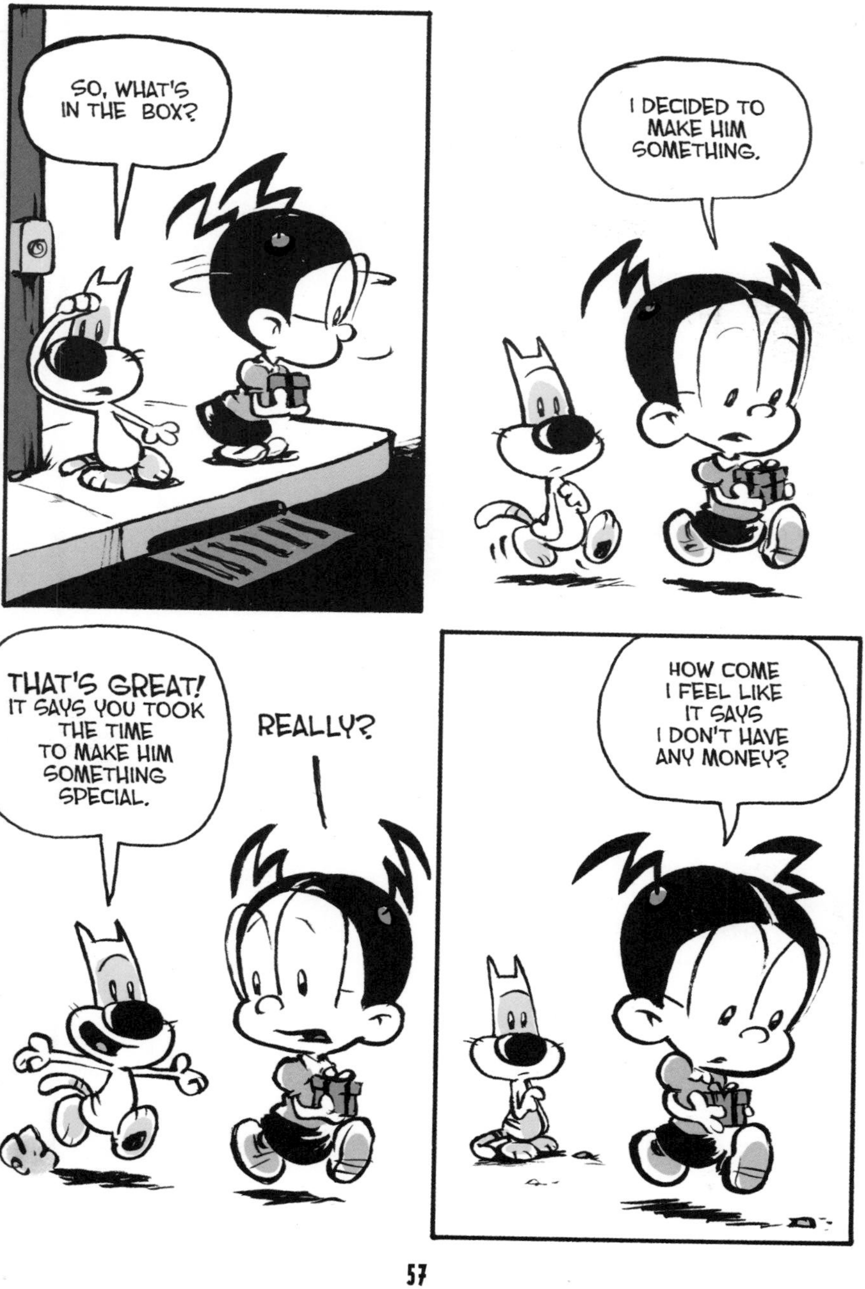
SO, WHAT'S IN THE BOX?
I DECIDED TO MAKE HIM SOMETHING.
THAT'S GREAT! IT SAYS YOU TOOK THE TIME TO MAKE HIM SOMETHING SPECIAL.
REALLY?
HOW COME I FEEL LIKE IT SAYS I DON'T HAVE ANY MONEY?

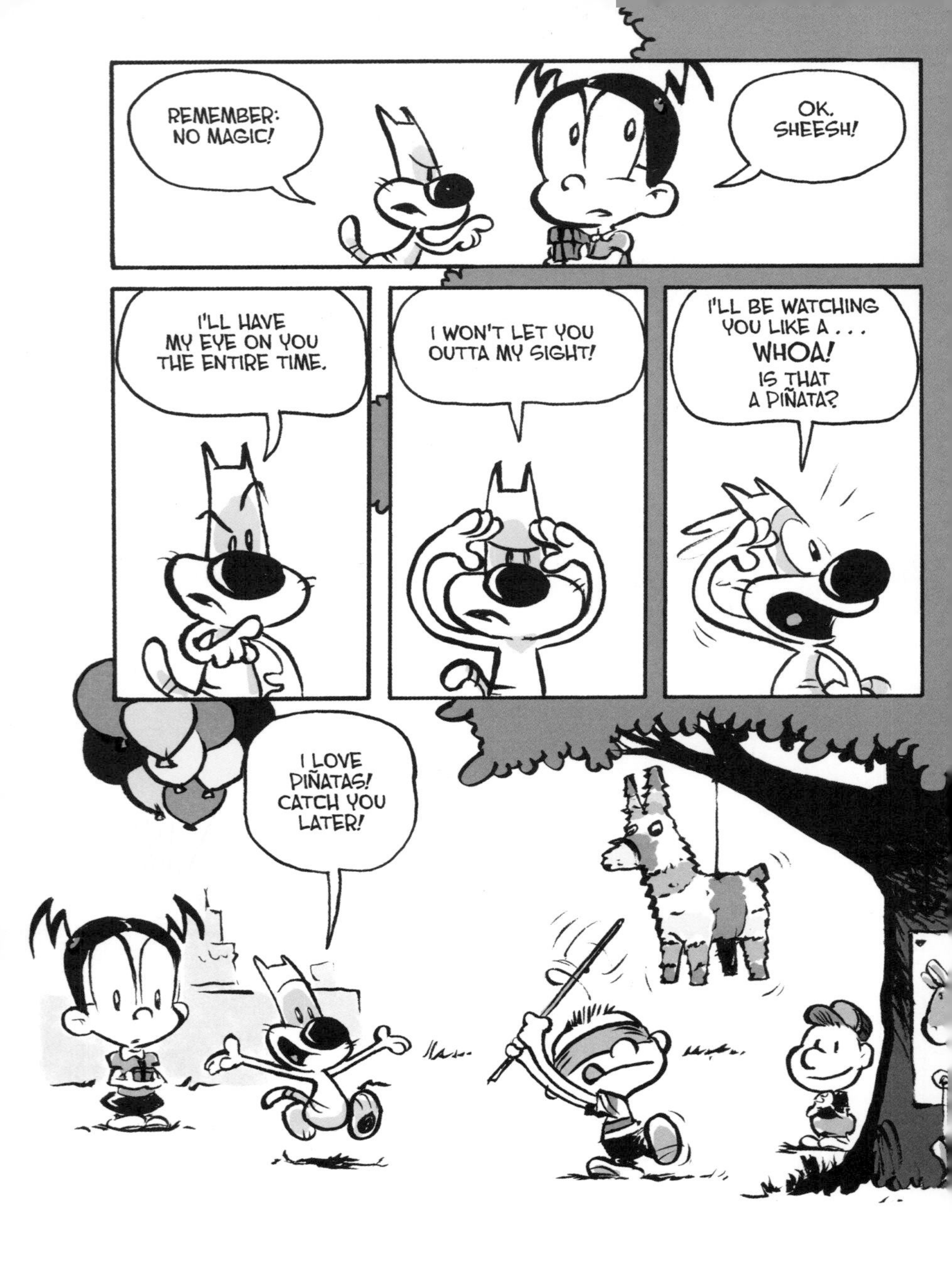
REMEMBER: NO MAGIC!
OK. SHEESH!
I'LL HAVE MY EYE ON YOU THE ENTIRE TIME.
I WON'T LET YOU OUTTA MY SIGHT!
I'LL BE WATCHING YOU LIKE A . . . WHOA! IS THAT A PIÑATA?
I LOVE PIÑATAS! CATCH YOU LATER!

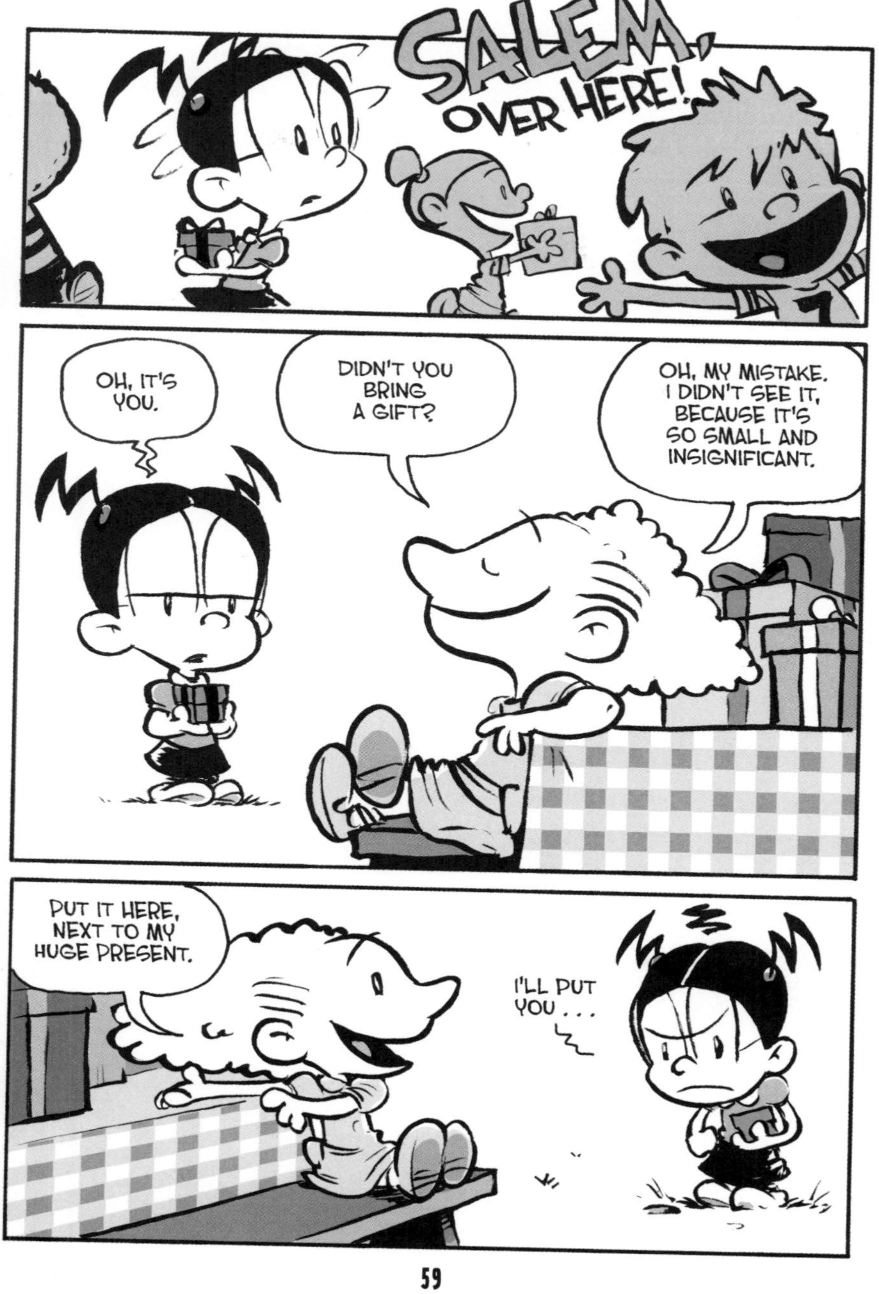
SALEM, OVER HERE!
OH, IT'S YOU.
DIDN'T YOU BRING A GIFT?
OH, MY MISTAKE. I DIDN'T SEE IT, BECAUSE IT'S SO SMALL AND INSIGNIFICANT.
PUT IT HERE, NEXT TO MY HUGE PRESENT.
I'LL PUT YOU . . .

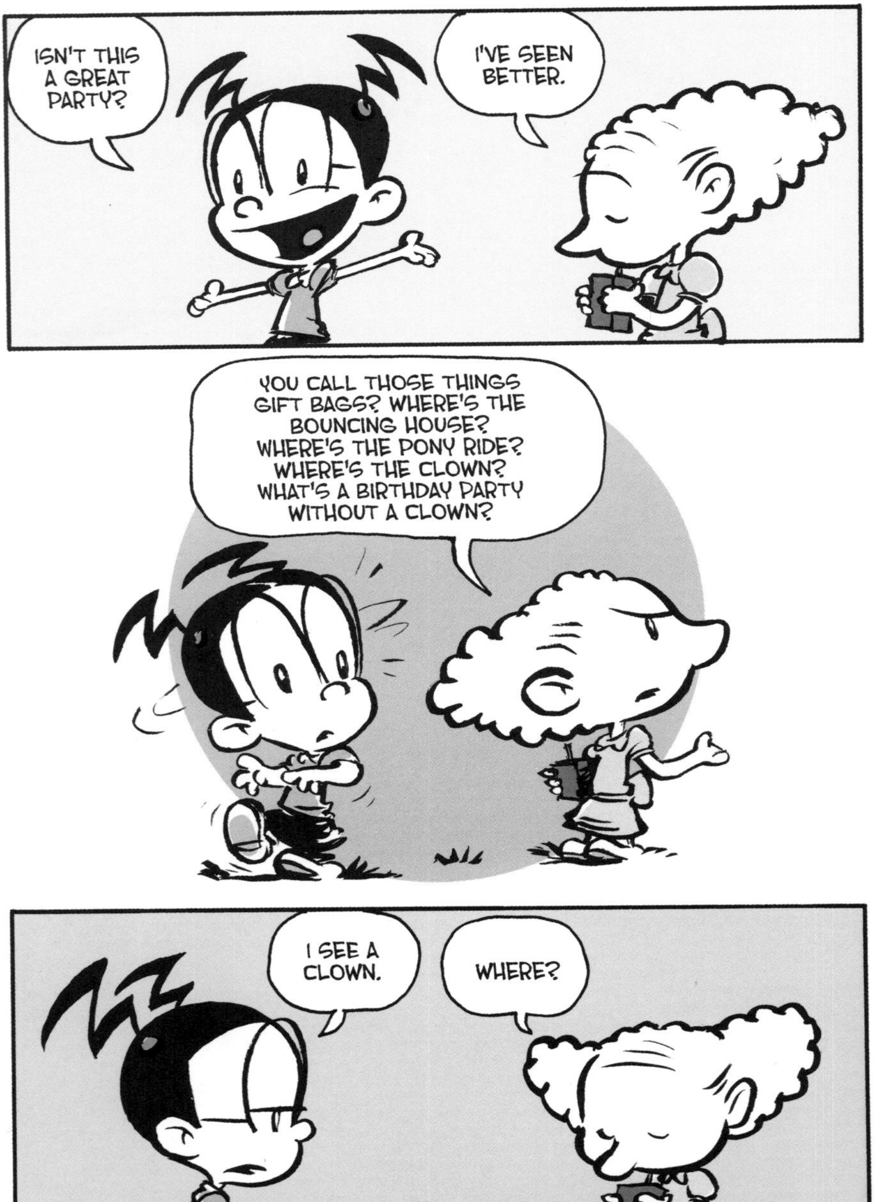
ISN'T THIS A GREAT PARTY?
I'VE SEEN BETTER.
YOU CALL THOSE THINGS GIFT BAGS? WHERE'S THE BOUNCING HOUSE? WHERE'S THE PONY RIDE? WHERE'S THE CLOWN? WHAT'S A BIRTHDAY PARTY WITHOUT A CLOWN?
I SEE A CLOWN.
WHERE?

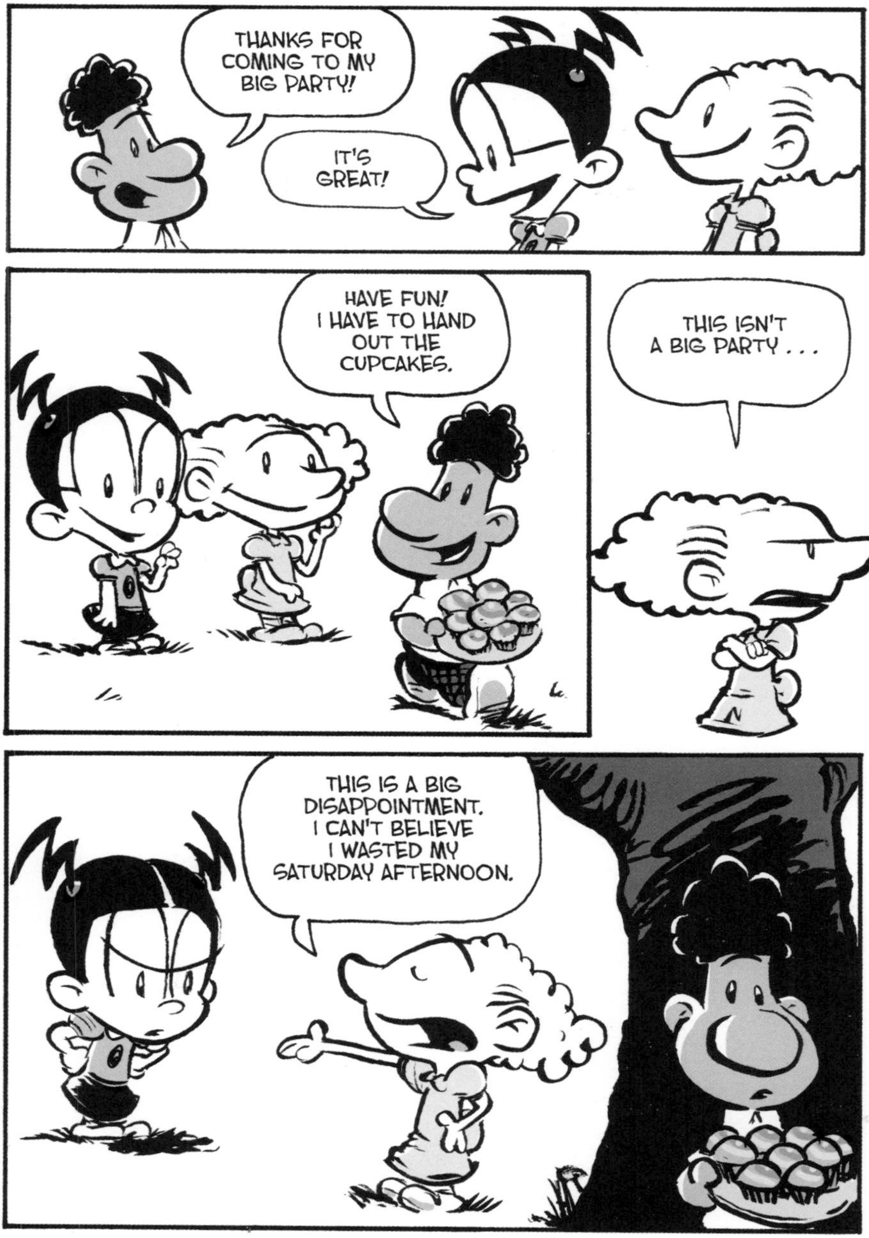
THANKS FOR COMING TO MY BIG PARTY!
IT'S GREAT!
HAVE FUN! I HAVE TO HAND OUT THE CUPCAKES.
THIS ISN'T A BIG PARTY . . .
THIS IS A BIG DISAPPOINTMENT. I CAN'T BELIEVE I WASTED MY SATURDAY AFTERNOON.

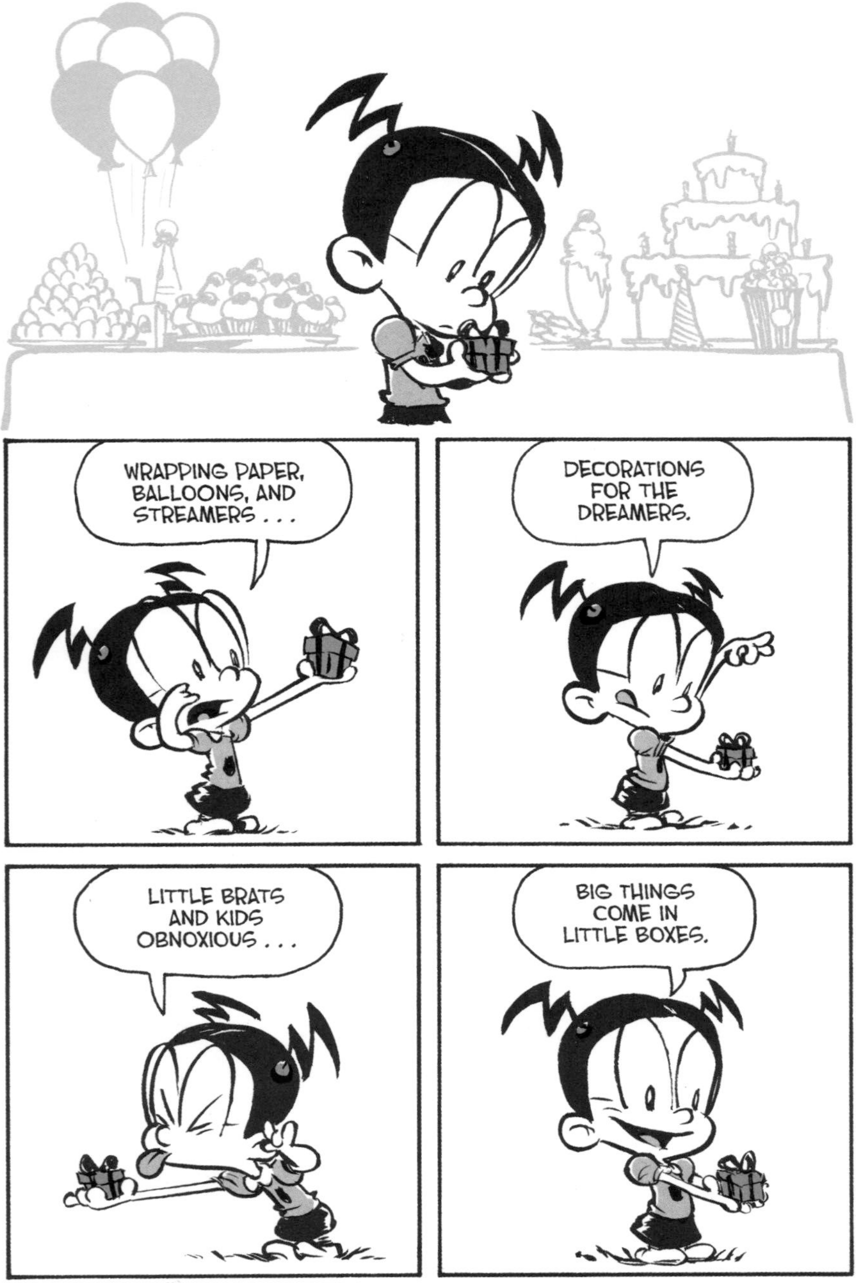
WRAPPING PAPER, BALLOONS, AND STREAMERS . . .
DECORATIONS FOR THE DREAMERS.
LITTLE BRATS AND KIDS OBNOXIOUS . . .
BIG THINGS COME IN LITTLE BOXES.

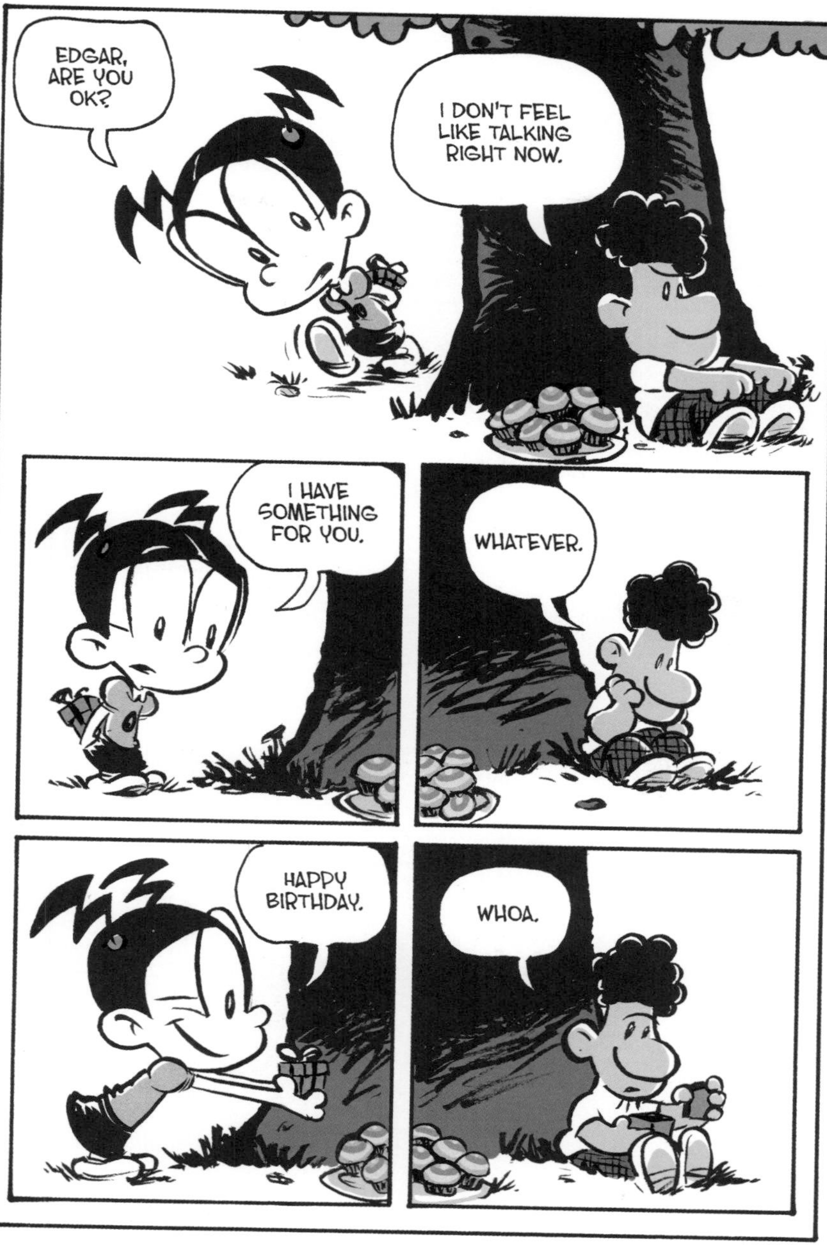
EDGAR, ARE YOU OK?
I DON'T FEEL LIKE TALKING RIGHT NOW.
I HAVE SOMETHING FOR YOU.
WHATEVER.
HAPPY BIRTHDAY.
WHOA.

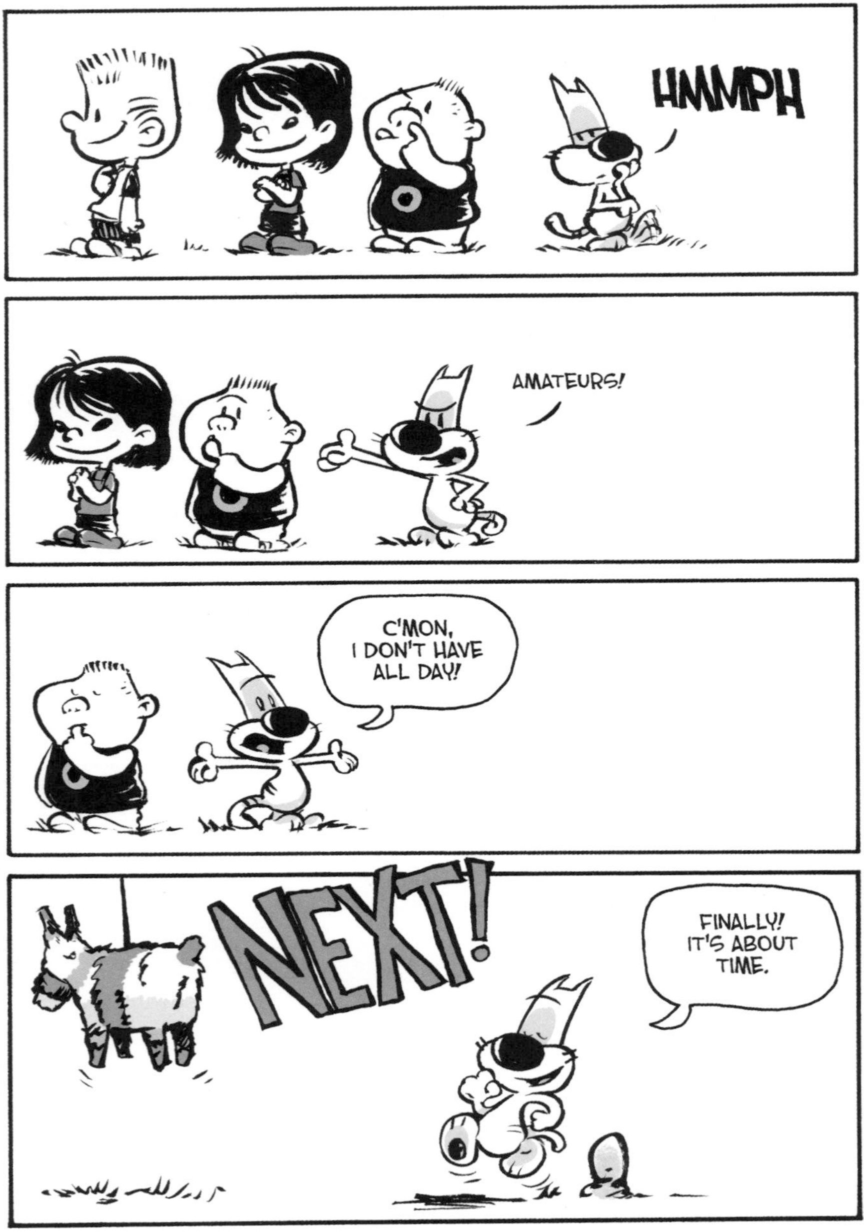
HMMPH
AMATEURS!
C'MON, I DON'T HAVE ALL DAY!
NEXT!
FINALLY! IT'S ABOUT TIME.

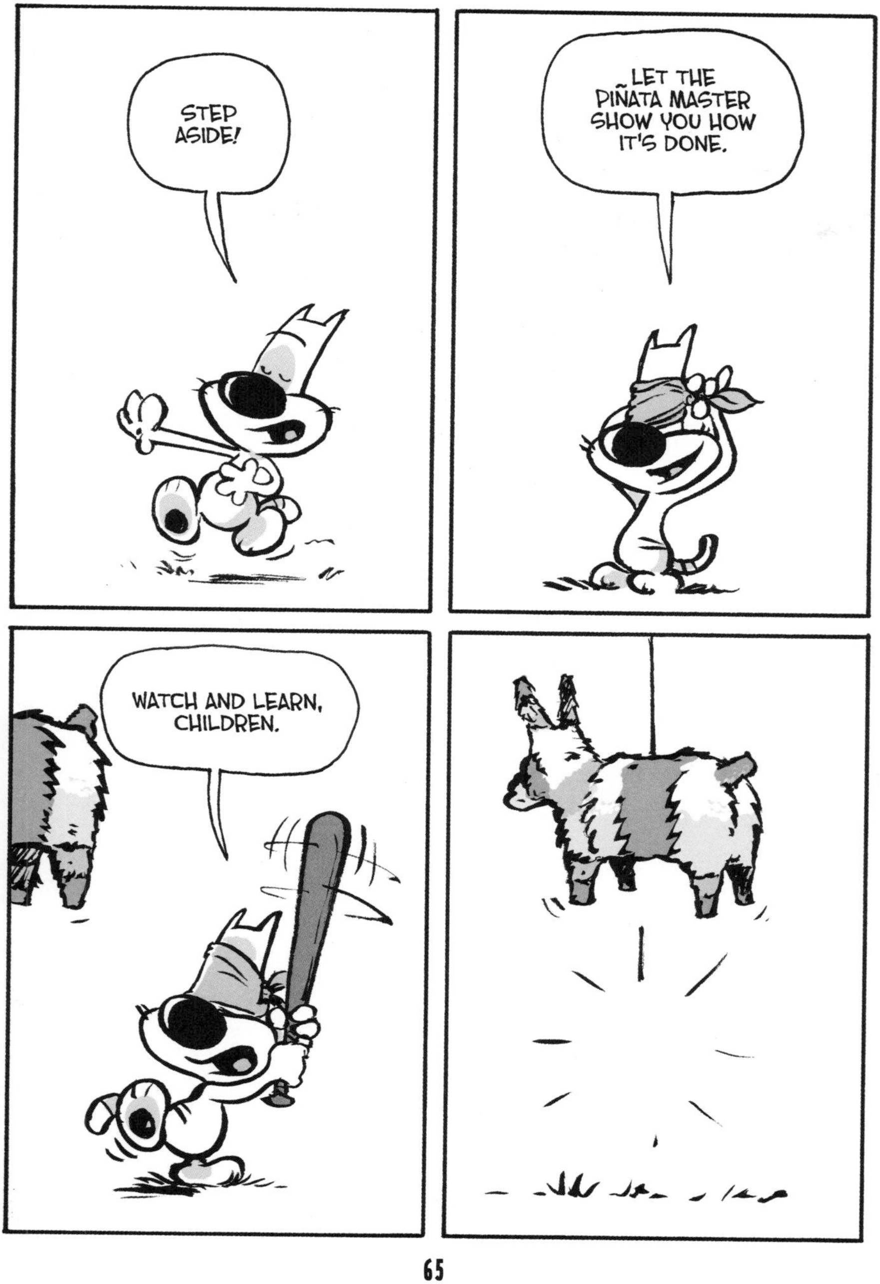
STEP ASIDE!
LET THE PIÑATA MASTER SHOW YOU HOW IT'S DONE.
WATCH AND LEARN, CHILDREN.

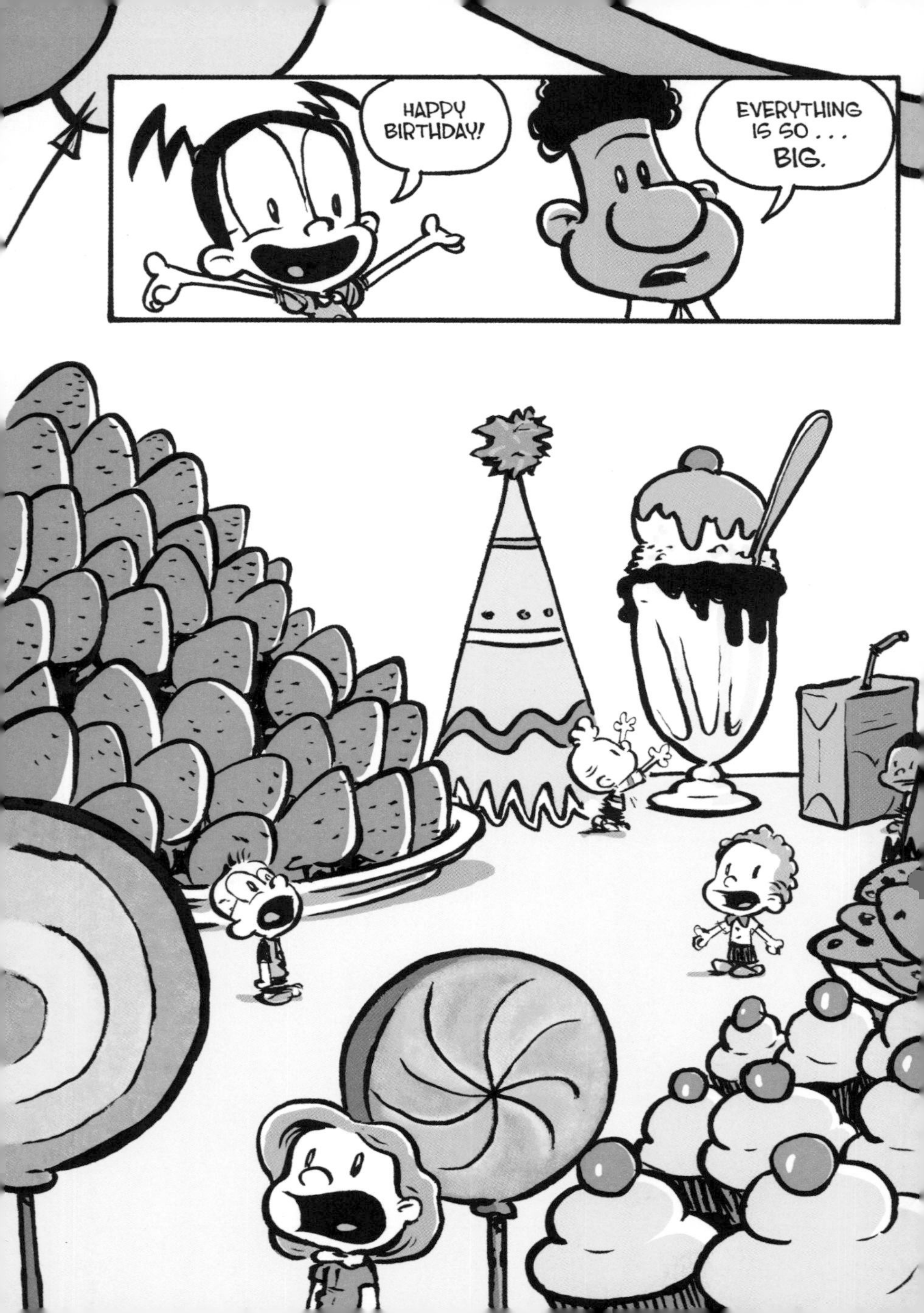
HAPPY BIRTHDAY!
EVERYTHING IS SO . . . BIG.

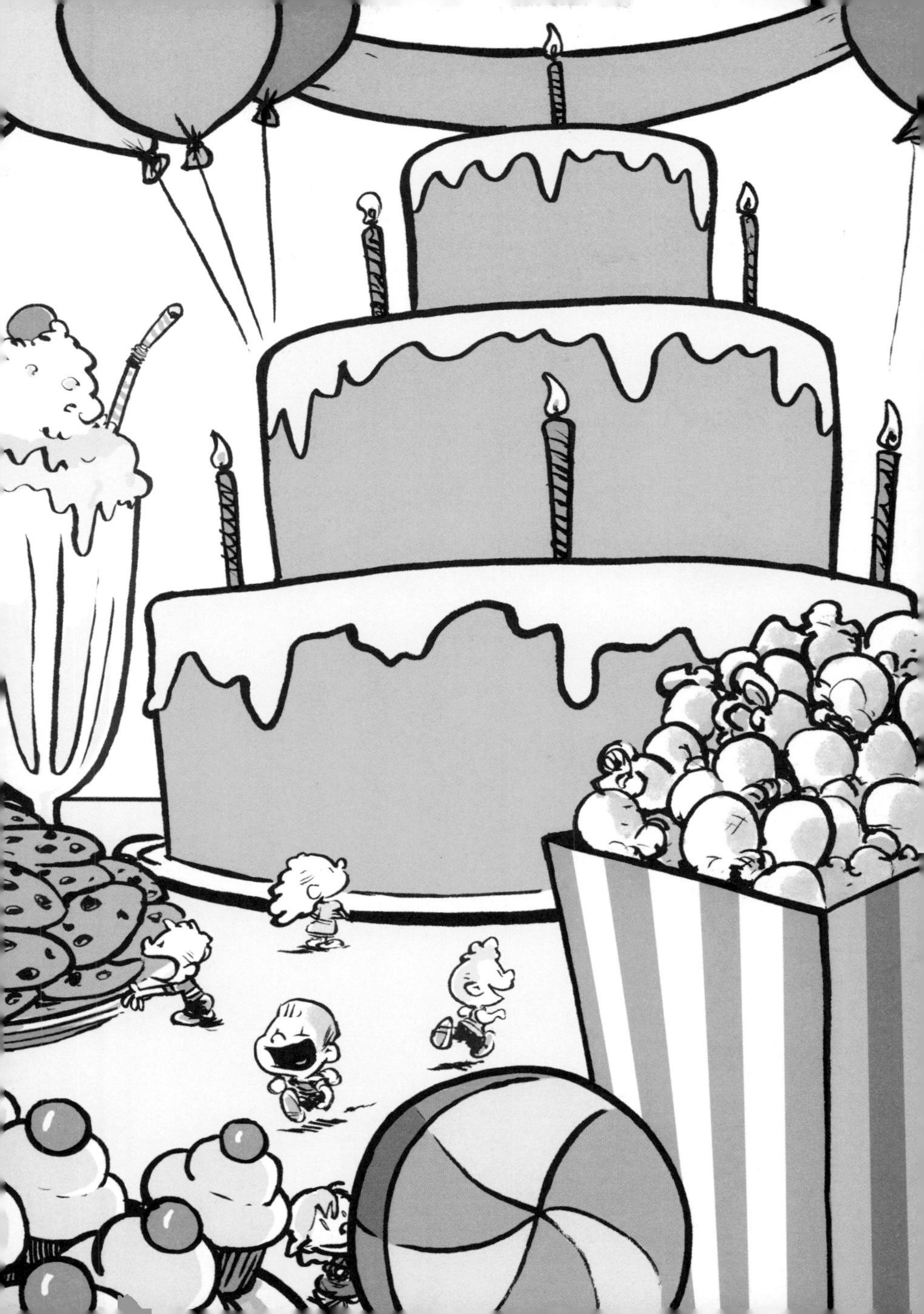

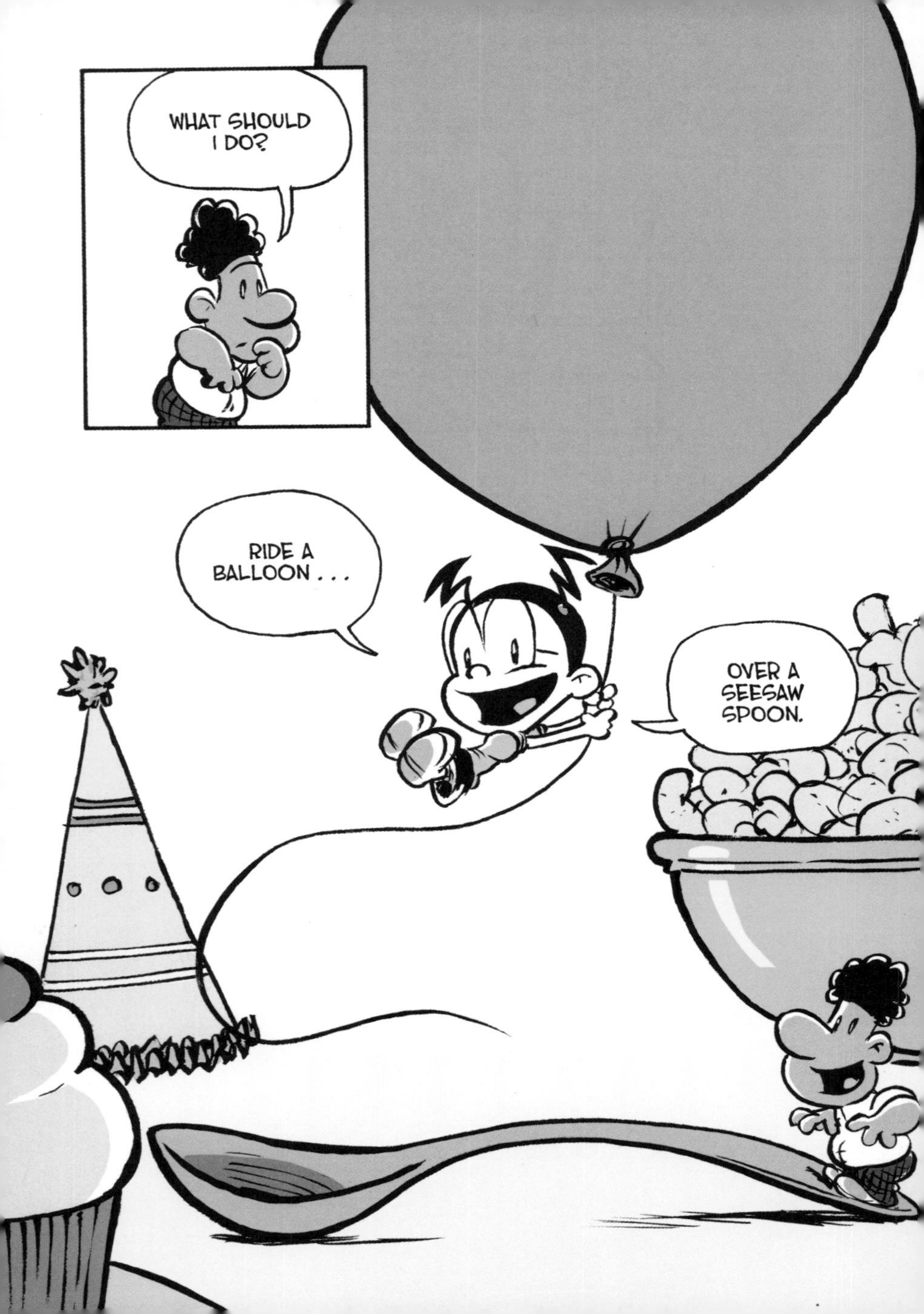
WHAT SHOULD I DO?
RIDE A BALLOON . . .
OVER A SEESAW SPOON.

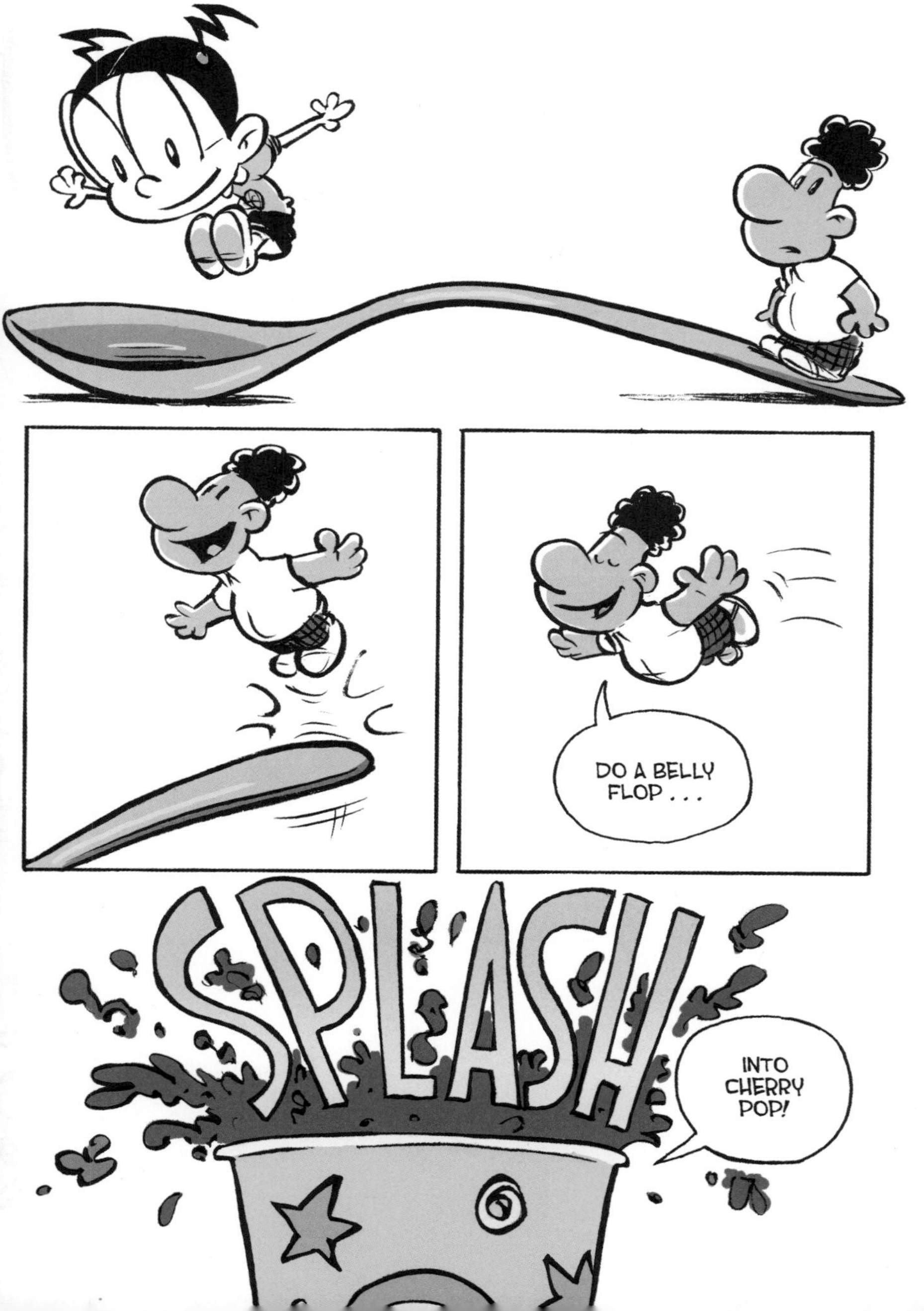
DO A BELLY FLOP . . .
SPLASH
INTO CHERRY POP!

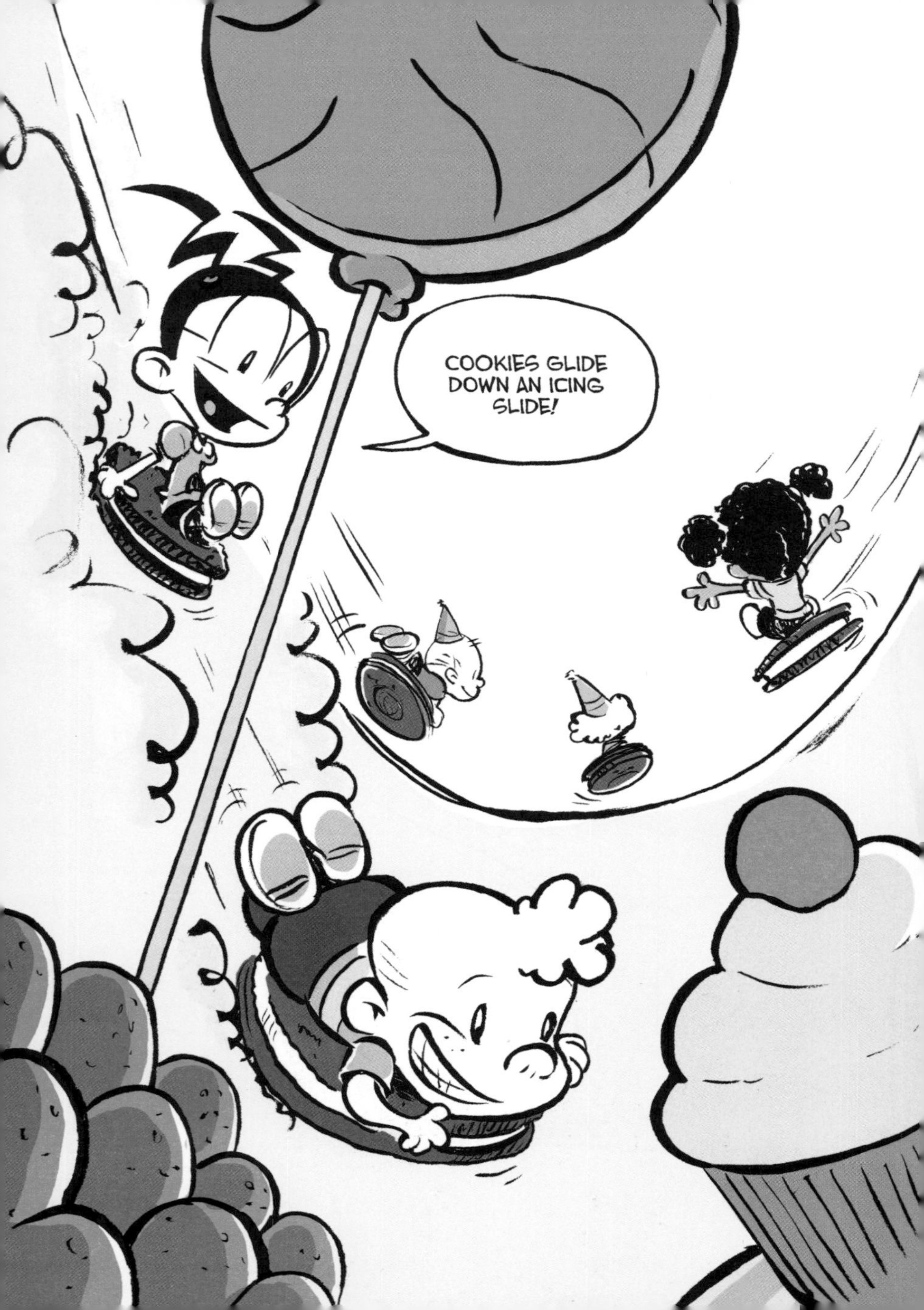
COOKIES GLIDE DOWN AN ICING SLIDE!

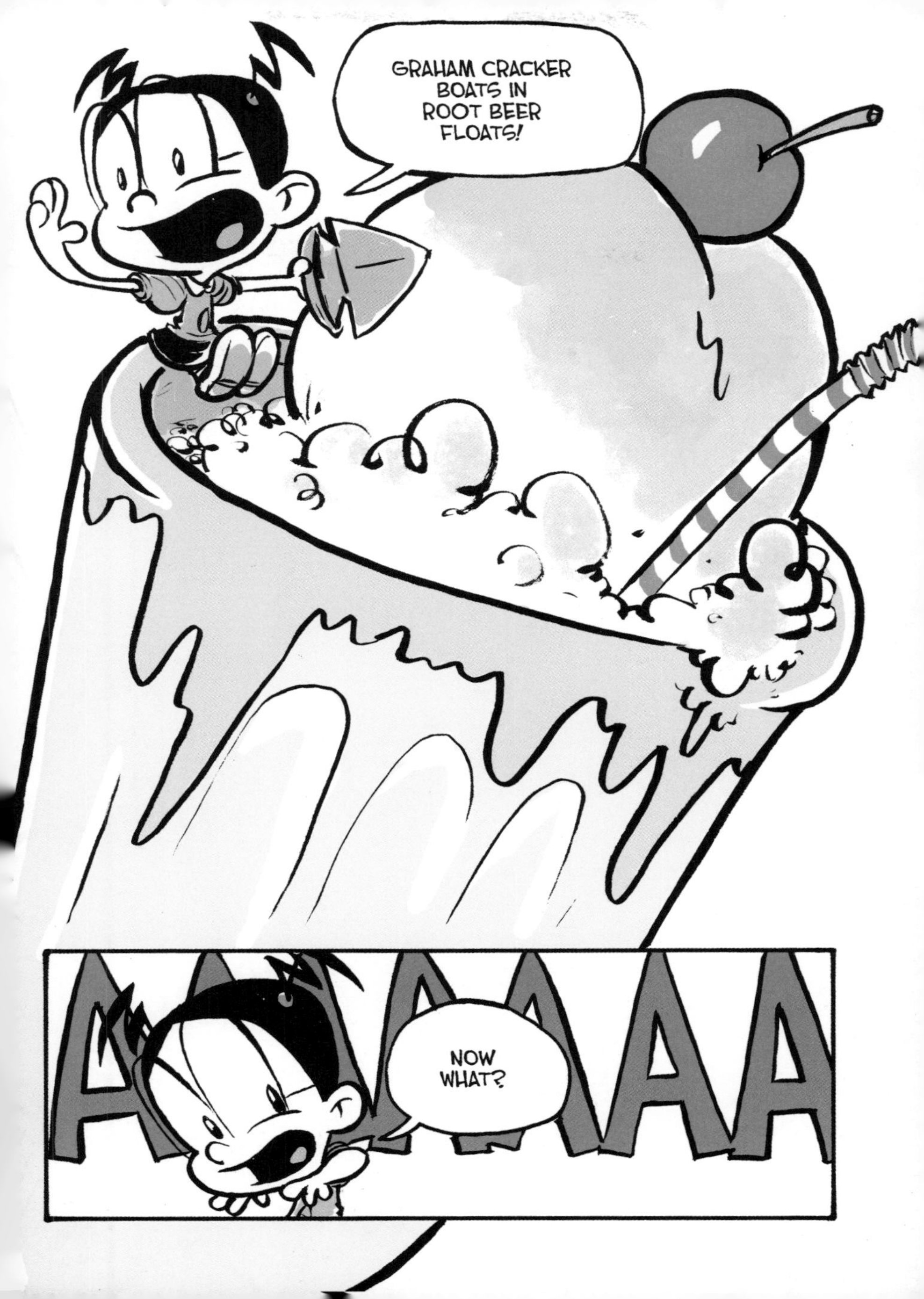
GRAHAM CRACKER BOATS IN ROOT BEER FLOATS!
AAAAAA
NOW WHAT?

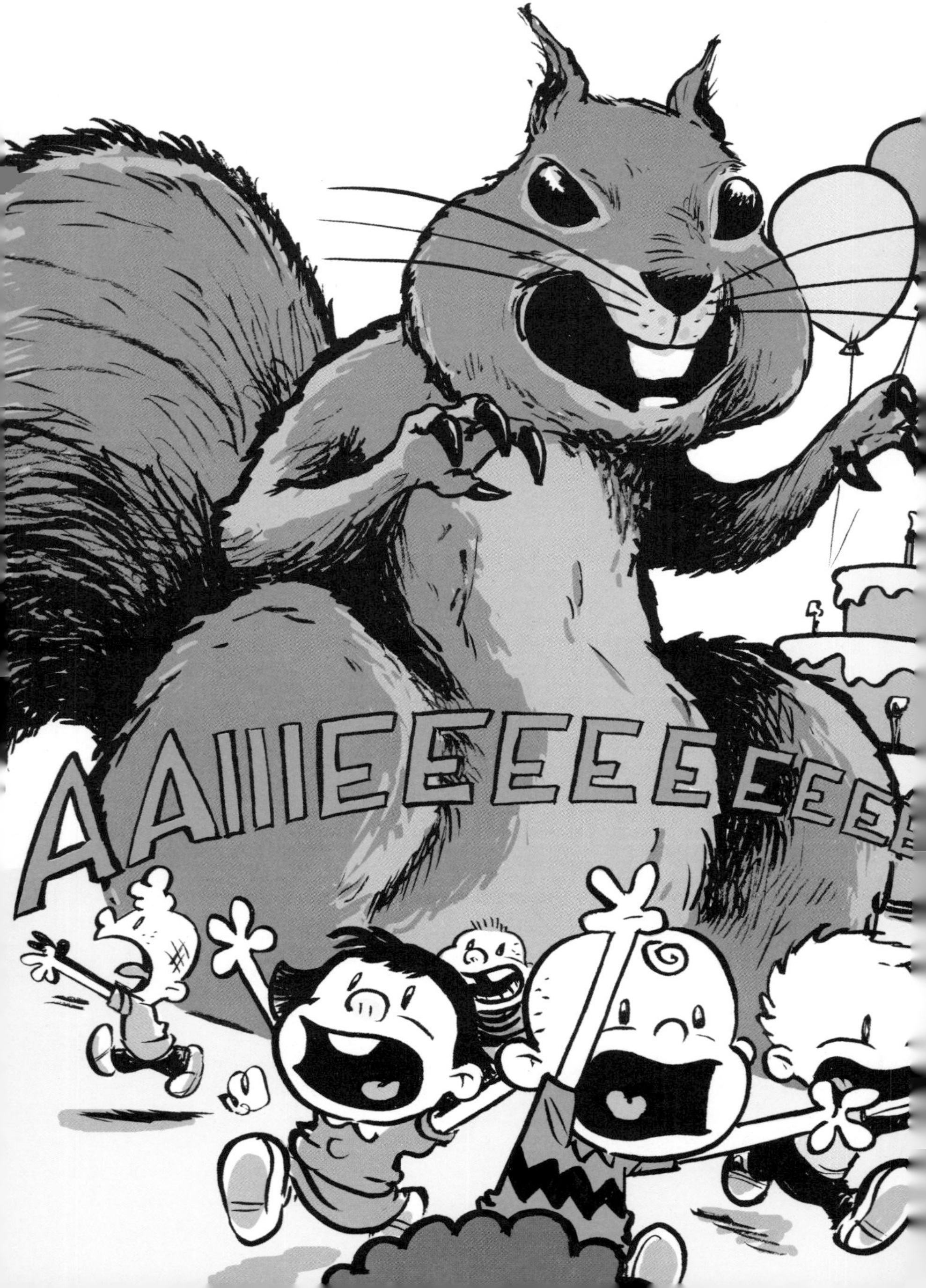
AAIIIEEEEEEEEE

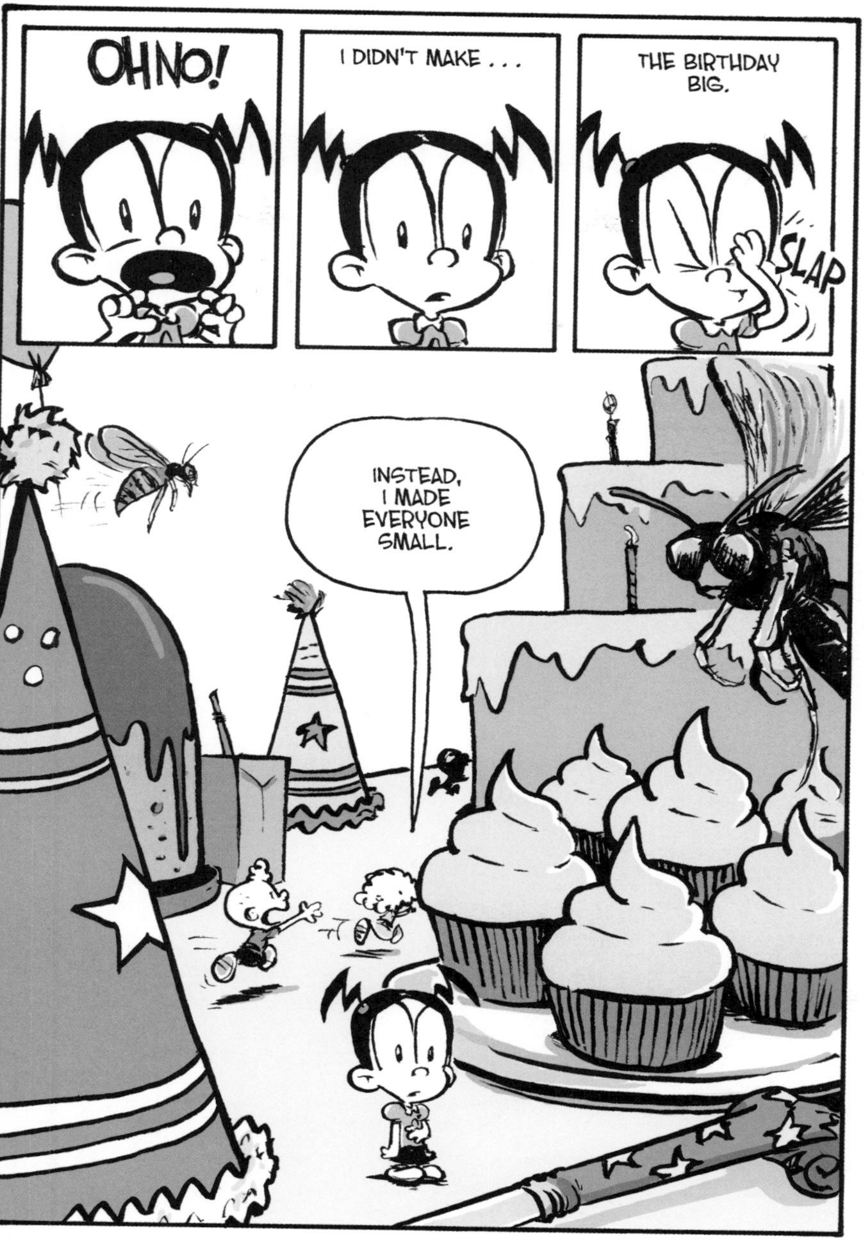
OH NO!
I DIDN'T MAKE . . .
THE BIRTHDAY BIG.
SLAP
INSTEAD, I MADE EVERYONE SMALL.

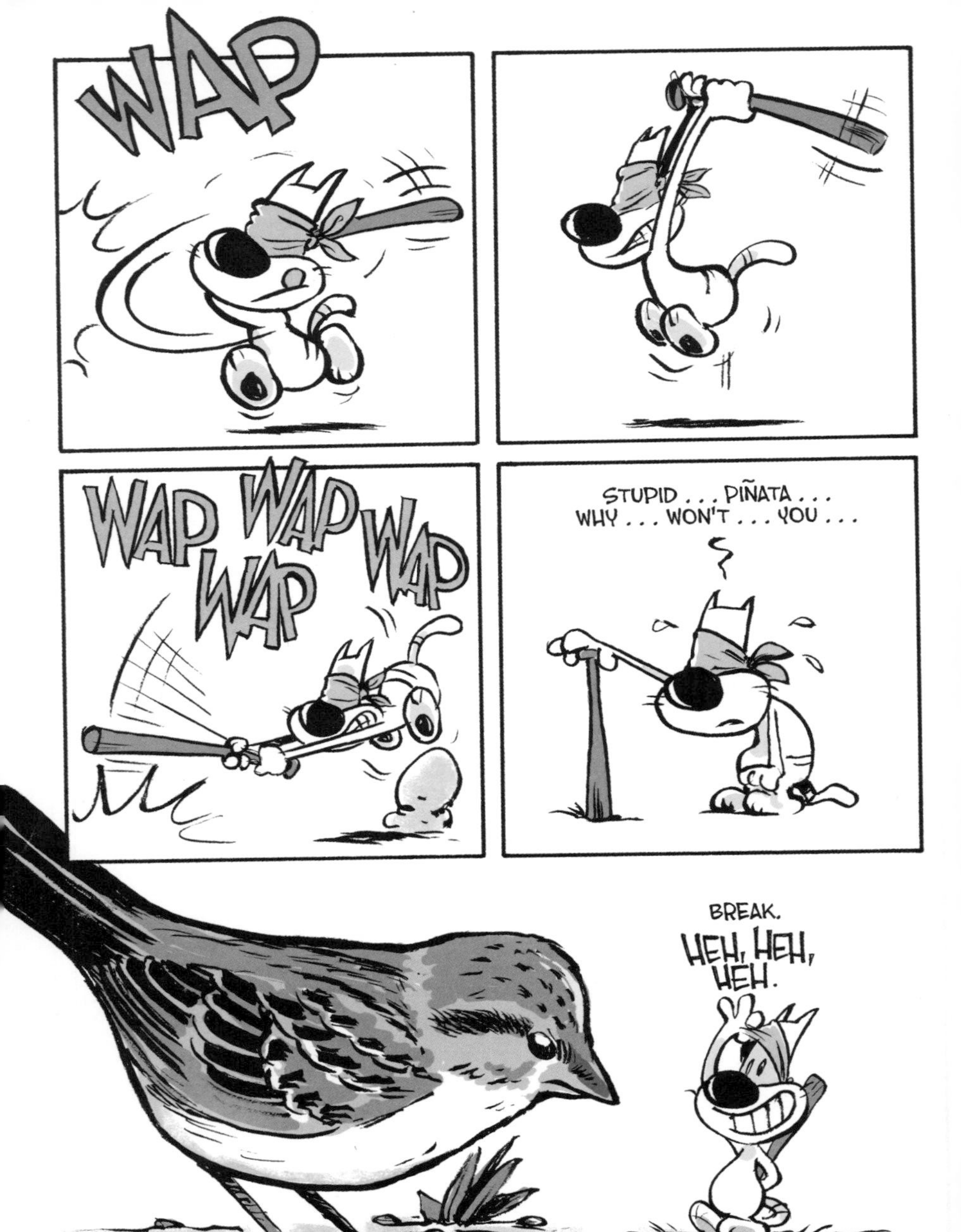
WAP
WAP WAP WAP WAP
STUPID . . . PIÑATA . . .
WHY . . . WON'T . . . YOU . . .
BREAK.
HEH, HEH, HEH.

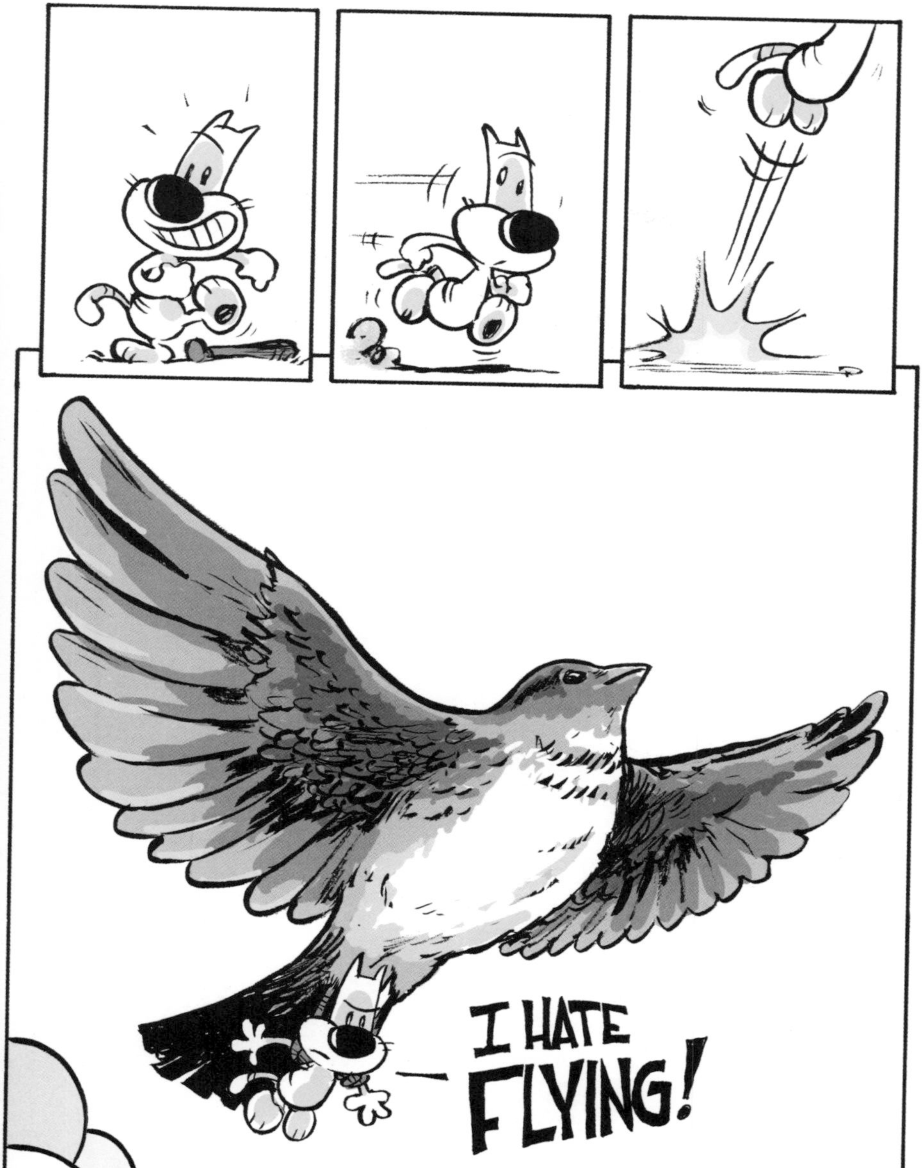
I HATE
FLYING!

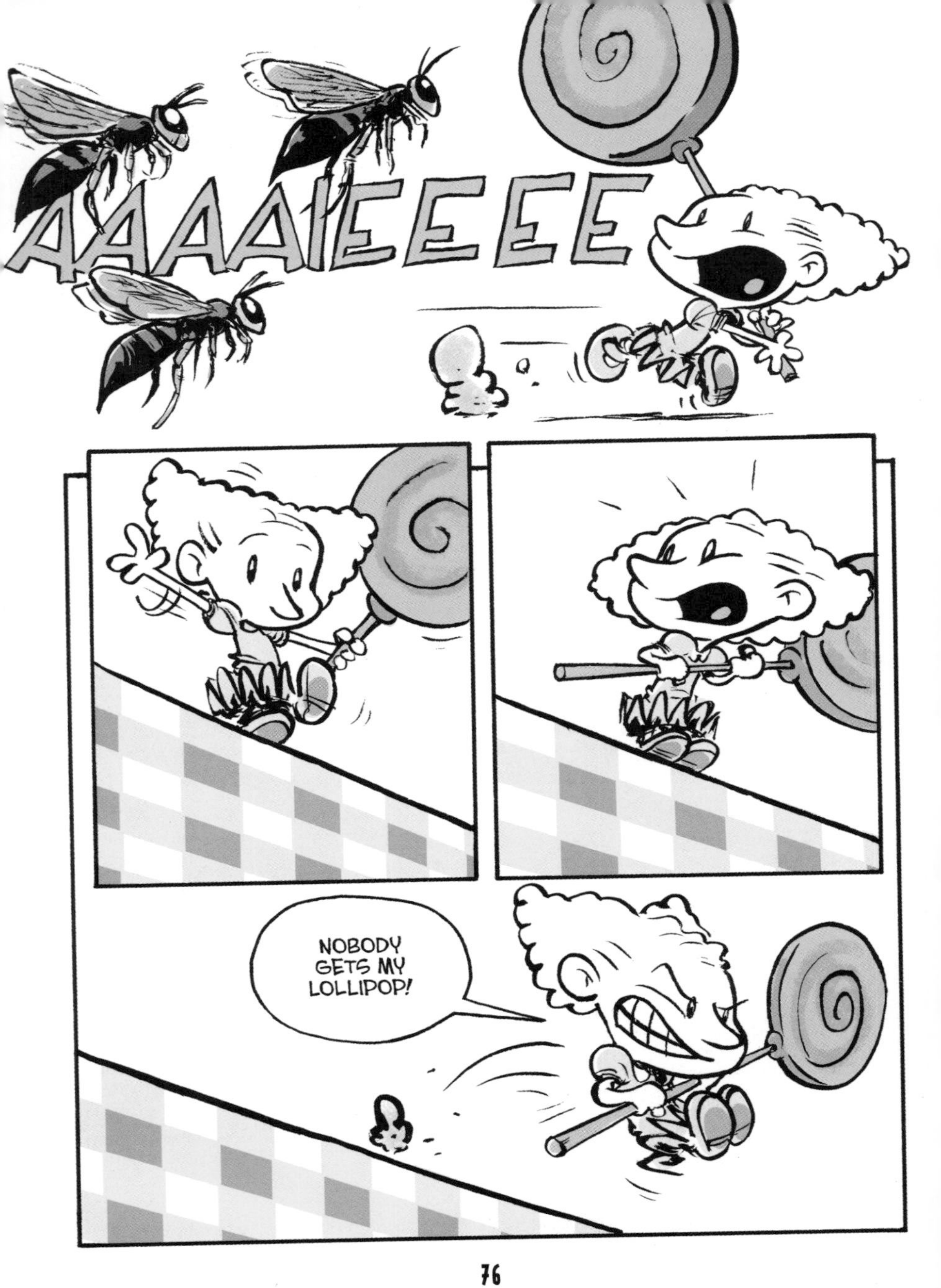
AAAAIEEEEE
NOBODY GETS MY LOLLIPOP!

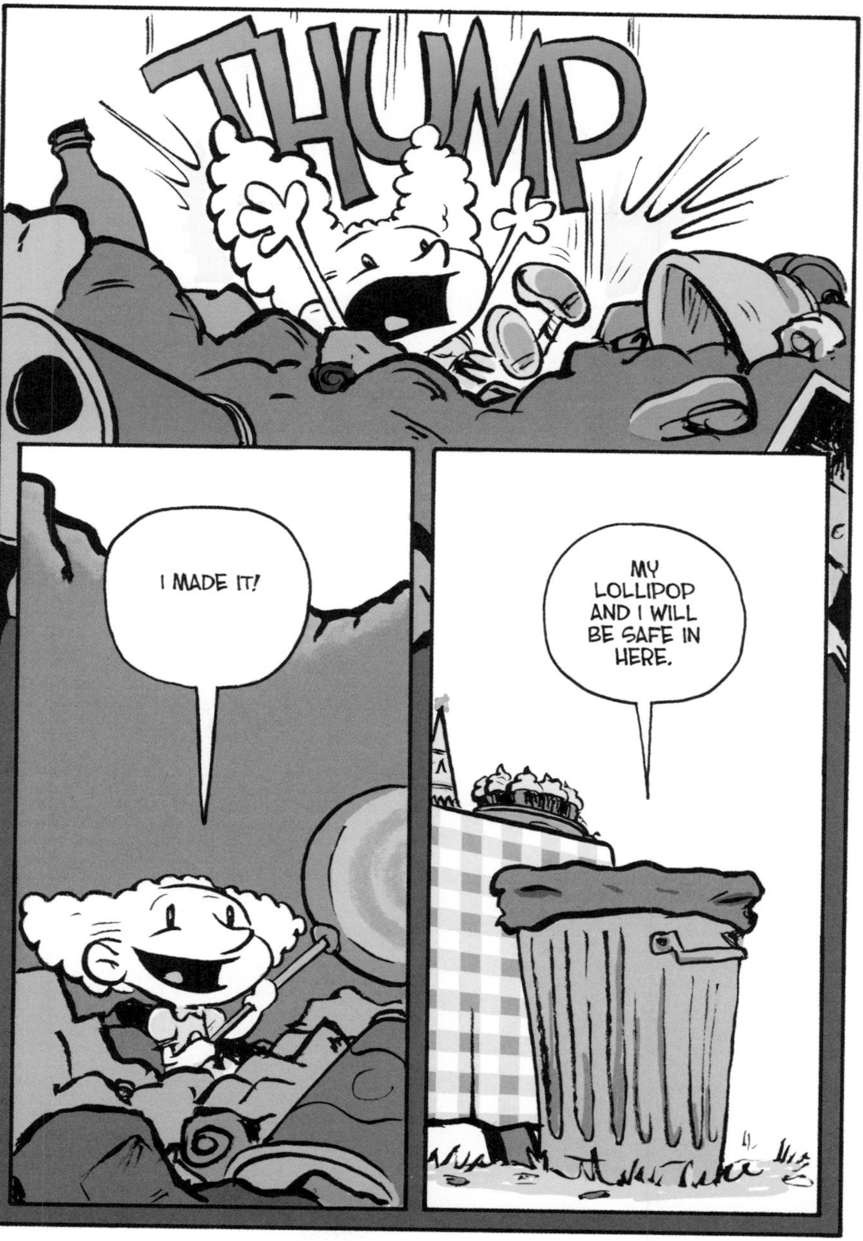
THUMP
I MADE IT!
MY LOLLIPOP AND I WILL BE SAFE IN HERE.

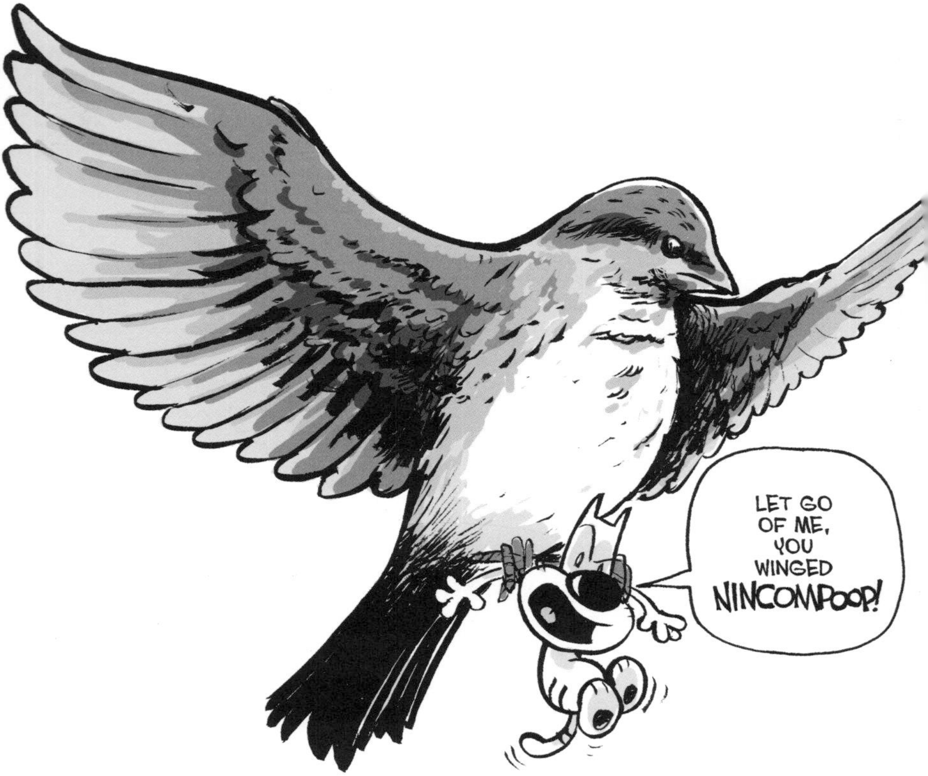
LET GO OF ME, YOU WINGED NINCOMPOOP!

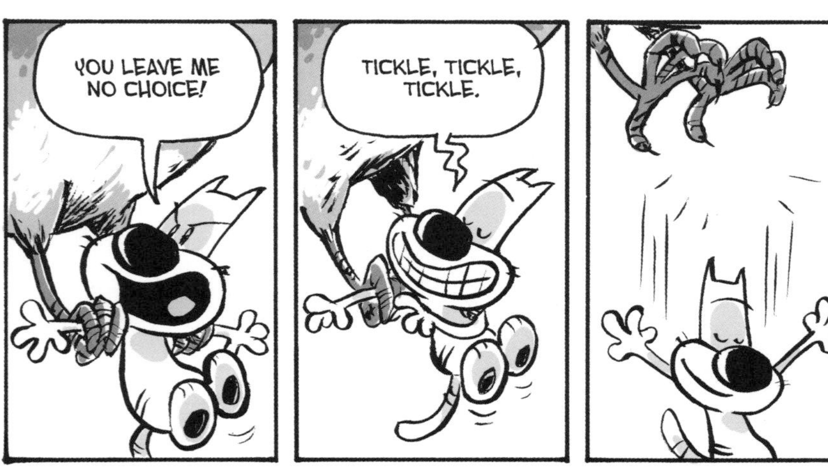
YOU LEAVE ME NO CHOICE!
TICKLE, TICKLE, TICKLE.

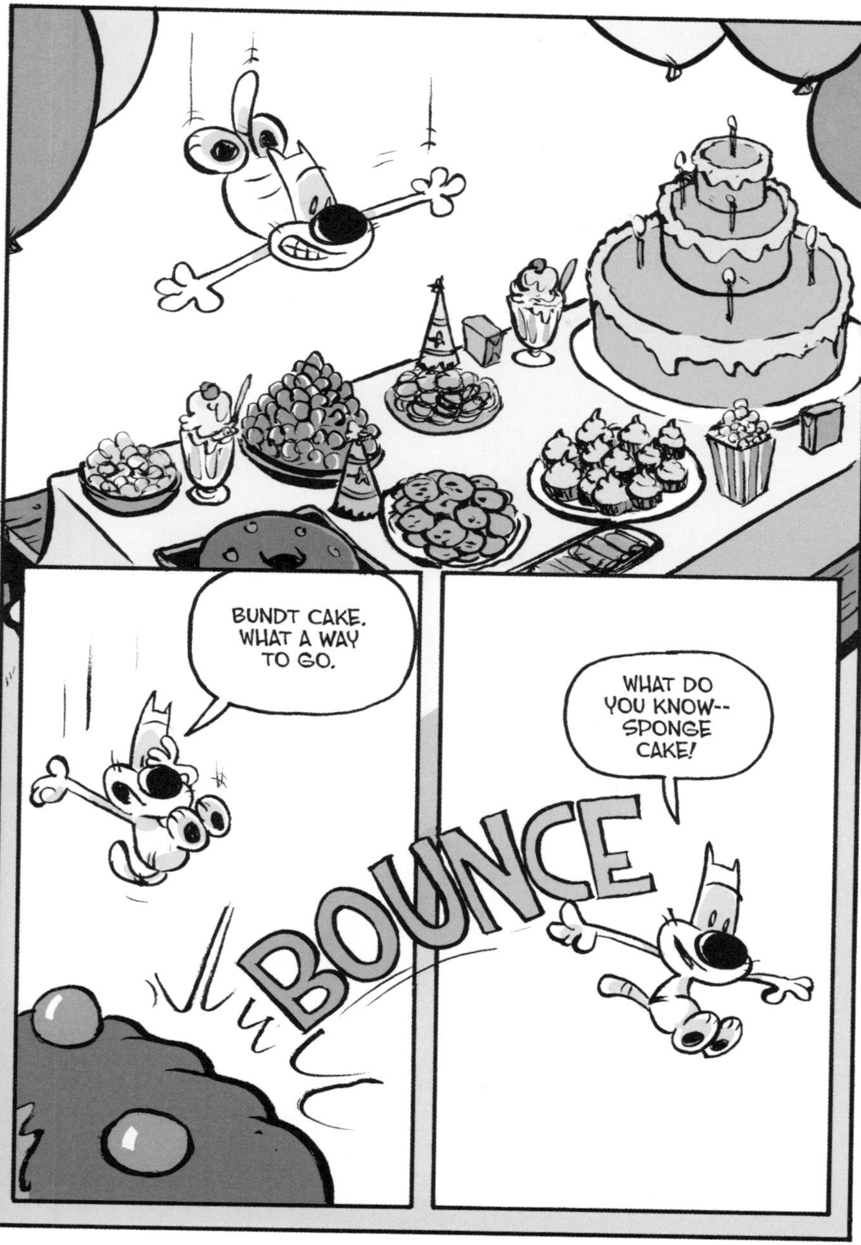
BUNDT CAKE. WHAT A WAY TO GO.
WHAT DO YOU KNOW-- SPONGE CAKE!
BOUNCE

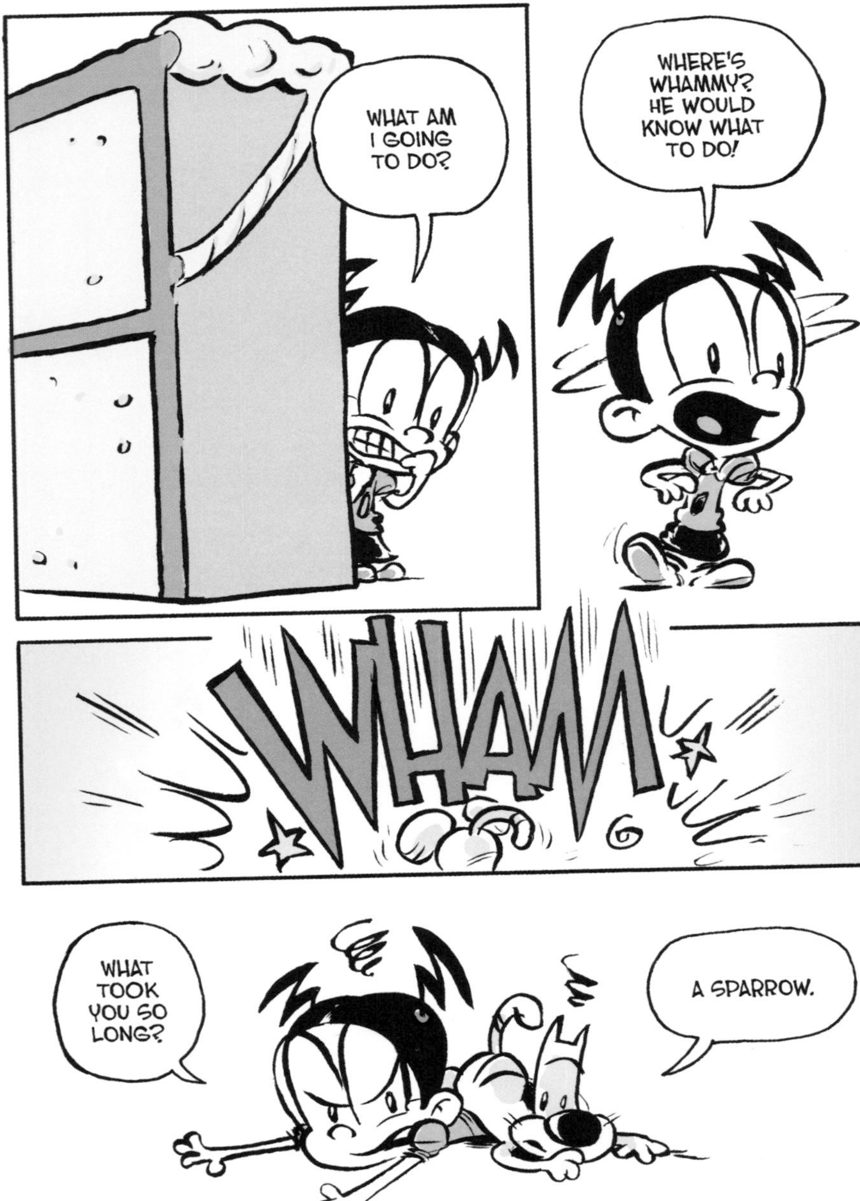
WHAT AM I GOING TO DO?
WHERE'S WHAMMY? HE WOULD KNOW WHAT TO DO!
WHAM
WHAT TOOK YOU SO LONG?
A SPARROW.

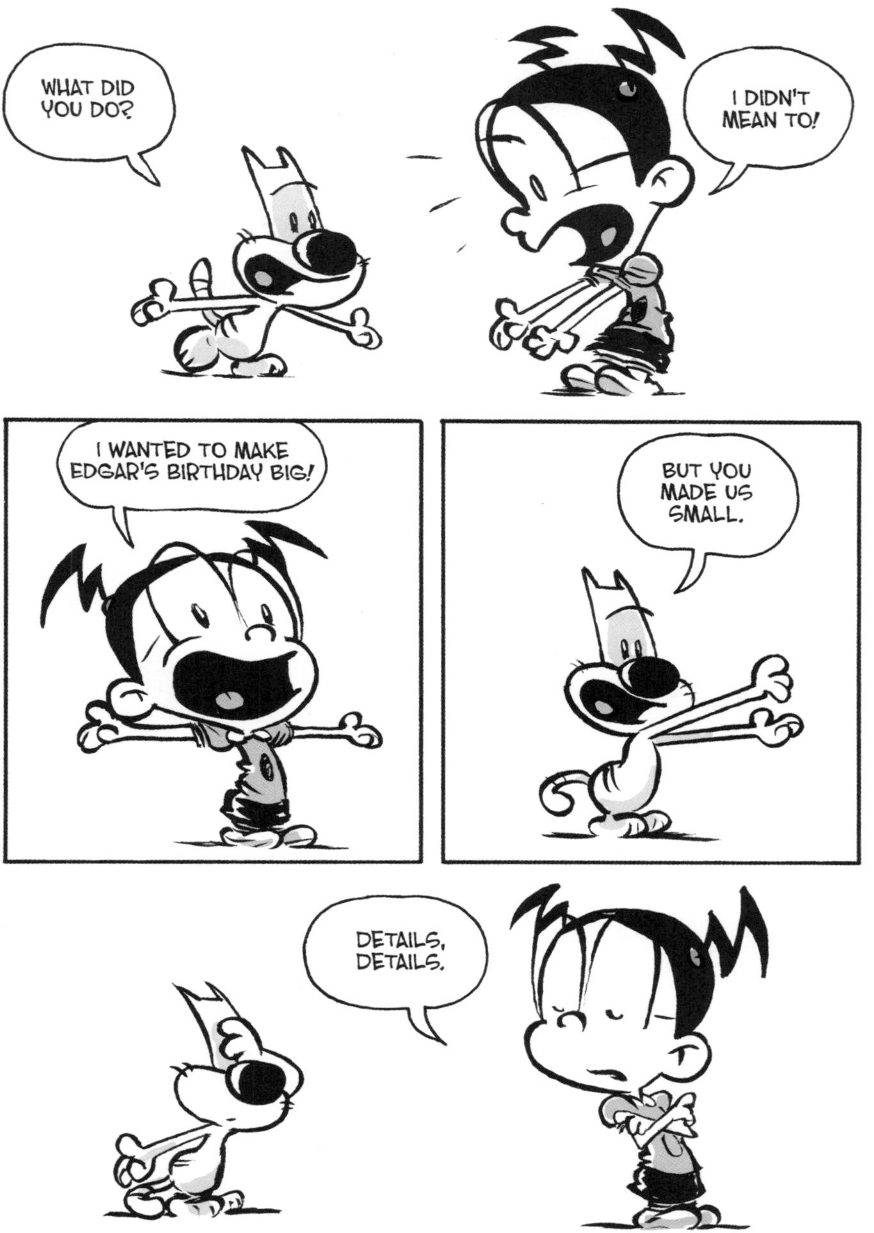
WHAT DID YOU DO?
I DIDN'T MEAN TO!
I WANTED TO MAKE EDGAR'S BIRTHDAY BIG!
BUT YOU MADE US SMALL.
DETAILS, DETAILS.

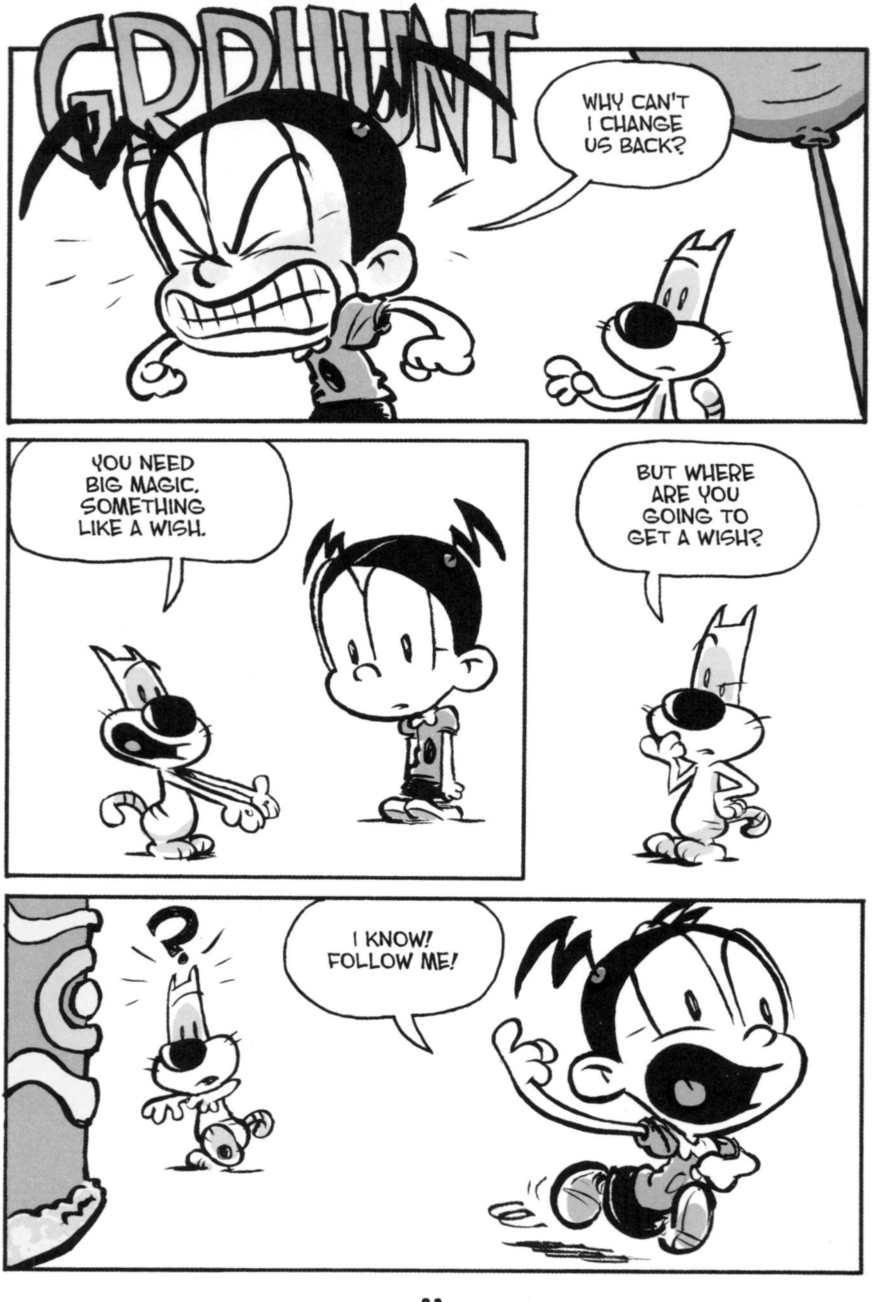
GRDHUNT
WHY CAN'T I CHANGE US BACK?
YOU NEED BIG MAGIC. SOMETHING LIKE A WISH.
BUT WHERE ARE YOU GOING TO GET A WISH?
?
I KNOW! FOLLOW ME!

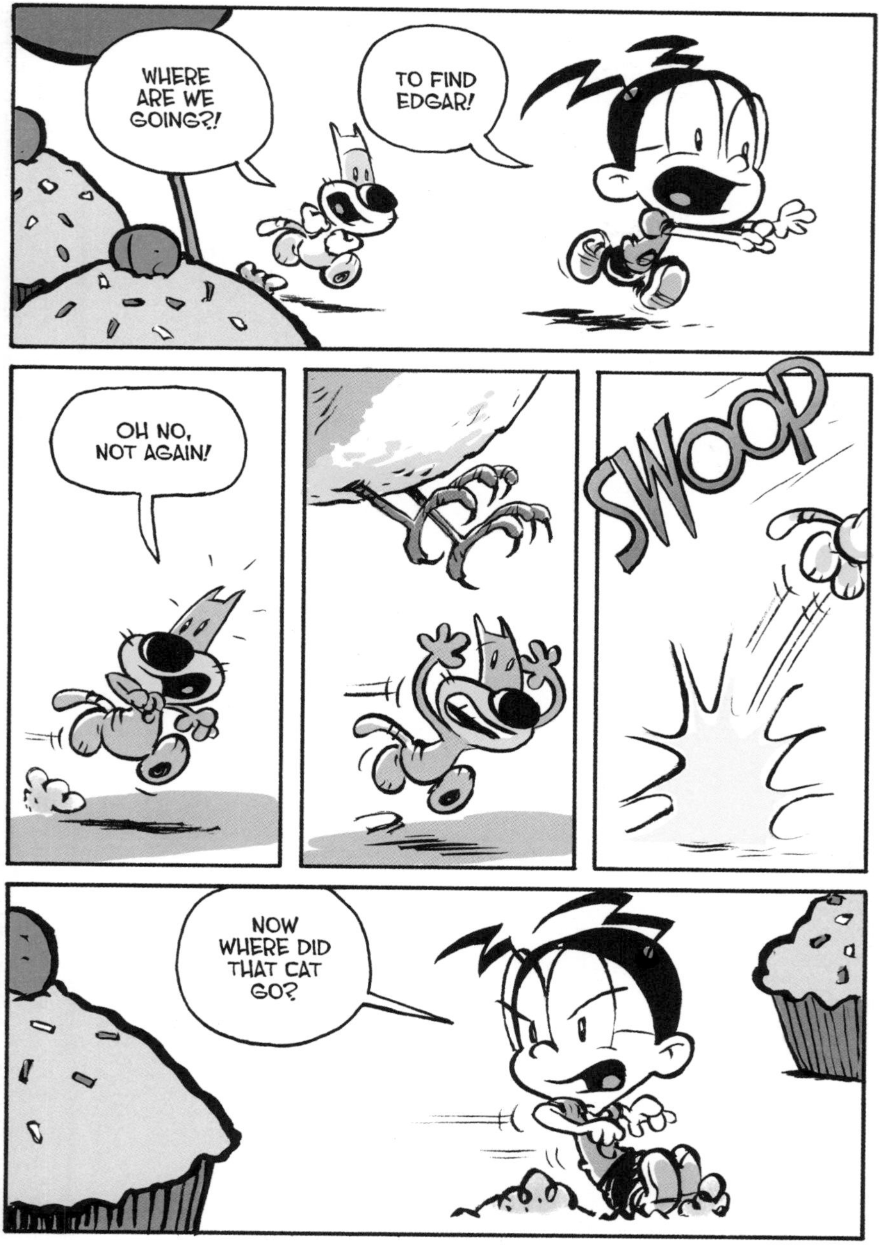
WHERE ARE WE GOING?!
TO FIND EDGAR!
OH NO, NOT AGAIN!
SWOOP
NOW WHERE DID THAT CAT GO?

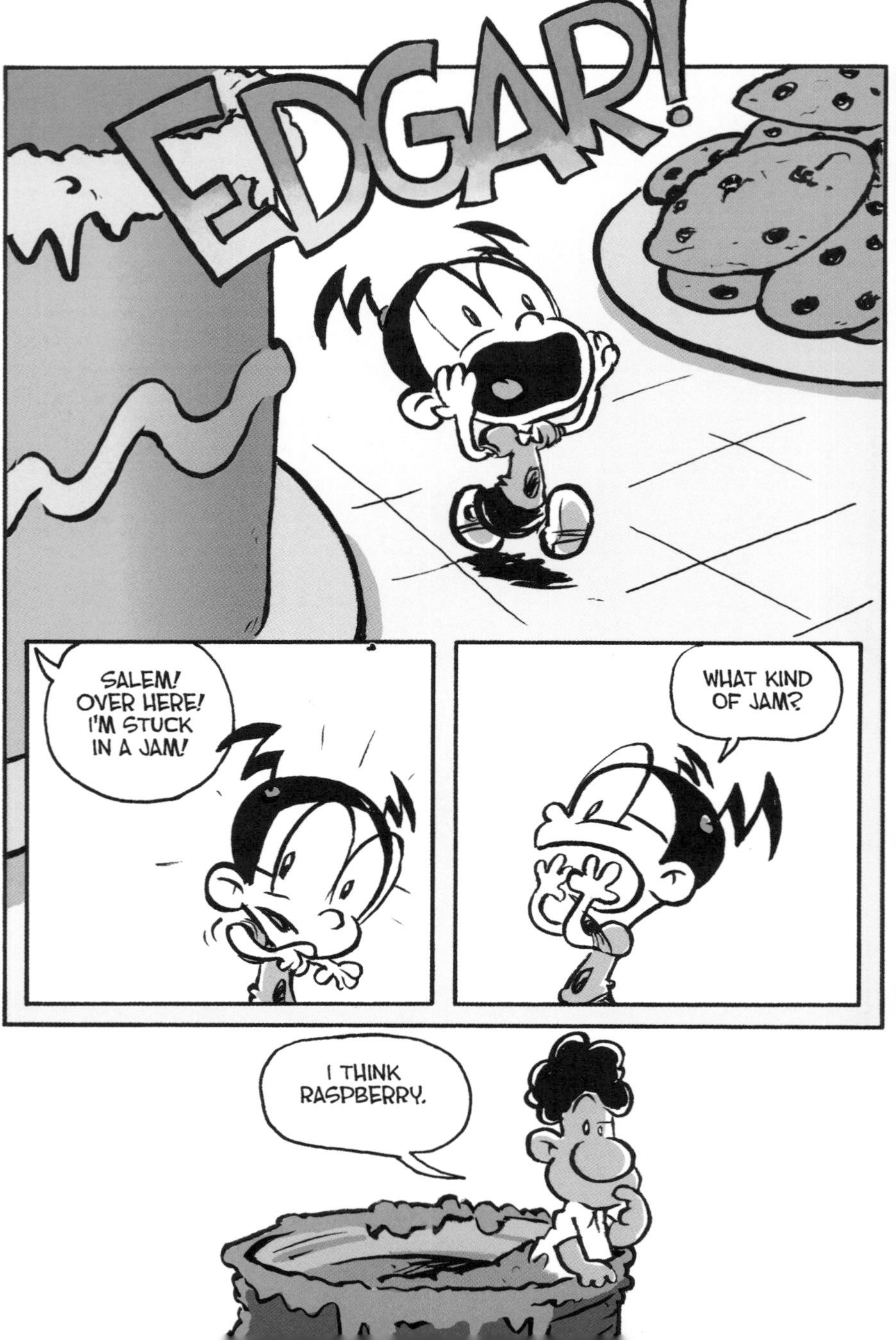
EDGAR!
SALEM! OVER HERE! I'M STUCK IN A JAM!
WHAT KIND OF JAM?
I THINK RASPBERRY.

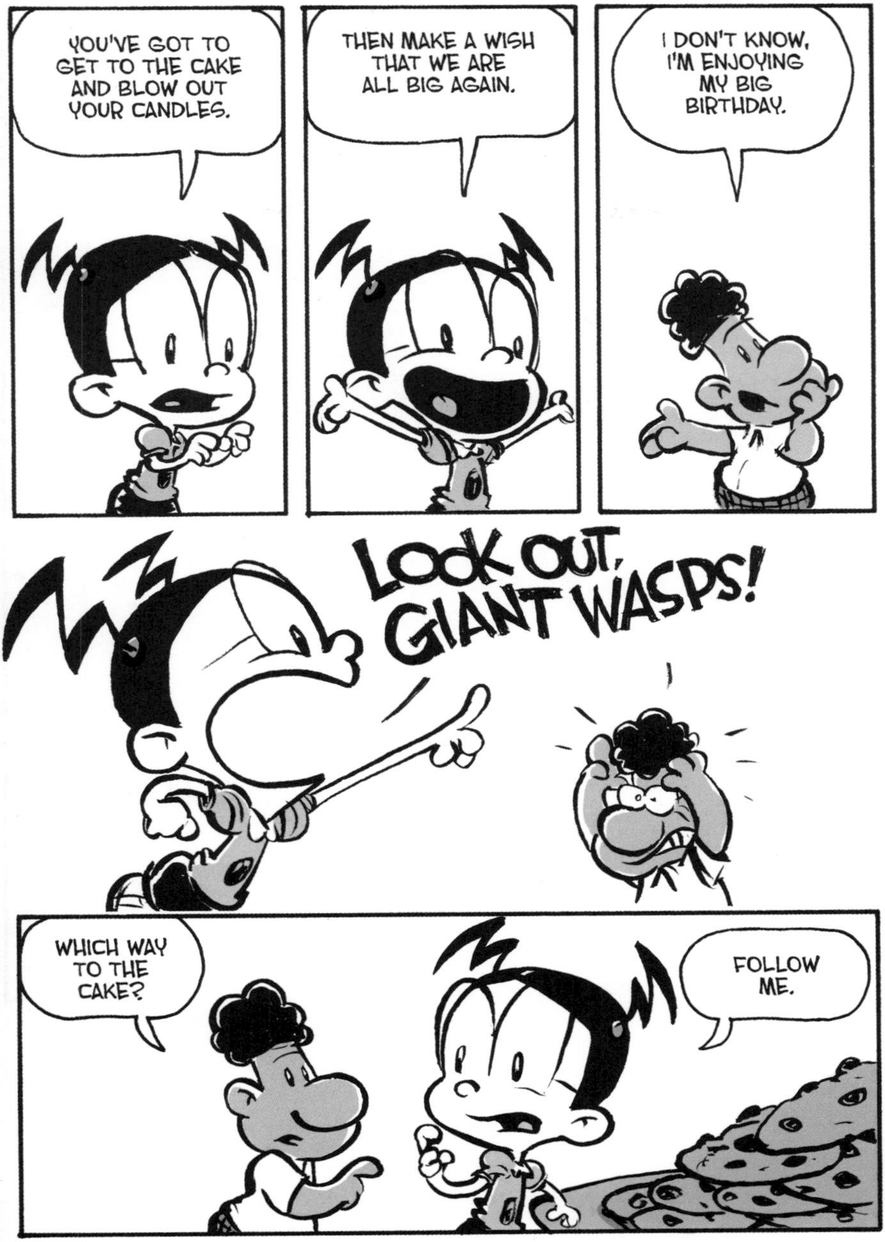
YOU'VE GOT TO GET TO THE CAKE AND BLOW OUT YOUR CANDLES.
THEN MAKE A WISH THAT WE ARE ALL BIG AGAIN.
I DON'T KNOW, I'M ENJOYING MY BIG BIRTHDAY.
LOOK OUT, GIANT WASPS!
WHICH WAY TO THE CAKE?
FOLLOW ME.

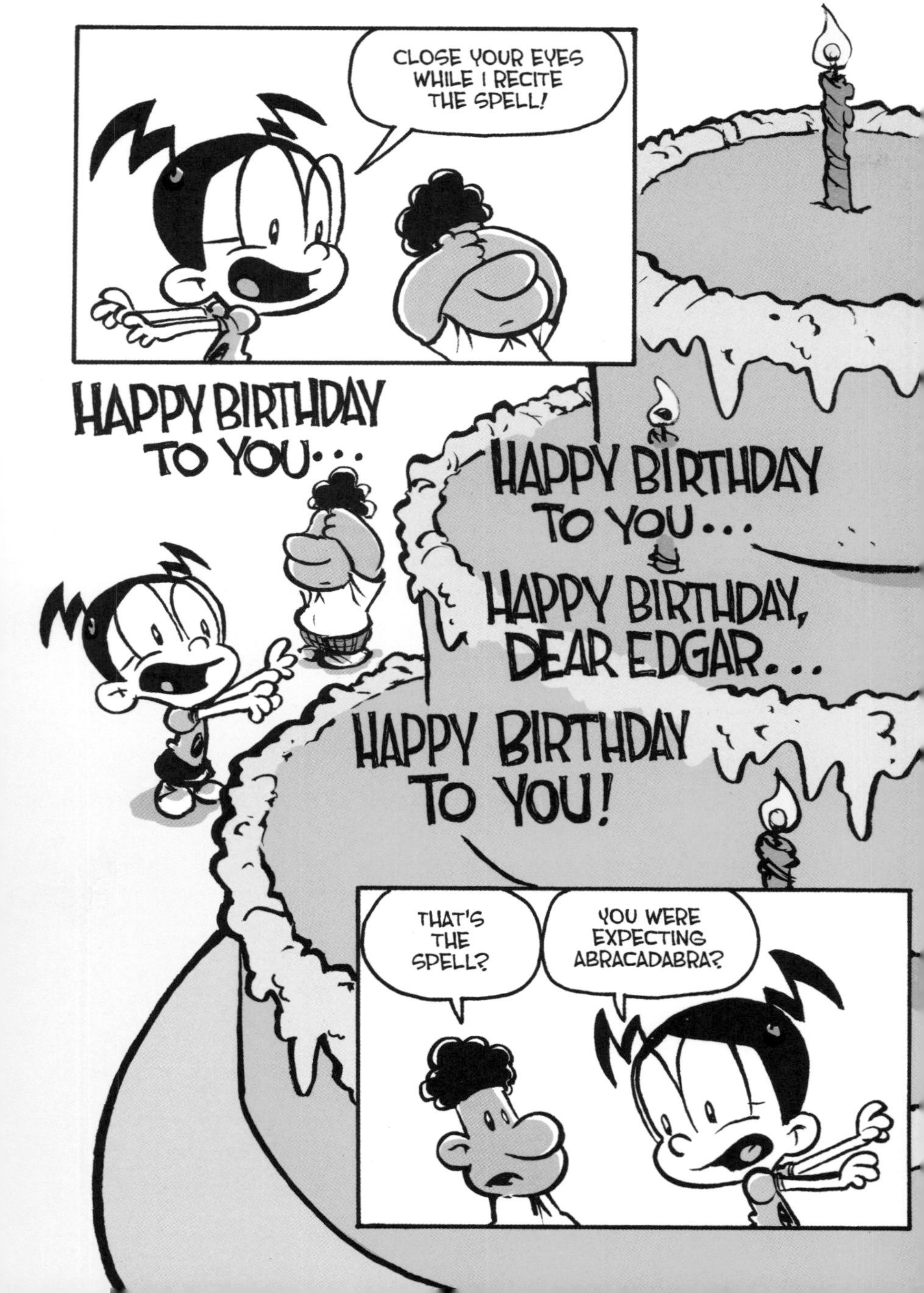
CLOSE YOUR EYES WHILE I RECITE THE SPELL!
HAPPY BIRTHDAY TO YOU...
HAPPY BIRTHDAY TO YOU...
HAPPY BIRTHDAY, DEAR EDGAR...
HAPPY BIRTHDAY TO YOU!
THAT'S THE SPELL?
YOU WERE EXPECTING ABRACADABRA?

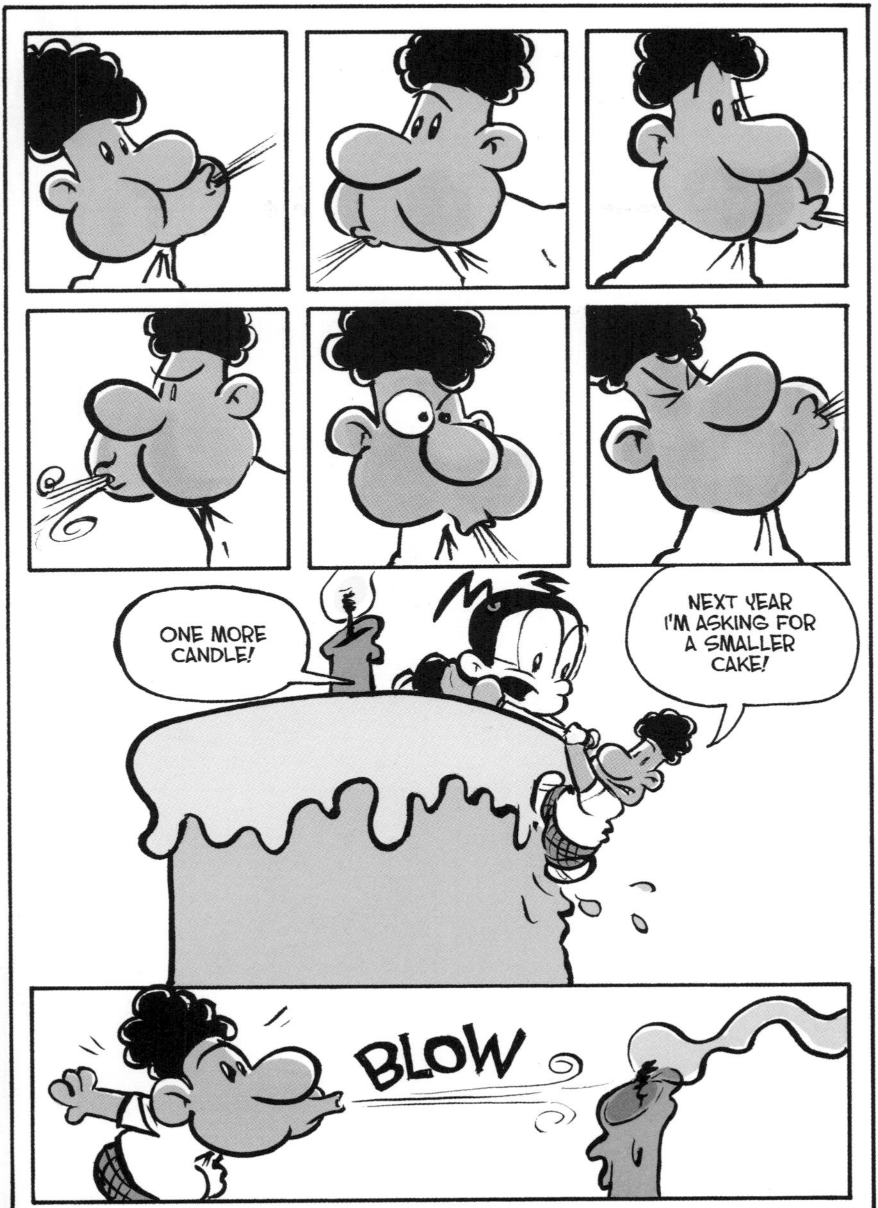
ONE MORE CANDLE!
NEXT YEAR I'M ASKING FOR A SMALLER CAKE!
BLOW

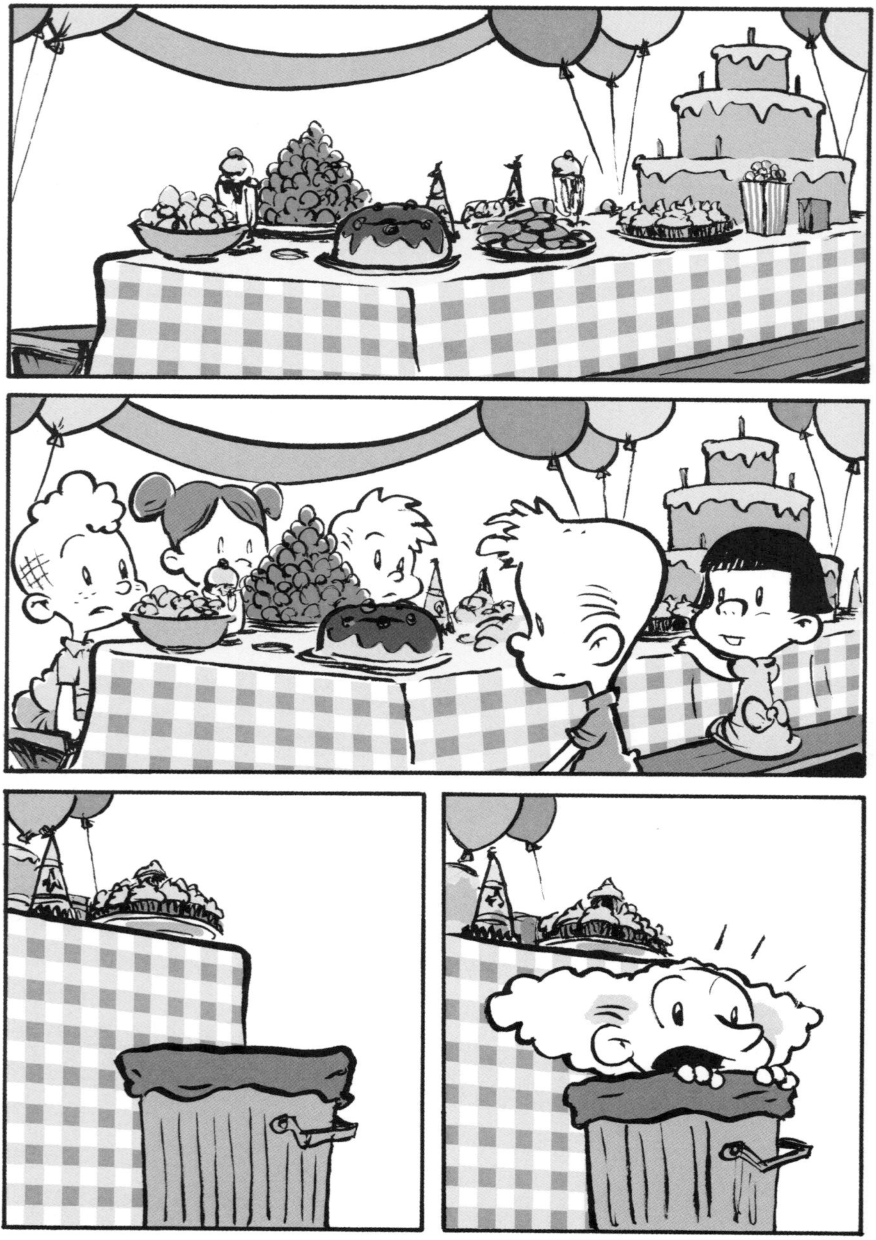

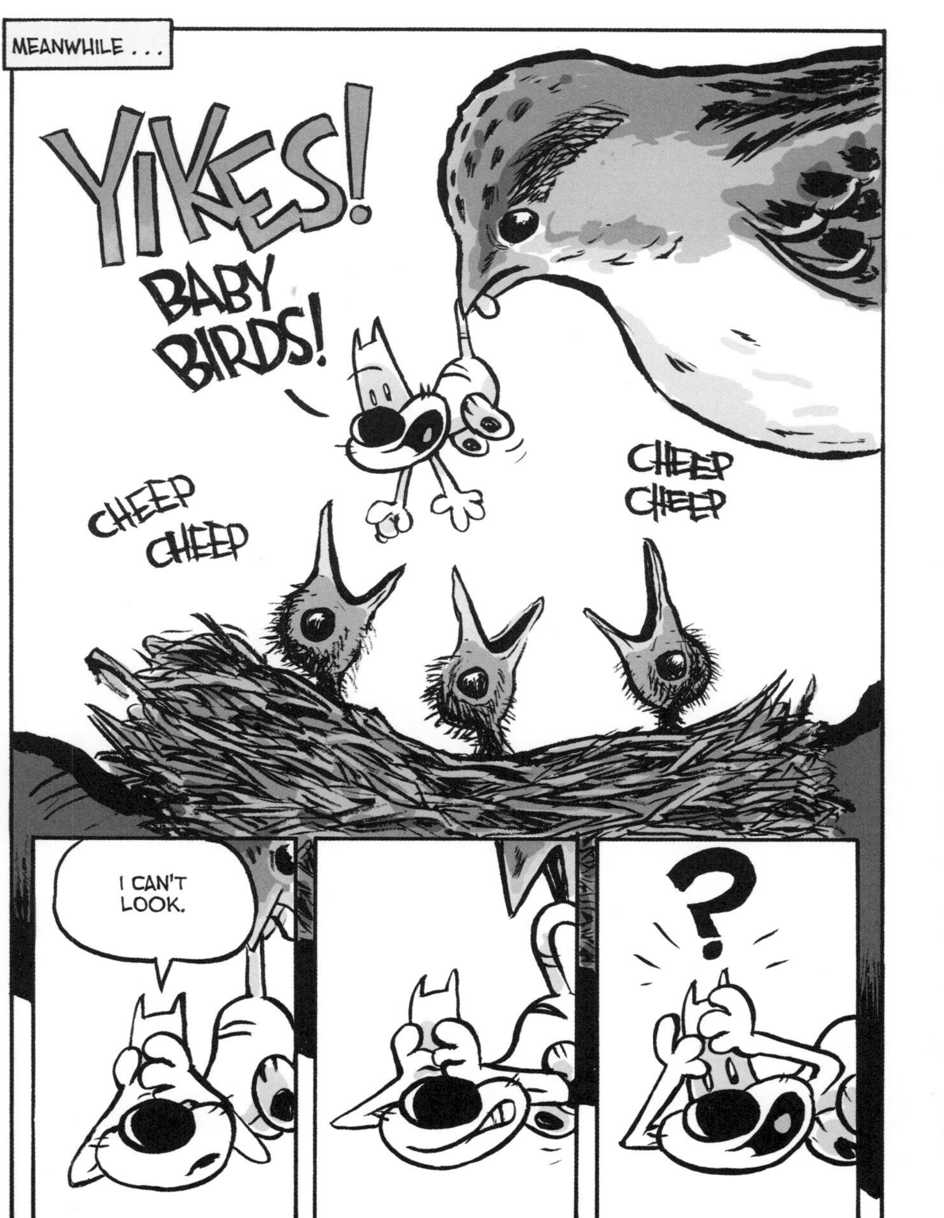
MEANWHILE . . .
YIKES!
BABY BIRDS!
CHEEP CHEEP
CHEEP CHEEP
I CAN'T LOOK.
?

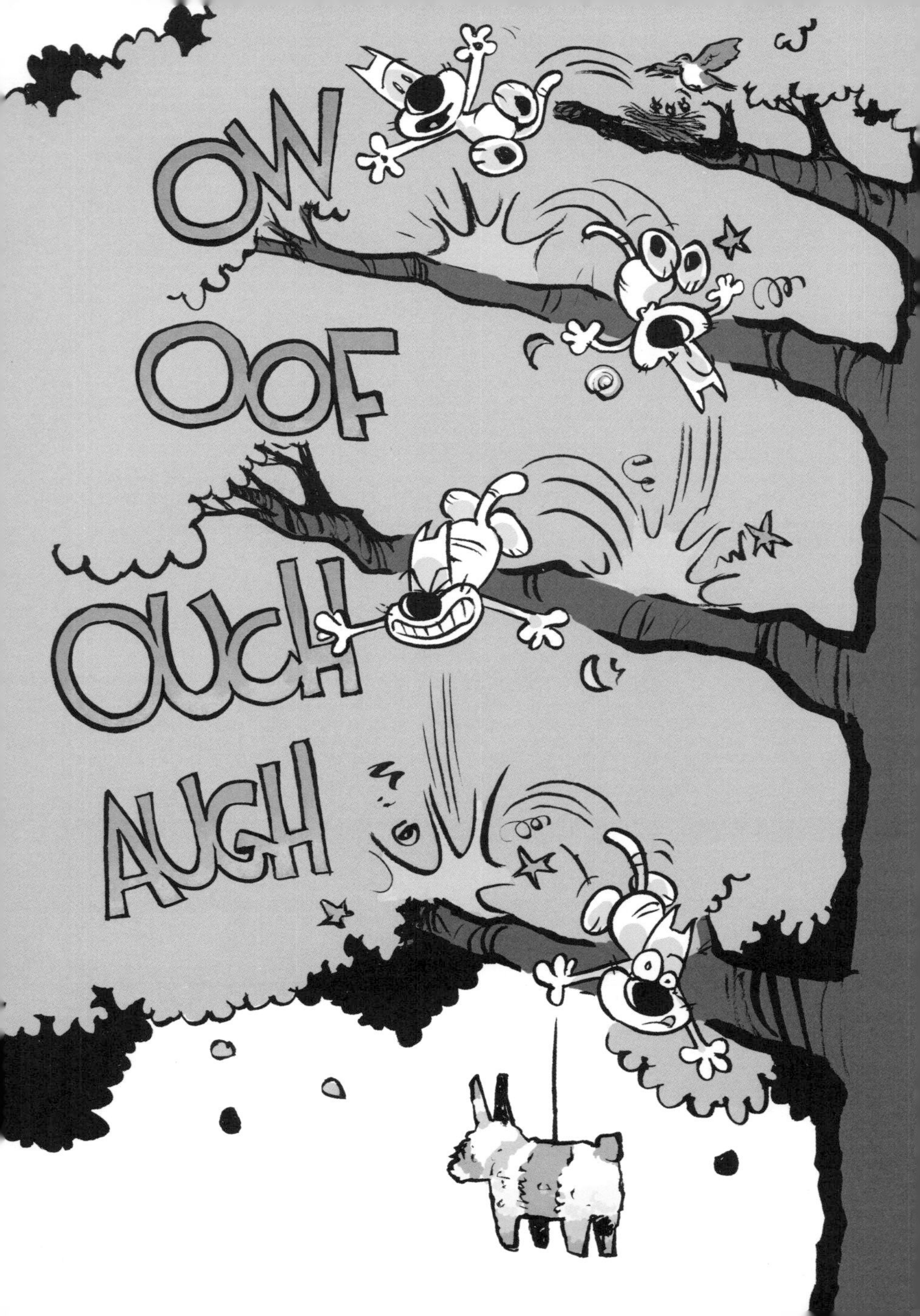
OW
OOF
OUCH
AUGH

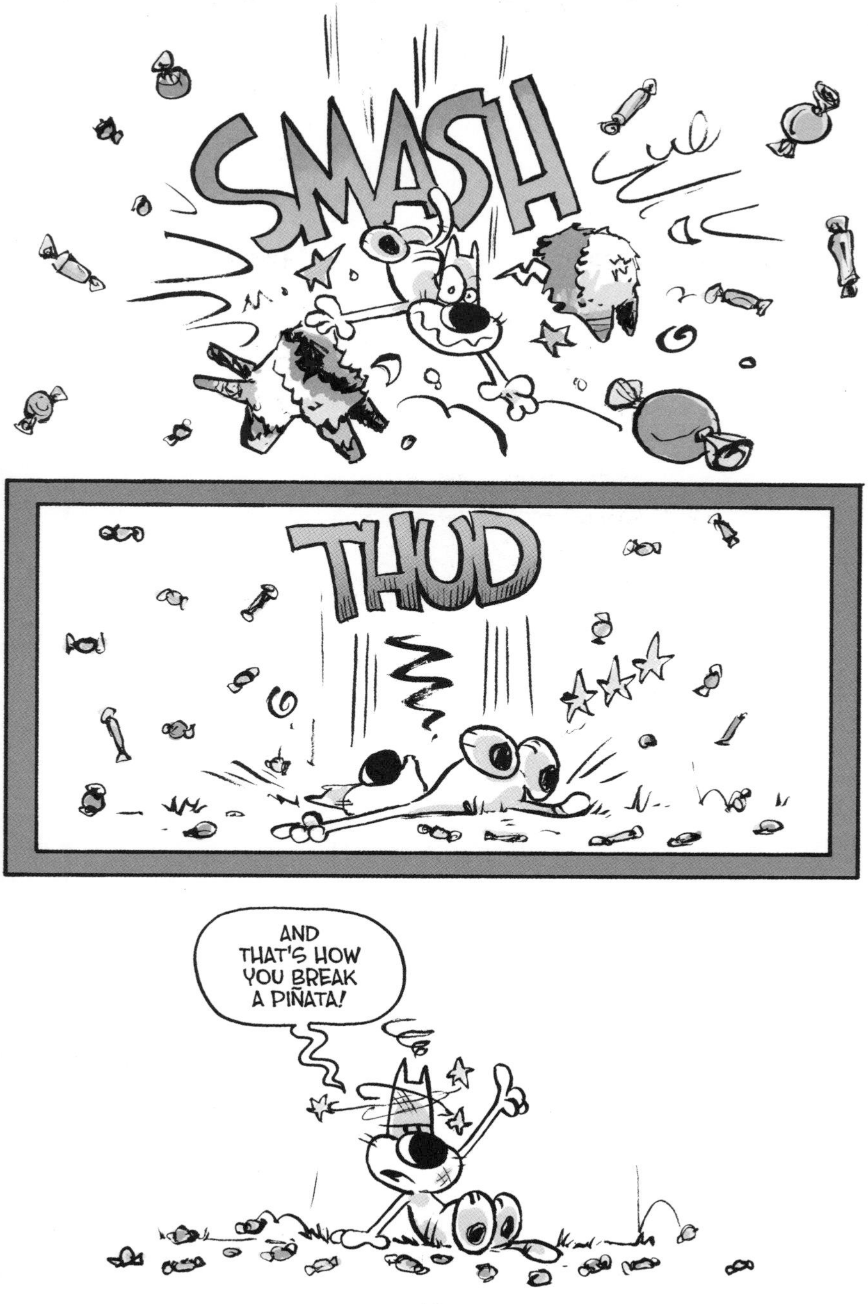
SMASH
THUD
AND THAT'S HOW YOU BREAK A PIÑATA!

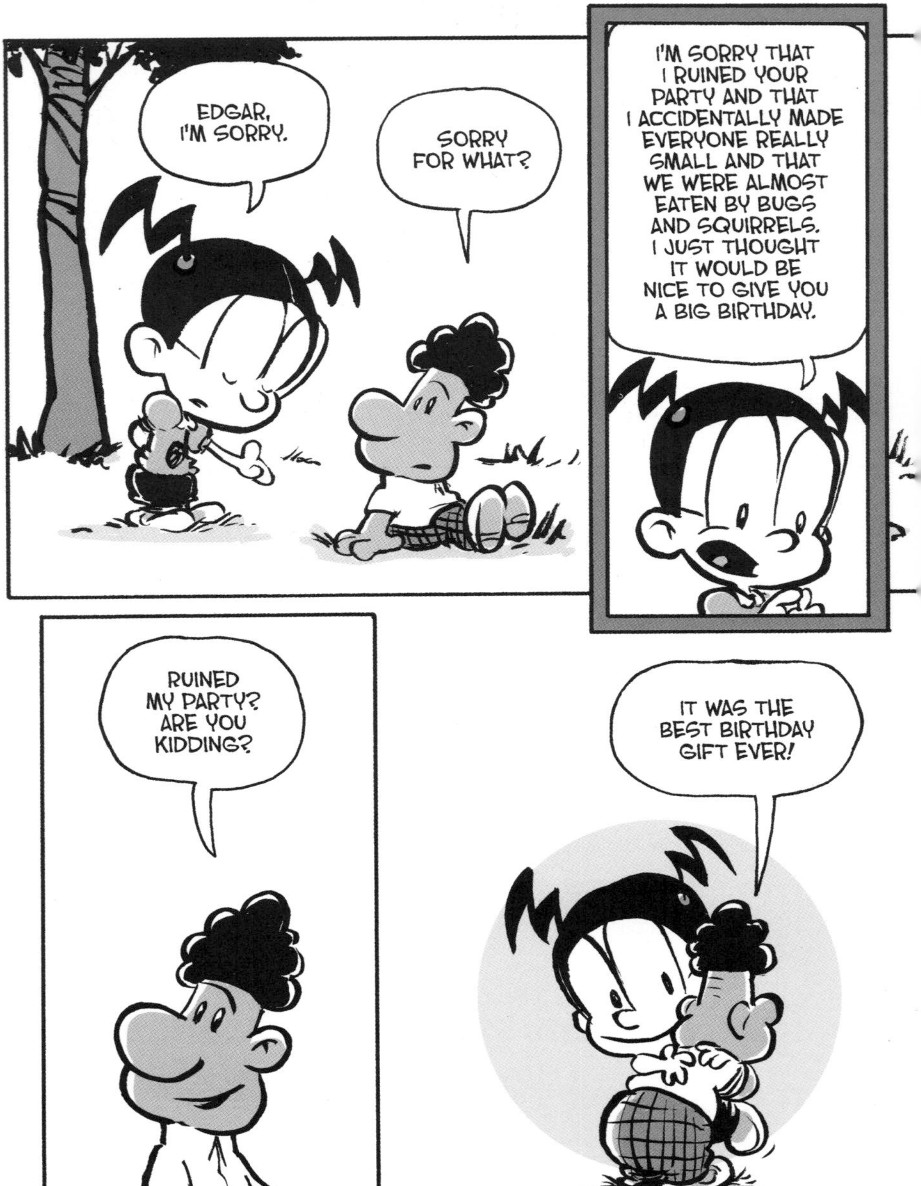
EDGAR, I'M SORRY.
SORRY FOR WHAT?
I'M SORRY THAT I RUINED YOUR PARTY AND THAT I ACCIDENTALLY MADE EVERYONE REALLY SMALL AND THAT WE WERE ALMOST EATEN BY BUGS AND SQUIRRELS. I JUST THOUGHT IT WOULD BE NICE TO GIVE YOU A BIG BIRTHDAY.
RUINED MY PARTY? ARE YOU KIDDING?
IT WAS THE BEST BIRTHDAY GIFT EVER!

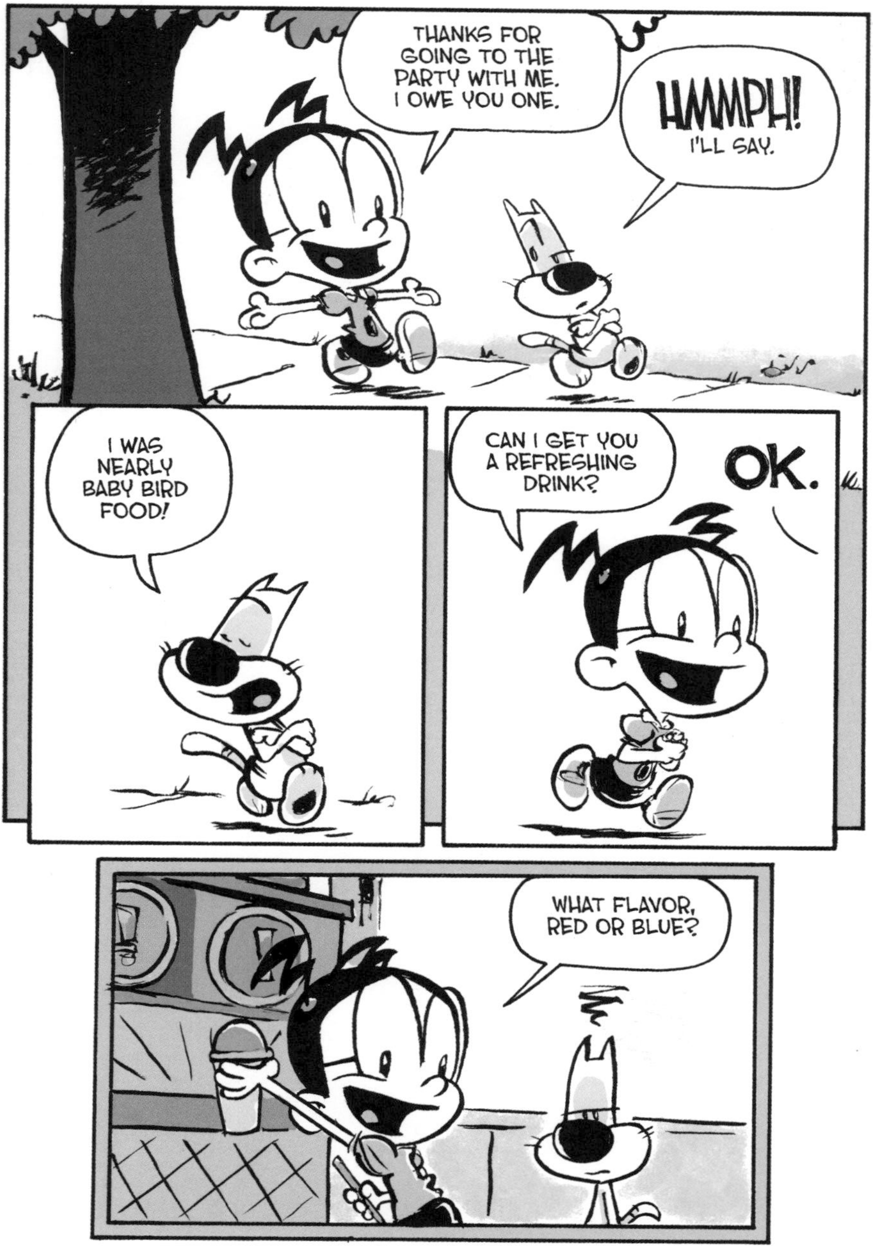

THANKS FOR GOING TO THE PARTY WITH ME. I OWE YOU ONE.
HMMPH! I'LL SAY.
I WAS NEARLY BABY BIRD FOOD!
CAN I GET YOU A REFRESHING DRINK?
OK.
WHAT FLAVOR, RED OR BLUE?

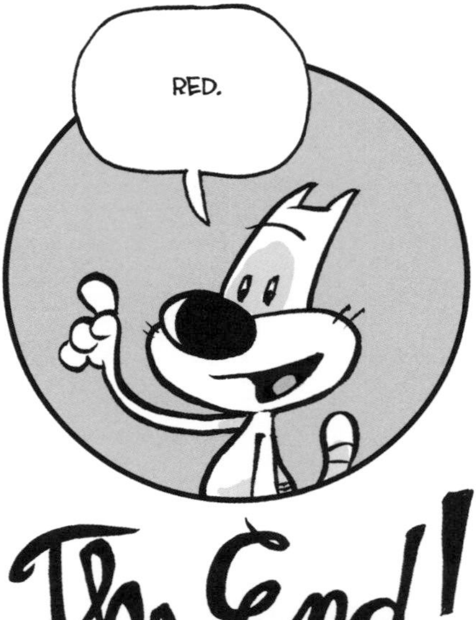
RED.

The End!

Getting to Know FRANK CAMMUSO

FRANK LIKES
1. SPENDING TIME WITH HIS FAMILY
2. PIZZA (ALL KINDS)
3. MAKING COMICS
4. READING COMICS (WHEN HE GETS A CHANCE)

FRANK DISLIKES
1. TUNA FISH
2. MAYONNAISE (ALL KINDS)
3. SHOVELING THE DRIVEWAY
4. BULLIES

FUN FACT: DID YOU KNOW THAT FRANK CAMMUSO ONCE GOT SICK AFTER DRINKING A SLUSHEE?

SPECIAL THANKS TO . . .

Ngoc and Khai, Kathy Leonardo, Nancy Iacovelli, Tom Peyer, Judy Hansen, Charlie Kochman, Maggie Lehrman, Sara Edward Corbett, Katie Fitch, Chad Beckerman, and finally to Hart Seely and Janice Whitcraft, who always enjoy a big party.

For more fun stuff about Salem & Whammy check out my website at . . .
www.cammuso.com

A Really BIG
Thank You!
(I hope you had fun too!)